Survival is a Dying Art

An Angus Green Novel

Neil S. Plakcy

Samwise Books

Copyright 2020 Neil S. Plakcy.

This book is a work of fiction. Names, characters, places, and incidents either are products of the author's imagination or are used fictitiously. Any resemblance to actual events or locales or persons, living or dead, is entirely coincidental. All rights reserved, including the right of reproduction in whole or in part in any form.

Reviews:

"The most interesting part of the book concerns Angus's developing friendship with an older gentleman, Tom, who becomes integral to solving the case. Most readers will look forward to seeing a lot more of Angus" – *Publishers Weekly*, November 2016

"Neil S. Plakcy's *The Next One Will Kill You* is best described as exhilarating, escapist entertainment. The novel's exciting and fun nature generates from the fact that it never takes itself too seriously and the fact that Plakcy manages to avoid allowing the players to sink to stereotypical caricatures is a testament to his faith in the original concept." – BOLO Books, October 2016.

Reviews

"The most interesting part of the book concerns Angus's developing friendship with an older gentleman, Tom, who becomes integral to solving the case. Most readers will look forward to seeing a lot more of Angus"

Publishers Weekly, November 2016

"Neil S. Plakcy's *The Next One Will Kill You* is best described as exhilarating, escapist entertainment. The novel's exciting and fun nature generates from the fact that it never takes itself too seriously and the fact that Plakcy manages to avoid allowing the players to sink to stereotypical caricatures is a testament to his faith in the original concept."

BOLO Books, October 2016

Chapter 1

Until the Nazis Came

Tom Laughlin and I were unlikely friends. He was in his late fifties, some thirty years older than I was. He had retired after a lucrative banking career in Boston, and I had only a year under my belt as a Special Agent with the FBI. He was about four inches shorter than my six feet, and his hair was dark and thinning, while mine was red and thick.

But we'd bonded as he helped me out with a case, and I was fascinated by his stories of being closeted for most of his life. He in turn was eager to hear what life was like for me, as the only openly gay agent in the Miami office.

Tom belonged to a gay book club, and he had invited me to join the group for dinner for my impressions of the book they were reading, which had an FBI angle, and I'd agreed. He met me at the front door of a casual restaurant on the second floor of a bland office building overlooking the Intracoastal Waterway in Fort Lauderdale.

I hugged Tom and smelled his lime after shave. He always looked so elegant whenever I saw him—he had a wardrobe of Brooks Brothers polo shirts and finely cut slacks that hugged his butt attractively. He led me to a big table outside overlooking the water, and introduced me to the half-dozen other men, all in their sixties or seventies, and we sat with them.

We were close to the Oakland Park Boulevard Bridge, and as soon as we ordered the bells there started ringing and the gates began lowering. A sport fishing boat with tall poles idled in front of us, churning a gentle wake as it waited to continue south. The name *High Risk* was painted across its transom.

Once the noise died down and we all had glasses of wine in front of us, we began discussing the book, a novelization of a real crime. It was about the exploitation of older men with AIDS who had sold their life insurance policies to a crooked company which defaulted on payments both to them and to the insurance companies, leaving them sick, impoverished, and uninsured.

We talked about the book for a while, and then Tom asked me, "How realistic is this crime, Angus?"

"I don't have much experience with fraud cases, but I'm afraid it rings very true to me," I said. "After I finished the book I looked up the files on the case the book is based on, and while the author changed some things for dramatic effect, the real crime was very similar."

One of the older men, a retired doctor, said, "I knew one of the men who sold his life insurance policy," he said. "He was HIV positive, and very quickly his case turned into full-blown AIDS. He couldn't work and had no medical insurance to pay for drugs. But he did have a hundred-thousand-dollar life insurance policy, and he found a company that would buy it from him for twenty-five grand. The broker made a deal with my friend to pay him over time, so he could pay his bills."

"Twenty-five thousand dollars isn't a lot of money, though," Tom said.

A big private yacht pulled up at the dock below us, and I reflected that twenty-five thousand dollars would barely cover its operating expenses for a year.

"It isn't," the doctor said. "The broker sold my friend's policy to investors for fifty grand and was supposed to use that money to pay the premiums until my friend died, as well as give him a cash payment every month to cover his living expenses. But my friend never collected the whole amount. He was able to get some experimental drugs, but suddenly the broker stopped paying him, and he slid backwards. He developed a secondary infection and died."

"That's the way the system was supposed to work," I said. "The business model was based on people with AIDS dying quickly, before they used up all the benefits they were due. But as more drugs came on the market, people were living longer, and even the legitimate brokers ran out of money to pay the insurance premiums."

I picked up my glass of white wine and took a long sip. "The Ponzi scheme the book describes is a classic one, where they recruited healthy people to take out policies, and sold them to pay the policy obligations they already had."

"And the gay men got screwed," the doctor said. "They'd sold their only viable asset for pennies on the dollar, and when the broker defaulted, they had nothing."

"This is emblematic of the problems facing our generation," another man said. He was a real estate agent with a big personality. "Many of us were shunned by our families when we came out. We didn't have the opportunities younger people have to get educations and good-paying jobs, so we never made that much money while we worked. And then we lost so many of our friends and lovers to AIDS. Now we're on our own without pensions or savings accounts or kids to look after us."

There was a general assent among the men at the table, and I felt guilty about the opportunities my generation had because of the pioneering work these men, and others like them, had done.

"A lot has to do with how soon we came out," another man said. He'd been introduced as Frank, and I had the sense that he and Tom were friends outside the book group. "I was too scared to come out when I was young, and I covered it up by working my ass off. I made money, yeah, but I never had the life I could have had."

The doctor nodded. "I married my high school sweetheart because I couldn't see any other path," he said. "She worked to put me through college and medical school and gave me two wonderful children. For years I knew that I was gay, but I couldn't abandon her after all she had done for me. It wasn't until the kids were grown that I finally told her."

I couldn't imagine how painful that must have been for both him and his wife. "Fortunately, she understood, and I was able to keep my relationships with my sons, and now I'm loving being a grandfather. But I know a lot of other men in similar situations who've been shunned by their exes and their kids."

The conversation wandered off onto tangents, and I was amazed at how many different paths these men had taken to get where they were. Tom insisted on paying for my meal, and then asked if I had a moment to speak with him and Frank.

Frank ordered us glasses of Scotch from the bar, and the three of us moved over to stand at the railing overlooking the waterway. It had gotten dark by then, and the only boat moving was a small powerboat with *Fort Lauderdale Police* along the side and a big searchlight at the prow.

Frank was a couple of inches taller than I was, close to my boyfriend Lester's height of six-foot-two but much skinnier. His gray hair was close-cropped and there were crow's feet around his eyes, but I could see he'd been quite handsome when he was younger.

"I was surprised when Tom told me that you work for the FBI," Frank began. "I wasn't aware they'd lifted the rules against homosexuals in sensitive positions."

"That happened long before I joined the Bureau," I said. "Now there are gay men and women at the highest levels. Even so, I'm the only openly gay special agent in my office." I took a sip of the Scotch, feeling the warmth on my tongue and the back of my palate. Smooth. "How can I help you?"

"I'm afraid someone might be trying to scam me, and while I

don't want to be taken advantage of, I do want to buy what he says he's selling."

"Slow down, Frank," Tom said. "Go back to the beginning."

Frank pursed his lips and thought for a moment. "Okay. My family are Italian Jews. Centuries in Venice. Did you know that the word ghetto originated there? It means foundry, and the Jews were segregated in the neighborhood where the iron works were located."

"Not quite that far back," Tom said. "Start with your father and his brother."

"Sorry." Frank grinned sheepishly. "I get distracted by all the history. My father and my uncle were born in Venice right after the turn of the century. When he was in his twenties, my father came to the United States, but my uncle Ugo stayed in Venice. He was gay, and he had a lively group of friends, so he had no desire to leave."

"Until the Nazis came," I said.

"Until the Nazis came. And by then it was too late."

We were all quiet for a moment. I imagined that being both gay and Jewish had made Frank's uncle a prime target.

"My uncle had a bureaucratic job with the city of Venice, and he made a good bit of money, which he apparently spent on art. The crown jewel of his collection was a painting called *Ragazzi al Mare*, Boys by the Seaside. By a painter named Mauricio Fabre, part of the Macchiaioli movement."

"And?" I asked.

"I didn't even know the painting existed until my father passed away," Frank continued. "When I was sorting through his effects, I found an 8-millimeter movie my uncle made that showed the painting, and a letter from my uncle describing it that included a carbon copy of the sales ticket."

"I still don't understand what you want from me," I said. "I don't know anything about art."

"Sorry, I'm getting there," Frank said. "A few months ago, I started looking around online to see what might have happened to the painting. I discovered that it had been confiscated by the Nazis, but then it disappeared. I put up a bunch of posts on art and auction sites asking for information, and eventually a man contacted me, saying that he knew where the painting was, and he could get it to me – for a fee."

I nodded. "And you're afraid he's scamming you."

"Exactly. I did my own research on him and I discovered that he owns a pawn shop in Fort Lauderdale. That made me concerned. I don't want to be involved in anything shady, and the very fact that he runs an operation like that makes me distrust him.'"

"What's his name?" I asked.

"Jesse Venable. Do you think you can check him out, see if he's legitimate? His company is called Knight's Pawn, and they have a couple of operations in bad parts of Fort Lauderdale."

I agreed, and we finished our Scotch as people partied on that fancy yacht moored below us. When it came to say goodbye, I kissed Tom's cheek and hugged him, then shook Frank's hand, but the two of them seemed unsure what they were supposed to do. I wondered about their relationship – just friends? Or did one of them want something more?

Once again, I considered myself lucky that I had been out of the closet for years and had built up the ability to sense someone's interest in me, and jump in if I felt the same way. I was lucky, too, that I'd met Lester, a bouncer at a bar in Fort Lauderdale, and started a relationship with him.

Whatever Tom and Frank wanted from each other, I hoped they could get it. And maybe by helping Frank track down his uncle's painting, I could pay back Tom for the favors he'd done for me in the past.

Chapter 2

Trader Tom's Market

The next morning I ran Venable's name through our computer system. I wasn't surprised to see him come up in several investigations, one of them run by Vito Mastroianni. When I arrived at the Miami office the year before, I had been assigned to the Violent Crime Task Force, which investigated everything from kidnapping to bank robbery to gang violence. I'd had the opportunity to work on several different cases involving jewelry theft, child pornography and the hijacking of armored cars.

I had often worked with Vito, a barrel-chested guy in his mid-forties who had been a cop in New York City and then an agent for DEA before joining the Bureau a dozen years before. If I was going to do any research on Venable, I knew I had to clear it with Vito first, so I walked down the narrow hallway to his office.

Vito's case involved the sale of stolen gold coins alleged to have come from the wreck of the Atocha, a Spanish treasure galleon that had sunk off the Florida coast in 1622 carrying millions of dollars' worth of silver from Peru and Mexico, gold and emeralds from Colombia, and pearls from Venezuela.

The investigation records I read surmised that coins stolen from an exhibit about the ship had passed through Venable's operation on their way out of Florida, but there was no concrete evidence, so the investigation had been put on hold.

"You worked on a case with a guy named Jesse Venable, didn't you?" I asked from the doorway.

He motioned me to the seat across from him. "What do you know about Venable?"

"I met with a guy last night who's suspicious of him, and asked me to look into him." I told him about the painting and the connection to Venable.

"You're sure this is the same Venable who runs the pawn shops?"

"That's what the man told me. Are you working on something with him now?"

"It's highly confidential."

I was accustomed to that. Since joining the Bureau, I'd learned that most information was on a need to know basis—and that ninety-five percent of the time, or more, I didn't need to know it.

"However..." Vito began, and I sat forward in my chair. "There is maybe something you could do to help me with Venable."

Vito crossed his hands over his ample chest. "Nearly two billion dollars in fake merchandise is sold in the U.S. each year, costing the global economy untold billions," he began. "Jesse Venable, in addition to his pawn shops, owns a booth at Trader Tom's Market where he sells knock-off belts, purses and sunglasses. I think a lot of that stuff is stolen, but Venable is a slippery character, and so far all I have on him is a series of complaints and rumors."

"So that's what you're investigating now?" I asked. "His flea market booth?"

"Not completely. But if you find something there I might be able to use it in my other case. How would you feel about taking a trip to the flea market this weekend? You've got an honest face, so I don't think anyone will peg you as a cop. I can get you some cash, and I'd like you to buy a couple of items you think might be counterfeit, to establish your cover as a shopper. But your real target is going to be Venable's booth."

It sounded like a fun way to spend a Saturday, so I agreed readily. "In the meantime, will it screw anything up for you if I look into this painting thing for my friend?"

"As long as you don't contact Venable or any of his associates without checking with me first."

I agreed, and spent the rest of the day, and the following one, researching counterfeit items in preparation for my visit to Trader Tom's.

The top ten counterfeited brands included a few I expected, like Adidas, Burberry, Lacoste and Reebok. The presence of Viagra, Microsoft and Benson & Hedges on the list was surprising, though. I was amazed at how many ways there were to tell counterfeit items, from improper stitching down to the wrong font used on a label.

For each brand on my list, I began to memorize tell-tale details like poor stitching, crooked labels, or misspelled brand names. For example, the rivets on some designer jeans incorporate the company's name. If the jeans use generic rivets, then they're fake.

The same was true for zippers and other hardware. I familiarized myself with the fonts used in the inside labels for a dozen commonly counterfeited brands, as well as the kind of cord or twine used for exterior hang tags.

Vito was right about my honest face; though I was twenty-six, my red hair and pale skin made me look younger and less like a Federal agent. Saturday morning, I dressed like a tourist for the excursion, in a brand-new T-shirt that read "I only drink water that's been through a brewery first." I'd bought an oversized one to cover the government-issued Glock in a thumb holster attached to the belt of my board shorts. I put a dab of zinc oxide sunscreen on my nose to sell the story even better.

When I walked into the market late that morning, I had a wad of cash in my wallet and a shopping list of brand name merchandise in my pocket. Too bad I wouldn't be able to keep anything I bought.

But then, it wasn't my money either.

The aisles of Trader Tom's outdoor flea market were narrow and crowded and the smell of sweat mingled with scented candles and the aroma of hot dogs on the grill beside a vat of poutine, a Canadian treat of French fries smothered in gravy. On the booth's speaker, Celine Dion insisted that her heart would go on.

The next booth sold t-shirts printed with sayings like "Jamaican Me Crazy" and "Herb is the Healing of the Nation" with a big marijuana leaf in the center. Jimmy Cliff competed with Celine, telling me I could get it if I really wanted. It was South Florida in a nutshell. Sunburned tourists mingled with Haitian hotel maids still in their pink uniforms, everybody out to get a bargain.

Seeing those women made me wonder if bargain-hunting was part of my genetic makeup. After my father died, my mother was left with two boys, ten and five, and no skills beyond homemaking. She had begun cleaning houses for rich people in Scranton, where we lived, and she shopped at flea markets and thrift stores to stretch every penny. But those markets of my youth were nothing like this one.

Back then, most of the vendors had been local people cleaning out their attics, craftsmen who made silver jewelry or handmade soap, and jobbers who bought remaindered items from retailers. At Trader Tom's market, these were regular retail operations, selling produce, cut flowers, clothes, handbags, sunglasses and fine jewelry.

As I strolled through the market, I was stunned at how many fakes I could recognize. At a sunglass booth, I bought a pair of gold-framed Ray-Bans in the Aviator style with green flash lenses that complemented my fair coloring. Fake, of course, though I hoped I'd be able to keep them.

Then a pair of bright red Nike Air Huaraches in my size. I knew from my research that the real ones were made to order and cost about a hundred fifty bucks, so I was pretty confident that the ones I paid forty-nine dollars for were knock-offs.

Someone jostled me as I walked past a cosmetics counter, and instinctively I reached for my wallet, which I was carrying in the front pocket of my shorts. My hand brushed someone else's hand, but when I turned the guy had slipped away. I wanted to go after him, but I wasn't there on a pickpocket detail, and it was more important that I stay focused on my mission.

I had learned from my research that nearly thirty thousand shipments of counterfeit goods were seized every year, but untold thousands more slipped past inspections and made it to markets like Trader Tom's. And the criminal gene didn't discriminate—I bought merchandise from a rainbow selection of vendors, from an African with skin so black it looked like the darkest of nights to a plump South Asian woman in a sari to a young man with close-cropped blond hair and a Russian accent.

I deliberately saved Venable's booth until I was hot and sweaty and burdened down with bags. The guy manning it was in his early twenties, with a neatly trimmed mustache and beard and a man-bun of dark hair. My gaydar pinged and I figured a little flirtation might get me results.

I took the last swig from a bottle of cold water I'd bought, tossed it into a big metal bin, and walked forward. "You look like you've had a good shopping day," the guy said as I stopped in front of his booth.

"I have. But I still need a belt," I said.

He looked at me, and my skin tingled as his eyes traveled up and down my body. "You're a twenty-eight waist, aren't you?" he asked.

"More like thirty," I said. "But I like being flattered."

"Then I'm the right guy to sell you a belt." He stuck his hand out. "I'm Larry."

"Andrew," I said. It was the standard name I used when I didn't want to give my own. That way I'd hear the beginning "An," and be able to respond.

Larry pulled out a black leather belt embossed with the Coach logo. "Try this on."

I liked the way it fit, but it didn't have any of the tell-tale signs of a knockoff. "Not quite what I was looking for," I said. One of the complaints we'd had involved a Louis Vuitton belt a customer alleged to have bought from the booth which turned out to be fake. "I was hoping to find a Louis V, but I haven't seen anything here."

Larry looked around. "I might have something for you," he said. "I haven't put them out yet because they're for a special client." He leaned down and picked up a box of coiled belts, and began lifting them out, one by one. "Here's a thirty-inch," he said.

It was a beautiful belt, a pebbled dark brown with four-pointed gold stars and the LV logo in gold metal as a buckle. I tried it on, and it fit beautifully. "How much?" I asked.

"For you? I can make a special price." He picked up a sheet of paper, and while he calculated I examined the belt carefully. For the price Louis Vuitton charged at retail, customers expected perfection in every detail. I found a minor irregularity in the stitching near the buckle, though, which was what I expected from a fake.

"I can do one-twenty-five," Larry said, which was still a hell of a lot less than the five-hundred-dollar retail price.

"Let me see what I've got left," I said. I fanned out six twenties in front of him. "I've only got a hundred-twenty left," I said, though I had some more in my pocket. "Can we make a deal?"

"What's five bucks between friends," he said. "Sure."

We weren't exactly friends, and I wasn't going to ask the guy out on a date when he might be the subject of a Federal investigation, but I agreed readily and handed him the cash. He slid the belt into a cloth sack with a drawstring. Another indicator it was fake: the real belt would have come in a brown box.

I thanked him and walked away. Mission accomplished: I'd established that Venable's booth sold counterfeit merchandise. I walked back through the narrow aisle with a sense of accomplishment.

Then I heard the shouting.

A pimply-faced guy with a pouf of black hair was yelling at a heavy-set man behind a display of running shoes – the booth where I'd bought the fake Nikes earlier that day. "You sold me a fake, asshole! I want my money back!"

"You think you were getting real Adidas for the price you paid?" the man said, in a heavy French accent. Given the local population of French Canadians, he was probably from Quebec. He pointed to a sign on the table. "No refunds."

"I should call the cops on you," the young guy yelled. He turned to the crowd that had gathered, blocking the narrow aisle. "This guy's a thief!"

The Canadian man came around from behind his booth. "Get the fuck away from here before I beat your skinny ass."

"You tell him!" a man said from a neighboring booth.

"Give him his money back!" a woman shopper called.

"You think you can come to this country and rip off real Americans!" the young guy said. "We ought to send your ass back to Canada."

Several people in the crowd applauded, though others shifted uncomfortably.

"You're a little piss-ant," the Canadian said. He waved his hands at the kid. "Now shoo!"

The kid must have thought the man was going to hit him, because he swung back. He was surprisingly strong, and he hit the Canadian square on the chin with his fist. The Canadian fell to the ground and the sound of his head hitting the pavement was gruesome.

"Holy shit," someone in the crowd said.

The kid stood there for a minute staring at the man on the ground, his mouth agape. Then he turned to run—but a security guard had just muscled his way through the crowd and he grabbed the kid by the arm.

Someone called 911 on a cell phone, and a woman in a hijab said, "I'm a doctor." She squatted beside the Canadian and took his pulse. "We need 911 right away. Can someone call?"

The crowd was stunned for a moment, then began to buzz. There were plenty of witnesses, so I slipped back the way I had come, passing Larry's booth. "What was all the fuss?" he asked.

"Kid who bought counterfeit shoes confronted the vendor," I

said. "Took a swing at him, knocked him to the ground. The vendor hit his head, but there's a doctor with him."

Larry's eyes opened wide and I could see him putting the pieces together. Whatever Venable was paying him to run the booth wasn't enough to risk getting hurt like that. He slid a rolling metal grille down over his booth with a clang, and I ducked out a side exit into the hot humid sunshine.

Chapter 3
Burning Love

When I returned home that afternoon, I turned my attention to Frank Sena and his uncle's painting. I emailed Frank and asked him to scan or photograph the documentation he had, including the segment of his father's will which established him as the legal heir.

Then I went to an art history website to learn about the Macchiaioli. The term had some negative connotations -- it implied that the artists' finished works were no more than sketches. The name also referred to the phrase *darsi alla macchia*, meaning to hide in the bushes, which tied in with the artists' desire to paint outdoors -- what was otherwise called by the French term *en plein air*.

It was interesting to read that their works also commented on socio-political topics, including Jewish emancipation, prisons and hospitals, and women's conditions such as the plight of war widows and life behind the lines.

By then it was early evening, and I put aside my research and headed west to Eclipse, a gay bar on the edge of Wilton Manors to meet up with Lester, my personal hunk of burning love. He was a former high school gym teacher and bar bouncer, six-two and two hundred fifty pounds of muscle and sex appeal.

He was a bouncer at a different bar when I met him, and after we dated for a while he told me that I inspired him to want to make something more of his life. He had connected with a company that made small batch whiskey, and was hired as a brand ambassador, traveling from bar to bar chatting up owners and staff and making specialty cocktails.

When I walked into Eclipse, I leaned over and gave Lester a peck on the cheek. He comped me a Lion's Tail, a mix of whiskey, bitters, lime juice and simple syrup, and I stood by the side of the bar and watched him work. For a big guy, he moved with surprising grace, opening cartons of whiskey, handing bottles to the bartenders, even cleaning up the bar back when he wasn't busy.

I didn't want to stand around doing nothing, so I began taking photos of the drinks and posting them to Lester's social media accounts. Pictures went up to Instagram and Snapchat and Pinterest, Facebook and Twitter and even LinkedIn, along with the appropriate locations and hashtags.

When Lester came over I showed him what I'd done. "We make a great team, G-Man," he said, and he kissed me. "Thanks for all that. I can finish up here in about fifteen. Then you want to go back to my place? Or yours?"

"Mine would be better," I said. "I have some research going on I need your help with."

"You got it, babe." He kissed me once more, a little more forcefully this time, and went back to work.

At just over six feet, I was a bit shorter than Lester, slim to his bulk, but we fit together very well. My red hair and fair skin complemented his shaggy brown locks and Mediterranean complexion. When I was with him, I didn't have to be a Federal agent, charged with protecting the population. I could just be Angus Green, boyfriend.

He finished as promised and he followed me back to my place in his SUV, leased by his employer so he'd be able to carry all those boxes of whiskey from bar to bar.

My roommate's car wasn't in the driveway. Jonas had begun dating a guy a few weeks before, and he was spending a lot of time over at his new friend's place, which was fine with me.

Lester and I tumbled into my bed as soon as we could, and worked off all the sexual tension generated by spending time in a bar full of cute guys and testosterone. Just before I fell asleep I remembered my dinner with Tom and Frank. They had been awkward together at the restaurant, as if they were on the verge of a dating relationship, and maybe if I worked with them on the search for the painting, I'd be able to nudge them closer.

The next morning, Lester and I were both up early, and we went for a long, sweaty run around my neighborhood. We passed a few older men walking dogs, heard the hum of air conditioners, and waited to cross the street between a line of cars waiting to park at one of the Pentecostal churches.

I went into the shower first, while Lester made us breakfast smoothies of orange juice, bananas, pineapple chunks and strawberries. By the time he finished his smoothie and took a shower, I had my laptop open on the kitchen table.

Lester had a love of art, and we'd spent some time at street fairs, buying small pieces and admiring larger ones. I opened my laptop to the documentation Frank had emailed me. "You think you can help me make sense of some of this stuff?" I asked Lester, turning the laptop to face him.

His hair was damp, and he was freshly shaved, wearing only a pair of boxers, and I really would have preferred to jump his bones, but I needed his help. I opened a page I'd bookmarked about the Macchiaioli and showed it to him. He read for a couple of minutes, then turned back to me. "You've heard about the Impressionists, I'm sure," he said.

I nodded.

"These guys used a lot of the same techniques, similar color palette and optical effects. Some critics called them "failed Impressionists" because they weren't as good as the French guys."

"Which is probably why you hear about Manet and Monet and those other guys, but not these artists."

"That's part of it. But they were more like early Modernists, who had these big ideas about how painting can capture the essence of a moment." He switched screens to the photo of *Ragazzi al Mare* that Frank had sent me. The painting depicted five young men, all nude, enjoying life at an ocean beach. One young man stood in a somewhat classical pose, while another appeared poised to jump into the water. The other three were in various stages of repose on the sandy shore.

It looked Impressionist, with the blurriness that I had learned was characteristic of the style in my one art history course at Penn State, and I understood the connection Lester had made to those more famous painters.

"See how this one guy is about to jump into the water?" he said, pointing to a boy on the left side. "You can almost feel the movement coming."

"That's very cool."

"And there's a reason why most of these guys are naked," Lester said.

"Not just because Fabre was queer? I read this biography of him that said he never married. That plus all the naked guys in his pictures sent my gaydar pinging."

Lester elbowed me. "You are such a horndog. This article says that his work focused on the male nude as a response to the overwhelming presence of female nudes in classical art. He felt that there was no reason why the male body couldn't be as sensual as the female."

We talked about Fabre some more. He preferred rich flesh tones, the vibrant blues of the Mediterranean and the brilliant yellow of the Tuscan sun. Many of his works had been painted at the seaside. His most famous, which was at the Uffizi Gallery in Florence, was of a beautiful sunset on a beach on the Ligurian coast. A single bather stood by the water, nude, and according to the records was a sailor from the nearby naval base at La Spezia.

But we couldn't find any specific information on *Ragazzi al Mare*. Eventually Lester had to leave for a Sunday afternoon tea dance at a bar in West Palm Beach, and I called Tom to tell him what I'd found.

"Why don't I call Frank and see if the three of us can get together," he said. "Then you can tell us both at the same time. And I have to admit I've been trying to come up with an excuse to see him outside the book group."

"Sounds like a plan." While I tidied up the house and waited for Jonas to return, Tom called Frank, and then called me back with a plan to meet at Frank's that evening. "He wants to show you the film he found of his uncle's apartment in Venice, which shows the painting on the wall."

He hesitated. "And he suggested that three of us should stay for dinner, if that's all right with you."

I loved the tentative sound of Tom's voice. "I'd be delighted," I said.

By the time Jonas got back, I'd stripped and remade my bed and run a load of laundry. Since I was about to walk out the door, all l I had time for was a quick fist-bump and a promise to get together one night that week.

It wasn't far from Wilton Manors, the inland suburb of Fort Lauderdale where Jonas and I rented a small house to Galt Ocean Mile, but it was another world from my neighborhood of run-down single-family houses to the line of elegant high-rises with water views to die for. Most of the traffic was coming the other way, cars and SUVs leaving the beach after a day of swimming and sunning, and I cruised easily up the bridge over the Intracoastal Waterway and turned left onto A1A, the divided four-lane road that paralleled the beach.

I found Frank Senna's building and parked in a guest spot out front. I checked my hair in the rear-view mirror, smoothed my collar, and marched in to the concierge desk, where I gave my name and was directed to an apartment on the eleventh floor.

Frank let me in and shook my hand once again. "Thanks for coming by," he said.

Frank's apartment looked like it had been decorated by a professional, though I'd learned not to underestimate the gene that some gay men had for fashion and design, which seemed to have skipped me. The leather sofa shone, as did the matching club chair. Built-in cabinets along one wall showed off a collection of small artifacts,

Tom was standing by the sliding glass doors that led to the balcony, a crystal lowball glass in his hand. As usual, he looked casually elegant, and I hoped that when I reached his age I'd look as good.

I crossed the room and hugged Tom hello. I smelled his lime after shave as our cheeks touched. "Can I offer you a cocktail?" Frank asked.

"Whatever Tom's having," I said. "I trust his taste."

"Scotch rocks it is then," Frank said. "I'm pouring Glenmorangie, if that's all right with you. I have a few other choices if you'd rather something else."

"I tended bar all through college, and had the chance to taste a lot of single-malt scotches. Glenmorangie is one of my favorites."

"You are clearly a young man of discerning taste." He poured me a glass, and I inhaled the rich peaty scent before I sipped it.

"I probably don't have much to tell you that you don't already know," I said. "But I did some research on Fabre and the Macchiaioli. I couldn't find any information about the current location of the painting."

"Let's start with the movie I have," Frank said. "And then I can show you how this man Venable got in touch with me."

Tom and I sat on the sofa and I told him about my counterfeiting case as Frank bustled around, getting out an old eight-millimeter projector and closing the vertical blinds. As he lowered the lights, I felt like I was in old-timey movie theater, waiting for the main attraction.

The projector clicked and clacked as it displayed the movie against the closed verticals. A dapper man in his early forties waved at the camera. He wore a white double-breasted suit with a dark shirt and a white tie, and he had a light-colored beret perched jauntily on the side of his head.

"That's my Uncle Ugo," Frank said.

The eight-millimeter movie was jerky and in black and white, but Ugo Sena was handsome, and there was something engaging about his attitude. I leaned forward as he took us on a tour of his apartment. The centerpiece was a large painting on the wall above a chesterfield sofa with rolled arms.

I recognized it as *Ragazzi al Mare*, and marveled at the ability to have such a large, famous painting in your apartment. Of course, back then, Fabre wasn't well-known.

Frank's uncle panned the camera around the room, and I noted a couple of other smaller paintings on the wall. The film ended and the room was shrouded in darkness. Then Tom turned on the lights.

"What do you think was the purpose of that movie?" I asked Frank.

"From what I can make out, it was a way to show my father that Uncle Ugo was doing well in Venice and had no desire to leave."

"And the painting above the sofa, that's *Ragazzi al Mare*?" I asked.

"So the documentation I have states. I found several documents in my father's apartment that my uncle sent him. He had the dealer who sold him the painting make a duplicate copy of the bill of sale, and he sent it to my father along with the movie. He was so proud."

He showed me the originals of the materials he had scanned and sent to me, starting with a piece of thin onion-skin paper titled *Fattura di Vendita* in a gothic-style script. "Here's the bill of sale." The whole document was in Italian, so I had to take Frank's word for it, though I knew that if my brother Danny was there he'd be able to translate for me. He'd been studying the language in preparation for a summer study program in Italy.

"There's my uncle's name," Frank said, pointing to the name Ugo Sena after the word *Acquirente*. "And there's the name of the painting."

Then he showed me a light blue aerogram, a flimsy piece of paper designed to be folded up and air mailed. It was written in an elegant cursive hand, again all in Italian. "This is where my uncle describes buying the painting," Frank said. He showed me printed photos of the front and back of the painting that looked like the ones I'd found online and looked at with Lester.

"Your father had no other siblings?"

"Just the two of them. And I'm an only child So that means the painting is mine."

He sniffed the air, and I realized that there was a wonderful aroma coming from the kitchen. "I've made my grandmother's eggplant parmigiana for dinner," Frank said. "Over dinner I'd like to talk to you about how to approach this Venable, and make sure he has the painting."

The food tasted as good as it smelled – slices of eggplant layered with mozzarella and tomato sauce, accompanied by homemade garlic bread and a green salad. Though Frank had invited me over to hear what I had learned about the painting, had he prepared dinner not just to thank me, but to keep Tom there as well?

Frank described how Venable had contacted him in response to a post Frank had made on an art search website, and the way they'd gone back and forth about the details of the artwork. I asked Frank to copy out any messages he'd received from Jesse Venable about the painting, and email them to me.

"I want this painting back," Frank said. "I don't care if I have to pay for it. To me, it's a way to give the finger to the Nazis, all these years later. They tried to wipe out the Jews, but I'm still here. They stole this painting because it belonged to a Jew, because the subject matter was decadent. Getting it back is like saying to the world that we survived—Jews and gay men."

"I get that," I said. "They took away your uncle and they tried to take this painting, which obviously meant a lot to him."

"Angus and I have had several conversations about how different his experience has been from that of the men of our generation," Tom said to Frank. "He never had to hide his sexuality from his family or his employer."

"Well, I wouldn't say never," I protested. "It's not like one day I realized, hey, I like boys better than girls and immediately jumped out of the closet. I had some angst along the way."

"Of course you did," Tom said. "But all teenagers go through something like that. I speak to my straight nephew, who's sixteen, and he's desperate to get a girl to have sex with him, worried he'll never lose his virginity. 'What if I get to college and I've never gotten laid, Uncle Tom,' he says. That is, right after making me swear not to tell my sister what he's said."

"And what do you tell him?" Frank asked.

"That his dick won't fall off if he waits until he's eighteen to have sex," Tom said dryly. "That self-love can be the highest love of all."

I snorted with laughter. "Does it work?"

"I doubt it. But it is fun to be the cool uncle that he can talk to about anything."

Frank stood and cleared the table. While he was gone, I leaned over to Tom. "I like him," I whispered. "He's good-looking and smart."

"You're not going to be my rival, are you?" Tom asked, with a twinkle in his eye.

"No, I'll stick to Lester. And I think he's interested in you, too. This dinner had to be as much for you as for me."

"We'll see."

Frank returned with three small glasses of grappa, an Italian brandy. "What do you think you can do to help me?" he asked, as he settled down across from us.

"This is my first look at art theft," I said, "so I have a lot of work to do in order to get up to speed on how to proceed. I can't tell you anything more than that Venable is a person of interest to the Bureau, so I'm going to have to move delicately."

We talked more over the grappa, and by the time I left Frank's condo I was determined to do what I could to help him out.

And who could resist the opportunity to give the finger to the Nazis, after all?

Chapter 4
Good Intel

Monday morning, I woke at seven and went for another run through my neighborhood. Then I drove to my office in Miramar, the western suburb of Miami where the FBI's field office was located. I went down to the lab, where they had sophisticated photography equipment, and a tech I knew, a Chinese-American guy named Wagon, got me set up with a white background and a digital camera on a stand.

I spent the morning photographing and categorizing everything I had bought.

Starting with the Ray-Ban sunglasses, I looked for the details that had alerted me to the possibility of fraud. The clue in this case had been the Ray-Ban logo on the earpiece, just in from the hinge. The logo on the real glasses was metal, burned into the plastic, but the logo on the Aviators I'd bought was a stick-on decal. Sure, the font was right, and unless you were familiar with the manufacturing you might believe, as the vendor had told me, that you were getting a great deal on a discontinued style.

I was able to zoom in on the logo, getting an excellent image of it.

I continued with each item, connecting it to the appropriate vendor, including the price and the details I found that indicated a fake.

I had to ask Wagon for help with the Louis V belt, because the irregular stitching was so tiny it was hard to get a good shot of. I'd worked with him a couple of times in the past, and loved the description he used of himself, as a nerd with a gun.

With all the photos complete, I returned to my office and began my report, which involved lots of typing and price searching. It wasn't very exciting, but after getting shot in my first big case in Miami, and putting myself into grave danger a couple of times, I was glad to have the opportunity to stay at my desk for a while and use the training I'd gotten at Penn State.

I paid special attention to the booth that Jesse Venable owned, describing it and recording as much as I could remember of my conversation with Larry—minus the flirting, of course.

I saved everything to a folder for the Violent Crimes Task Force. Since all the agents assigned to that task force had access to the root folder, I added special permissions to allow only Vito to see the contents, then emailed the link to him.

When I was finished, I read through the correspondence Frank had forwarded to me between him and Jesse Venable. Venable appeared to know several details about the painting, which made his claim more credible.

When I finished, once again I navigated the narrow corridors of our headquarters to Vito's office. "I uploaded my report on Trader Tom's and sent the link to you," I said, as I settled into the chair across from him. "I'm pretty certain that the belt I bought from Venable's booth is a counterfeit, and I identified a couple of other booths we could investigate further."

"Good," Vito said, without looking up at me.

"One more thing," I said hurriedly. "About that painting I was telling you about, that Venable has a lead on. I found it in a database of art confiscated by the Nazis during World War II. Then it got stolen, along with many other works, from the church in Venice where it had been stored. Since then, it's been listed as missing."

Vito finally looked up. "You think maybe Venable is dealing in stolen paintings now? Or just scamming this guy?"

"I don't know. But I'd like to keep looking, as long as it's all right with you."

"Remind me of what else you're working on."

"Tracking the money for the Male Power pharmaceuticals case." It was a locally-owned drug development company focused on generic equivalents to Viagra and similar products. The chief financial officer was accused of embezzling money from angel investors and parking it in his personal offshore accounts. "I've got subpoenas out for information, but I don't have anything else to do at the present."

"Then I can spare you for a while. Tread carefully. And you'll need to speak with Miriam Washington before you go much further."

"Who's she?" There were over a thousand employees in our office, from special agents to support and administrative personnel, and I only knew a few dozen.

"She's on the Art Crimes Task Force. Not her full-time gig, you understand, but she's the go-to person in this office with the specialized training to investigate art thefts. If there's a case there, she'll know it."

When I got back to my office, I looked up Agent Washington, and sent her an inter-office email and asked if I could meet with her to discuss a tip I'd received. While I waited to hear back from her, I read through a bunch of press releases on the Bureau's Art Theft Program, based at headquarters in Washington and comprised of sixteen special agents assigned to specific regions.

Was this a case for them? What would qualify this for their investigation? The theft had taken place in Italy, not in the United States. Did the FBI have jurisdiction because the potential buyer was a U.S. citizen? Or maybe she'd report the tip to someone in Italy who'd follow up on it.

Late in the afternoon I got a response back from Agent Washington. She was about to leave for a presentation that evening at the Fort Lauderdale Museum of Art. If I could stop by the museum, she could meet with me after her talk finished.

I wrote back and thanked her. Then I closed my computer and headed out. The rush-hour traffic was slow, and I was lucky to make it to downtown Fort Lauderdale in time. I parked at a garage and walked over to the art museum, where I followed the signs for the presentation on famous stolen paintings.

A couple of dozen folding chairs had been set up in front of a podium that held a laptop computer, with a folding screen behind it. I slid into a chair and the room filled up, mostly older men and women. Some looked like they'd come straight from work, while others wore the kind of clothes I associated with retirement communities – brightly colored track suits matched with expensive rings, watches and necklaces on both men and women.

When I was growing up in Scranton, women wore wedding rings and the occasional strand of pearls—usually fake, according to my mother. Back then, most men didn't wear jewelry beyond wedding bands or class rings. When I admired a man's heavy gold ring festooned with horse heads with tiny diamond eyes my mother told me that meant he was a gambler, and to watch out for men like him.

My memory was interrupted when a young African-American woman with dark hair in complicated cornrows, topped with a puff of what looked like white fur, stepped up to the microphone. I wondered, for a moment, if the museum had a salon attached that created hair art.

"Good evening, everyone, and thank you for coming out this evening," she said, leaning awkwardly into the microphone. "I'm from the museum's community outreach department and I'm delighted that we have an opportunity tonight to learn about some famous art crimes and how the FBI has solved them."

"Our special guest is..." She hesitated for a moment, and looked down at a card in her hand, and her complicated hairdo bobbed dangerously. "Special Agent Miriam Washington from the Miami Field Office, which covers nine counties in southern Florida. This office is also responsible for addressing extraterritorial violations of American citizens in Mexico, the Caribbean, and Central and South America."

I could tell from the baffled look on her face that she was reading from a script that she didn't quite understand. *Welcome to the club*, I thought. It had taken me a while to understand that meant we stepped in when Americans got in trouble in the tropical zones around us.

The young woman cleared her throat and continued reading. "Special Agent Washington holds a bachelor's degree in art history from Wellesley University, and master's and doctoral degrees in art history from Boston College." Her voice strengthened as she finally understood what she was reading. "She has also received specialized training in art and cultural property investigations and has assisted in art related investigations worldwide."

She looked up at us and with relief said, "Please join me in welcoming Special Agent Washington."

The audience applauded and a statuesque black woman in her mid-forties stepped up to the podium. She wore a stylish suit in blood-red and matching pumps. "How many of you here have heard of the Isabella Stewart Gardner Museum in Boston?" she asked.

There was general agreement from the audience, and though the name was familiar to me because of the famous theft that had occurred there, I didn't know any details of the crime or the investigation.

Washington hit a couple of keys on the laptop, and the screen behind her came to life with a photo of the museum. Moorish arches looked out on a lavish garden and reminded me of pictures I'd seen of Venice – one of the many places I hoped someday to visit.

"I was fortunate to visit the Gardner Museum many times when I was an undergraduate," Washington said. "It was during that time, in 1990, when a theft from that museum rocked the art world."

She went on to describe the crime, and the FBI's investigation into it. "Altogether, thirteen pieces were stolen at an estimated loss of $500 million, making the robbery the largest private property theft in history. Despite our best efforts, most of the art work is still missing."

She went through a few screens of the missing pieces of art, and she was such a confident speaker, adding interesting details, that the audience was rapt, and so was I. She was clearly what Vito would call a smart cookie.

She flipped to another screen. "We have had some great success in our program, though," she said. She described the reasons why the FBI had been involved in the recovery of the golden armor of an ancient Peruvian warrior king, the Rodin sculpture that inspired the Impressionist movement, the headdress Geronimo wore at his final Pow-Wow and the rare Civil War battle flag carried by one of the nation's first African-American regiments.

The presentation took about twenty minutes, with another fifteen for questions and answers. Then the woman with the complicated cornrows returned to the podium and thanked her for a wonderful presentation, and the audience dispersed.

I went up to Special Agent Washington and introduced myself.

"My throat is parched," she said. "Mind if we do this at the café?"

"Not at all." We walked over to the café, adjacent to the bookstore by the front entrance, where I bought her a large iced tea and got a cappuccino for myself, and we sat at a table in the corner.

"You said in your email you got a tip about stolen art?" she asked.

I explained about Frank Sena and the story he'd told me about his uncle's ownership of *Ragazzi al Mare* before it was confiscated by the Nazis. "And the guy who says he knows the location of the painting is someone the Bureau's been interested in for a while."

"I don't know anything about that painting, but it certainly sounds worth looking into." She finished her tea. "What are you working on now?"

"I'm assigned to the Violent Crime Task Force," I said. "Working with Vito Mastroianni on a case that's on hold while I wait for documents to come in. But I feel a real connection to this situation, knowing the man whose uncle was murdered by the Nazis. And though I'm not Jewish, I am gay, and if I'd been in Italy then I would have been a target as much as Ugo Sena. It makes me want to see justice served."

"That kind of passion is important in a case, as long as you don't let it blind-side you." She paused for a moment, her lips pressed together. Finally, she said, "I'm in the middle of an investigation into pre-Colombian art that may be moving through Miami," she said. "So my plate is full. But I'd be happy to mentor you if you want to look into this situation. As long as you have Vito's OK."

I was excited. I felt a visceral connection to this case, and not just because I wanted to help Tom Laughlin get into a relationship with Frank Sena. Like I said to Special Agent Washington, the gay connection mattered to me, as it had in several other cases I'd worked.

"Vito sent me to talk to you, but I'll verify with him tomorrow. What would I need to do to get started?"

"First thing is to get up to speed on the period when the painting was created, and the painting itself. For example, there may be details provided by this intermediary that don't ring true. You know anything about art?"

"I took one art history course in college, but that was years ago."

"They have a good art history department at FIU. Call over there, see if you can talk to one of the professors. Get him or her give you some quick basics. Go online, learn about the painter, and the group he belonged to. Research past auction prices, where his other work is held—is it in museums? Private collections? Anything up for sale right now? You're going to need a whole dossier. And get copies of all this gentleman's documentation."

I was staggered by how much I had to learn. "I have everything except a copy of the 8-millimeter movie. You want me to report back to you when I've got the information?"

"Call it liaise rather than report back," she said. "We're not doing anything official at the moment. Though it's not often violent, for the

FBI's purposes art theft does fall under Violent Crime, so it shouldn't be that great a stretch for you to spend some time on this if Vito doesn't need you. But before you do anything else, forward me the documentation you have. Let's make sure we're starting from good intel."

Chapter 5

Hiding in the Bushes

Early the next morning, I had a Skype call scheduled with my brother Danny, who was on a summer study program in Florence. Because Italy was six hours ahead of Miami, I'd been having trouble connecting with him in the evenings. So as soon as I woke, I turned on my computer. We'd be able to talk while he was on a lunch break from his classes.

As I waited for the Skype software to initialize, I thought about the art theft case. I was intrigued to learn about a different kind of crime, and interested in learning more about art and art crimes because it tied in with Danny's interests. He was a rising senior at Penn State, majoring in art history with a minor in Italian. Both not very useful degrees career-wise, but I was happy he'd found something he enjoyed. And I knew from my own experience that as long as you knew how to read, think and communicate you could eventually find a path that suited you.

He'd tried to convince me to come join him at the end of his course and spend a week traveling around Italy together, but my student loan debt put the kibosh on that idea, even though I very much wanted to see him, and to travel to some of the exotic places I'd learned about from our dad.

When I was a boy, I used to sit on my father's lap and look through the atlas with him, and he'd point out all the exotic places he wanted to go someday. Pitcairn Island in the South Pacific, where the Bounty mutineers had landed. Mount Kilimanjaro in Africa, Red Square in Moscow. He loved places that had a history to them, places so different from Scranton, Pennsylvania, where he'd lived his whole life.

He'd never gotten to travel, though; he was always working to support us until he died when I was ten. Those memories were all I had of my father, along with a bunch of photographs my mother had saved, from his childhood and the years they'd been married. When I was a teenager I used to stare at those photos, forcing myself to remember the few moments we had shared together. He was a big man, tall and broad-shouldered, with dark hair and eyes, and every year I struggled to hold on to those fading memories.

Danny and I took after our mother, with her slim build and fair coloring, though Danny had our father's cleft chin. To keep his memory alive, I'd tried to position myself for the kind of adventurous life he'd longed to lead. And now that I had the chance to head to a foreign locale, I was stuck financially just the way my father had been.

I was determined to be upbeat when I spoke to Danny. I'd only spoken to him once before through Skype – between the time difference and his classes and my work schedule, it was hard to connect, especially as he didn't have Wi-Fi in the student apartment he was sharing with three other guys. Instead, we'd exchanged long emails.

My heart felt good when his face appeared on the screen. Danny looked a lot like me, though his hair was more gold than red, but we had the same square face, slim nose and dimpled cheeks. He'd gotten a bit of a tan and he was smiling broadly.

"Hey, bro. How's it going with that gorgeous Italian girl you've been crushing on?"

"I asked her out last week, but she shot me down. Has a boyfriend. But the good news is that I was totally able to communicate with her in Italian."

"I'm jealous," I said. "You can flirt in two languages now."

"You bet. Too bad I'm leaving here in two weeks."

I was delighted to feel he was finding his bliss. I'd struggled and sacrificed to make sure that Danny had what he needed when we were growing up, working two jobs in high school and college, buying him clothes that our mom and step-dad wouldn't, making sure he could go on school trips and had the entrance fees for Penn State. Seeing him happy made it all worthwhile.

"How are things with your boyfriend?" Danny asked.

"Lester? All good. We spent some quality time over the weekend, though he left today for a whiskey competition in California, so I won't see him for a while."

We talked for almost a half hour. I asked if he'd ever heard of Mauricio Fabre or the Macchiaioli. "Too recent for anything we're studying here," Danny said. "You have to be dead for at least a couple of hundred years to make it into our curriculum. But I can ask my professor if you want."

I said I'd email him the details, and told him about my visit to the flea market to track down counterfeit goods.

"The other day I was walking down the street and this guy was wearing a T-shirt that read 'University of Princeton,'" Danny said. "Like, he had no clue it was a fake. Just loved that it was American."

We finally ended the call. "I have a few days' vacation coming to me," I said. "Maybe I'll come up to Penn State and see you when you get back." That ought to be a cheap trip, especially if I flew to Philadelphia and then took the bus to State College, in the geographic center of Pennsylvania.

"That would be terrific, Angus. I haven't seen you in person since you left for Florida."

I agreed. It had been nearly a year, too long, and I missed him.

We ended the call, I showered and hurried to work, where I went over to Vito's office as soon as I could. I felt like an eager puppy dog—can I work with Miriam Washington? Can I, can I please? I had to rein myself in. I was a Federal agent, after all. I had been through Quantico. I'd had major roles to play in two big operations.

Before I could ask, though, he said, "I got permission to bring you into the loop about Venable," he said, as he motioned me to the seat across from him. "What do you know about Turkey?"

"The country? Or the Thanksgiving centerpiece?"

"Wiseass," he said, but there was no heat behind his words. "Right now, Turkey is number two in the world in the production of counterfeit goods, with a market of over ten billion dollars."

"Wow. I had no idea Turkey was involved to that degree."

"And unlike the shit they make in China, a fake Rolex will have a ceramic bezel, sapphire glass, stainless steel, a quality band, and a Japanese movement, all of it assembled in Turkey. In the bazaars in Istanbul, they make a practice of charging at least ten percent of retail because they have the quality."

"And you think Jesse Venable is importing these fake watches?"

"That's the intel I have. Turkey's a tough place right now," Vito said. "Lots of refugees from Syria and other trouble spots flooding in, looking for transportation to Greece. Looks like the guys who smuggle the watches are getting in on the lucrative business of smuggling refugees, since they already have the connections and the boats."

He shifted his computer screen so I could see the picture on it. A small boat was wrecked on the shore of what looked like an island. "Fifty Syrian refugees and twelve cartons of counterfeit watches were on this boat when it sank," he said. "Only two men survived, both of them passengers who were lucky enough to get free of the wreck and have the strength to swim to safety."

I didn't know what to say. Sure, I saw images like this on the news regularly, but they'd been so removed from anything encountered in my daily life.

"One of the guys who survived was smart enough to grab something from the boat to use as a bargaining chip with the authorities who showed up."

"What?"

"A shipment manifest for those twelve cartons of watches. Want to make a guess where they were destined?"

"The United States?"

"Keep going."

"Florida? Miami? Fort Lauderdale?"

"You're a sharp guy when you use your brain instead of running your mouth," Vito said. "Yeah, there was paperwork that indicated the watches were headed here. Of course, there's no name or street address. That would make it too easy."

"But you think they were going to Venable?"

"We suspect he received a similar shipment last year, but couldn't make anything stick. He's a very slippery fellow." He looked up at me. "What did Miriam Washington say last night?"

"She's willing to mentor me as I look for the stolen painting, as long as it's okay with you."

He nodded. "I want to go after Venable with everything we've got. We catch him with this stolen painting, then maybe we leverage him for information on these smugglers. Stop the flow of watches." He waited a beat. "And make a connection to these refugee smugglers that can save some lives while we're at it."

I let that sink in for a minute. I wasn't just looking for a single stolen painting to help Frank Sena. Whatever I discovered could save lives, too.

I had learned early on that any investigation the Bureau took on was an important one, even if I didn't fully understand the reasons. Every innocent victim needed to be helped, every criminal needed to be prosecuted.

Of course, the lines were never that clear, and I was learning to use my own judgment. But saving lives? That trumped everything.

As I walked back to my office, I felt a new urgency. I followed Miriam's suggestion and called the Department of Art + Art History at FIU. I introduced myself to the secretary and explained I was looking for a professor who knew something about Italian art from the late nineteenth century. "Closest we can probably come is Professor Jose Barry," she said. "He teaches our art history survey courses, so he has a pretty broad knowledge. He has office hours tomorrow afternoon from two to four." She gave me his office address, on the second floor of a building called Viertes Haus, or VH.

I was curious to learn as much as I could about the incident that Vito had mentioned, the crash of the boat carrying Syrian refugees from Turkey to Greece. I looked online and I was horrified to see how many similar incidents there were. People were paying over a thousand dollars each to cross the Aegean Sea. The winter months were particularly treacherous, and more than three hundred sixty people had lost their lives on such trips.

My roommate Jonas texted me as I searched, asking if I'd meet him at the gym after work, and I agreed.

When I went back to my search, I couldn't find any mention of an incident that combined smuggling goods with people in any of the mainstream media. I was frustrated, following every link I found through Google, Facebook and Twitter, until I stumbled on a gay news site that focused on international issues. There I read about a man named Elyas Ahmadi, who had dared to come out to a circle of family and friends in Damascus, where homosexuality was illegal and punishable by imprisonment, and ISIS rebels in the country had been videoed throwing gay men off buildings.

Someone had told the police about him, and Ahmadi had been arrested and tortured. He was released when his family and friends raised enough money to buy him away from the police, and then pay smugglers to get him to Turkey, and then onto a boat to Greece.

The boat had been hit by bad weather, however, and had crashed on a rocky shore. Ahmadi was one of only two men to survive.

Survival is a Dying Art

So far the details matched. Why hadn't Vito mentioned that the man who survived was gay? He certainly knew that I was.

However, his sexuality didn't matter to Vito, as long as Ahmadi had that manifest of stolen goods. I wasn't a hundred percent sure it was the same boat, because there was no mention in the article about any stolen watches on board. Ahmadi had been shipped to a detention camp on one of the Greek islands, hoping to establish an asylum claim based on his persecution in Syria and a fear for his life if he returned.

I shut down my computer for the night and drove home, thinking about how lucky I was to live in a country where I could be open about my sexuality. Sometimes life in Wilton Manors took a frivolous turn, with strippers and X-rated movie launches, and it was easy then to ignore those who lived in less tolerant places.

Jonas and I belonged to a gay gym a short drive from our house, and as I drove him there he bubbled over with excitement about his new boyfriend. "He's a phlebotomist, which is like one step removed from being a doctor. He knows so much about medicine and anatomy and all that stuff."

I knew that phlebotomist was a fancy name for someone who took your blood in a doctor's office, spending the day wrapping rubber bands around upper arms and asking you to squeeze a rubber ball. Not exactly life-saving, but I let Jonas have his moment. When I met him, he'd been overweight and perpetually sad-faced, the kind of guy other gay men avoided for fear his attitude might be catching.

With his shambling gait, the extra pounds that still remained on his waistline, and the hair already starting to sprout from his ears, he wasn't a catch, but in the last six months, he'd begun to work out more regularly, he'd lost some weight and gained some self-confidence. If the phlebotomist was helping with that, more power to him.

We worked the circuit more slowly than I would with Lester, stopping to comment on cute guys, and then we went out for sushi together. "What's up with you these days?" Jonas asked over rainbow and shrimp tempura rolls.

I told him about seeing Lester over the weekend, my call with Danny that morning, and the chance to get onto a new case at work. Of course I couldn't give him too many details, but he was more interested in talking about himself anyway.

I wondered how much longer we would live together. When I was assigned to the Miami office, I'd looked around for a gay neighborhood where I could live, and I'd landed in Wilton Manors, which wrapped around the western side of Fort Lauderdale. Or, as someone had told me, it hugged Fort Lauderdale's ass.

The house I shared with Jonas was a run-down ranch in a rapidly gentrifying part of town. The huge oak tree in the front yard kept the grass from growing, and the walls were painted puke green, but it was home. Our lease would be up at the end of the summer, and I assumed we'd have the chance to renew if we wanted. Our rent would probably go up a lot, if the landlord didn't sell the place as a tear-down.

But if Jonas was moving on with his blood-taking boyfriend, would that mean I'd be on my own? Was it too soon to consider moving in with Lester?

It was too much to consider, on top of my usual worries about paying my down my student loans, keeping things going with Lester, and doing a good job at work, so I pushed the idea away to focus on when I had to.

When Jonas and I got home, he went into his room to call his boyfriend, and I pulled out the big hard-bound text from my one college class in art history. There wasn't more than a couple of paragraphs about the Macchiaioli, all of which I already knew, but I did read some more about the Impressionists, and got some insights from that into what the Macchiaioli were trying to do.

The next morning, I had some follow up work to do on the Male Power case, and when I finished that I checked in with Miriam Washington. I found her in an office on the other side of the building. She wore another smartly tailored suit, this one in a navy blue, and a gold filigree necklace in complicated pattern that looked like it had been made by an artist.

Photos of famous paintings and other artwork were on her walls. "All of these stolen?" I asked, as I sat down across from her.

"Some recovered, others still in the wind," she said. "Vito agreed to let you work with me for a while?"

"He did. I did some research on the artist, the painting and the movement, and I have an appointment at FIU this afternoon with an art history professor."

"I did some checking myself," Miriam said. "If Venable really has a line on this painting, it's very interesting to officials here and in Italy. And I understand Vito has an interest in Venable, too, so we need to move very carefully."

I agreed to check back with her after I'd met with Professor Barry. Then I drove south to the FIU campus.

It was my first time there, and it took me a while to get my bearings. I discovered that Viertes Haus was German for "fourth house." Seemed weird to me, as I was looking for information on Italian art, but I went with the flow.

I found Dr. Barry's office and waited until he was finished with the student he was speaking with, a young woman with black hair streaked with neon green. When she left I stepped up and introduced myself.

Dr. Barry was a rotund guy in his mid-forties, and his office was decorated with Haitian landscapes in lively primary colors. I explained that I needed a crash course in the Macchiaioli because I was helping on an investigation into a painting from that group that had surfaced after years being missing.

"I read about them online," I said. "I know they were a group of Italian painters active in Tuscany in the second half of the nineteenth century, and I've read they were the Italian equivalent of the Impressionists, because they liked to paint outside. But I'd like to know a little more about them, and about one particular painter named Mauricio Fabre."

"I can tell you what I know," he said. "And then I can refer you to some sources." He sat back in his chair. "Let's start with some Italian history. Back in the 1800s, the northern provinces were under the control of Austria, and the Italians staged a series of revolutionary actions to retrieve control of their territory."

"Was that the Risorgimento?" I asked.

He nodded. "You know your history. Good start. Many of the artists who became part of the Macchiaioli had fought in various battles toward the unification of Italy, so that gave them more of a political bent than the Impressionists, and they brought that revolutionary outlook to their art. They felt a responsibility to reinvigorate Italian art and bring it back to the prominence of some of the old masters."

"Was Fabre one of those revolutionaries?"

"I'm not familiar enough with his background to say," Barry said.

"What about the name of the movement. Was that a revolutionary term?"

"The word '*macchie*' means patches or spots in Italian, and the Macchiaioli believed that little spots of light and shadow were the chief components of a work of art."

"Like the French pointillists," I said.

He nodded. "*Macchia* was commonly used by Italian artists and critics in the nineteenth century to describe the sparkling quality of a drawing or painting, so it was logical that the name would stick to them. Like the Impressionists, they weren't exactly welcomed by the powers that be, and they were ridiculed, and their early works received hostile reviews."

A student hovered in the doorway of Professor Barry's office, this one a skinny boy in drooping board shorts and an FIU T-shirt.

"Thanks for your help," I said to Dr. Barry. "Can you suggest any places I could go to look for more information?"

"There's a database called Oxford Art Online," he said. "You can get into it from the library here. They'll have more information on the Macchiaioli and on Fabre."

Survival is a Dying Art

I left Barry's office even more energized. I was going to learn everything I needed to know about this movement, this painting and this artist in order to get Frank Sena his uncle's painting back, then trap Jesse Venable and force him to tell us everything he knew about the smuggling of watches and immigrants.

Chapter 6
Agent Asshole

I ducked into the student union building to get a cold drink, and walked into the middle of some kind of summer festival. One student club was selling used junk for a fund-raising project, a number of vendors sold merchandise from silver rings to T-shirts, and the advising department was giving away literature on career options.

As I browsed, I spotted a display of Armani Exchange T-shirts in a variety of colors and sizes, and I was immediately suspicious. First-quality T-shirts went for fifty to sixty dollars, and these were on sale for ten bucks apiece. I picked one up, and it didn't feel like the quality I would have expected—the fabric was thinner and the label on the inside was held on only by a single thread.

They could be seconds, I reminded myself. Not necessarily counterfeit.

A South Asian girl with flowing brown hair picked up a shirt with the Armani eagle spanning the entire front. "Wow! These are cheap. Are they real?"

"No, they're imaginary," the woman behind the table said, without looking up from the laptop she was focused on. "And I'm a unicorn." Her blonde hair was pulled into a scrunchie, and her FIU-logo T shirt, with a growling panther leaping across the front, was wrinkled and spotted with some kind of stain. A baby of about a year old slept in a stroller beside her.

The South Asian girl snorted, but she couldn't seem to resist a bargain, and she slapped a ten-dollar bill on the table and walked away with a bright orange shirt.

A boy in a T-shirt that read *Team Fuck It Up* bought two shirts while I browsed, and the woman barely looked up. I remembered something I'd learned while researching fake Armani products for Vito, and I stepped away and pulled up a site on my phone. Sure enough, Armani Exchange was a separate brand, and never used the eagle with its wings spread, and certainly never with A|X on it instead of GA.

I went back to the table. "Good afternoon," I said. I pulled out my badge to show her but she didn't even look up, her head bowed as if she was zoned out.

"Whatever. You want a shirt, they're ten bucks."

"I don't want a shirt. And I don't want you to sell this counterfeit crap."

She finally looked up and saw my badge. "Who are you?"

"Read the badge, ma'am. Special Agent Angus Green from the FBI. I need you to shut down your operation immediately."

"The FBI? You've got to be kidding me."

"I assure you, I'm not kidding."

A group of students had gathered around to watch our interaction. The woman closed her laptop and stepped up to me. "Can I talk to you?" she asked. "Privately?"

I stepped around behind the table. "Look, I'm in a real bind," she said. "I teach at the community college, and we don't get maternity leave, so I registered for a sabbatical when I got pregnant. They never used to care if you published anything or came up with new teaching methods, so I didn't think twice."

I had no idea what her pregnancy and sabbatical had to do with fake T-shirts, but I listened.

"When I came back from my semester off, suddenly they were all 'what did you do to enhance student success while you were on sabbatical.' Like anything we do can help our students succeed when they don't give two shits about literature or writing essays."

"How does that connect to these shirts?"

"They garnished my salary to pay back the sabbatical leave money," she said, as if I was stupid and not following her. "And with a new baby I couldn't afford to lose that income. So my brother-in-law got me a couple of shipments of these shirts and I go around to fairs and sell them."

"But you know they're fake?"

"Of course. Where are you going to get a genuine Armani Exchange T-shirt for ten bucks? These students are as stupid as the ones at my college."

The little girl in the stroller woke up and started to cry. "It's just too much," the woman said, as she picked up the baby. "I have to teach the entire summer at slave wages and I still won't have paid back the money until sometime next year. It's not fair. I should have gotten paid maternity leave. Then I wouldn't be in this situation."

I felt sorry for the woman. It was obvious she was in a tough situation. But I couldn't ignore the way she was breaking the law, deceiving innocent students with shoddy merchandise, and cheating the manufacturer out of legitimate profits.

"Here's what I can do," I said. "You pack up and leave, and I won't have you arrested."

She opened her mouth to protest, then shut it again. "Fine. You're just another cog in the corporate oligarchy that is running this country into the ground. Asshole."

"Agent Asshole, if you please," I said. She put the baby back in her stroller and pulled a couple of boxes from beneath the table. I would have offered to help her pack up if she hadn't been such a bitch. Instead I watched as she packed, then carted the boxes out to her Lexus. Yeah, cry me a river about the money you cheated your employer out of.

As she backed away, she gave me the finger. I took down her license plate, and when I got back to the office that afternoon, I checked her out. She had been telling the truth, at least as far as her job at the community college.

"You've got good instincts, Angus," Vito said, when I stopped by his office to tell him about the incident. "She's small potatoes, but give me her information and I'll bring her in and question her. Maybe this brother-in-law of hers is a bigger fish, or can lead me somewhere."

"You don't want me to handle it?"

"You stick to this art case. I need anything you can get me on Venable."

"I had one more idea," I said. "A couple of weeks ago I found a gold bracelet with a broken clasp in a parking lot. I was thinking I'd take it in to one of Venable's Golden Ticket shops and see what his operation is like."

"If you want. Just don't do anything to spook him. We need to play the line out for a while, see what we can catch. And make sure when you write up your report that you note that the bracelet is yours, so the Bureau doesn't try to collect the money back from you."

Back at my office, I checked the price of gold. There had been a lot of fluctuation over the past couple of years, but it was close to its all-time high, over thirteen hundred dollars an ounce. I was excited at what my bracelet might bring, but when I checked the Golden Ticket website I realized I wouldn't get anywhere near that. The bracelet I had was fourteen karat, and pretty lightweight—light enough that the woman wearing it wouldn't have noticed it fell off when the clasp broke. So I wasn't going to get rich.

There was a Golden Ticket outlet on Sunrise Boulevard, not far from my house. I stopped at home, where I changed into shorts and a polo shirt, and then took the bracelet to the store, in a small strip mall. I was buzzed in by a uniformed guard, and the bracelet was weighed on a digital scale. The guy I dealt with showed me how much it weighed, then calculated what he could pay me. "A hundred twenty dollars," he said, and I agreed.

I had to provide my driver's license, which they photocopied, then sign a form and include a thumbprint, and then the man I dealt with went into the back to get the cash from the safe. I walked out happily, though I wondered how legitimate the operation was. I could have given them a fake license, for example. Did anyone check their records on the back end? Was there a way I could?

That would require a subpoena, of course. And in order to get one of those, I'd need to demonstrate evidence that a fraud was going on. Couldn't do that with what I had, so it looked like I'd need a golden ticket of my own before that would happen.

Chapter 7

An Important Work

Thursday morning I met with Miriam Washington. "I've been researching the painting and the artist, as you suggested, and yesterday I met with a professor at FIU to get his input."

"Ah yes, academia. There but for the grace of God go I."

"You have a PhD yourself," I said. "You ever think about academia? Should I call you Dr. Washington?"

"Please don't. I always worry someone will get confused and expect me to perform CPR or an emergency tracheotomy."

I laughed.

"My father's a minister and my mother's an elementary school teacher, and they wanted me to teach—they thought it was a safe, solid career. Needless to say they're not thrilled I carry a gun and track down criminals."

She sat back in her chair. "I wanted something more. I just didn't know what at first. While I was in graduate school I worked part-time at a gallery on Newbury Street in Boston. It was an elegant place, very high-end work, and I learned a lot about the business of art there. At one point, an agent from the Art Crimes Team came in to ask about a stolen painting he was tracking, and he and I had a great conversation. He suggested that I consider the Bureau."

"And you did?"

"Not right away. At the time, I just laughed. A black girl with a PhD in art history working as a Special Agent? The idea was ludicrous. Then I got a teaching assistantship and began working with undergraduates. After a few semesters of that the FBI looked better and better. I went back to that agent I'd met, and he mentored me, and here I am."

She went back to her computer. "Speaking of mentoring, let's look at the painting together. You're going to need some art smarts in order to carry off an interest that will get you the information you need."

She brought up a photo of a bronze sculpture on her screen, then angled it so I could see. "Look at this and tell me what you see."

"A naked man?"

"Yes. But what else?"

I leaned in close. "It's very sensual, isn't it?" I asked. "It's bronze, right? The bronze is so smooth it's almost like flesh."

"Good. Go on."

"The pose reminds me a little of the painting, *Ragazzi al Mare*. The guy on the left side of the scene, looking down at the other guys on the beach."

"As well it should," she said. "You have a good eye, Angus. This is Donatello's David, after his defeat of Goliath. This is actually the first free-standing male nude statue of the Renaissance. It embodies, literally, the revival of ancient Greece and Rome."

"So by mimicking the pose Fabre is trying to evoke that statue?"

"Absolutely. And what else?"

I thought for a moment. "If the Macchiaioli were trying to return to the era when Italian painting was dominant, then the painting is making a political statement, too, isn't it? Calling back to that classical form, but with new technique."

She nodded. "So you see why this is an important work. It's not just a pretty scene of good-looking naked men at the beach. It helps us understand Fabre, and the Macchiaioli movement."

"Which means that it's worth our while to recover it," I said.

"Exactly."

She pulled up the database of stolen art. "Here's the information on the painting," she said. "Painted in 1862, last known sale was to a man named Ugo Sena in Venice in 1941."

She hit a couple of keys on her keyboard and I saw the PDF Frank Sena had sent me, which I'd forwarded to her. "The paperwork your Mr. Sena provided matches that. According to the record, the painting was confiscated from Ugo Sena by the Nazis and stored at a church called Beata Vergine della Laguna, the Blessed Virgin of the Lagoon, on the Calle Ghetto Vecchio in Venice. It was coded JVV243. That means it was the 243rd piece of art confiscated from Venetian Jews – *Juden von Venedig*."

I had a brief shiver of recognition – the first two letters of the code matched Jesse Venable's initials. That led me to consider Frank Sena's uncle Ugo, losing everything he cared about, then being sent to a concentration camp and consigned to death. At the least the Syrian refugee who'd gotten off the sinking ship with the list of counterfeit watches had been able to escape with his life, even if just barely.

It made me that much more determined to get the painting back for Frank Sena – and at the same time, I hoped, prevent others from suffering the same fate as Ugo Sena and all those refugees fleeing war or discrimination.

Friday morning, I went for a long run around the neighborhood. I'd gotten accustomed to running with Lester, and I missed him. What did the cards hold in our future? I'd been a serial monogamist through college, dating guys who caught my fancy until the spark died out. My connection with Lester seemed deeper than any I'd had before, and I knew that I had to nurture it or it could fade away.

I spent the morning in a meeting with a few dozen other agents from the Violent Crime Task Force, as Vito shared the newest crime statistics in our region, which ran from Key West to Fort Pierce.

When we finally broke for lunch, I walked up to him, curious to show him I'd been able to find out the refugee's name without him giving it to me.

"Did Ahmadi give you anything more than just the manifest?"

"Who?"

I pushed forward. "Elyas Ahmadi. The gay Syrian activist who survived the boat crash."

Vito leaned forward. "How did you find his name? We haven't released any information on him."

"I did some research, found an article about a gay Syrian who survived a boat crash. The details seemed to match, but there was nothing in the article about counterfeit goods."

"Remind me never to play poker with you," Vito said. "You're a damn good bluffer. Yes, Mr. Ahmadi is the one who provided us with the manifest. In exchange for asylum, he also gave up the contact in Istanbul who arranged the trip."

"Where is he now?"

"Officially? In a camp in Greece. Unofficially, he's already been relocated to Amsterdam and given a new identity. His information led to the shutdown of a network of immigrant smugglers. Unfortunately, he didn't know anything about the watches."

"What's happening to refugees now? There have to be other smugglers, right?"

"Above my pay grade. All I'm focusing on, and you by extension, is making a connection between those smuggled watches and Jesse Venable." He glared at me. "Keep that in mind, Agent Green."

"I will."

I walked back to my office, thinking about the different dimensions of this case. Miriam had said that I'd have to sound knowledgeable about the painting. Was she assuming that at some point I'd have to meet with Venable myself and convince him? How would I? I couldn't reveal that I was an FBI agent; that would make him shut right up.

Could I meld my background with my brother Danny's? Say I

was an accountant—which was true. And that I worked for various clients, also true. After moving to Florida, I had begun to pick up a few freelance accounting clients, mostly gay guys I met through the bars who needed some help with paperwork and tax filing. I'd been filtering a lot of I made from them to Danny, to help with the cost of his summer in Italy, but once he was back at Penn State I might be able to use the money to pay my student loans down faster.

I could add in that I'd taken a bunch of art history courses in college, which was why Frank Sena had asked for my advice. I was sure I could get Frank to say that he hired me for some accounting work.

I had no undercover experience – but I knew someone who did. I'd worked with Special Agent Katya Gordieva on a previous case and she and I had become friends. With her experience digging into the Russian mafia while pretending to be a real estate agent, she'd be the perfect person to help me understand what I had to do.

I texted her and asked if she was available for drinks or dinner over the weekend, and while I waited to hear back from her, I looked up the Central Database of Holocaust Victims run by the Yad Vashem organization. There were over fifty pages of people with similar names, and it took a while until I found Ugo Sena's name on page forty.

Ugo Sena was born in Venice, Italy to Leone and Elena nee Richetti. He was a bachelor. During the war he was in Auschwitz, Poland. He was murdered in the Shoah. This information is based on a Page of Testimony submitted by his brother, Carlo Sena.

The simplicity of the report was horrifying. A person's life and death reduced to a few lines. And there were fifty pages of people with similar names.

It took me a couple of minutes to take all that in. I'd studied World War II, knew that millions had died, but it became more real to me seeing those names. Which I guessed was the purpose of the list.

I assumed that Carlo Sena was Frank's father, but wanted to verify it anyway. I found his name in a list of donations Frank had made to a gay synagogue in Fort Lauderdale, "In memory of Leone, Elena, Carlo, Rebecca and Ugo Sena." The only unfamiliar name was Rebecca, and I assumed that was Frank's mother.

I went back to the collection of text messages between Frank and Venable that Frank had sent me. Venable was very cagey—he never indicated that he had the painting or knew anything about his history. Just that he had an online contact who had listed the painting for sale along with a number of others. The vendor was cagey about dealing with people he didn't know, so for a fee, Venable could be Frank's intermediary, arranging to purchase the painting and have it shipped to the United States.

That was where Frank had left things. Venable never mentioned his pawn shop, his gold buyer business or his booth at Trader Tom's, never offered to throw in a very good fake Rolex made in Turkey.

Clues were falling into place. Everything that Frank Sena had told me so far was true. The painting was an important and valuable one, and Venable was connected to it. Could I leverage all of that to get Frank his painting back and put Venable in a position where he'd be willing to trade information about the smugglers for a lesser sentence, or his own freedom?

Chapter 8

A Little Excitement

I t was the end of the day before I got a text from Katya saying she was free that evening. Instead of sending texts ping-ponging back and forth, I called her. I can be old-school like that sometimes.

She was still living in Sunny Isles Beach, where her case had been centered, so we agreed to meet at a bar at the race track in Hallandale, halfway between her place and mine. An hour later, I drove in to the complex past a giant statue of Pegasus slaying a dragon. Working for the Bureau I felt like that big horse sometimes, my wings outstretched and a villain under my hoof.

Not that often, though.

Stores and restaurants had been built on either side of the grandstand, all of it in the faux Mediterranean style that was everywhere in South Florida. I parked in the garage and kept to the shady side of the street as I walked over to the bar. Though it was early evening, the sun was sharp, the temperature in the eighties and the humidity high.

I took a seat as far from the big TV screens as I could get, ordered a draft of raspberry wheat beer, and turned to the door to wait for Katya Gordieva.

She was a beautiful woman with fair skin, honey blonde hair and a luscious figure, and several men at the bar looked up when she walked in. She had been a special agent not much longer than I had, first in an undercover operation among the Russian Mafia in New York, then a similar one in Sunny Isles Beach.

We hugged and kissed, and she settled onto a bar stool beside me. After she'd ordered a vodka tonic, she turned to me. "I hope you have something entertaining to talk about, because I'm bored. Working in the office isn't as interesting or challenging as being out in the field."

"That's what I wanted to ask about," I said. "I may have an opportunity to go undercover and I need your advice."

"Dish," she said, as she lifted the highball glass to her lips.

I told her about Jesse Venable, the pawn shops and the flea market booth, and the painting confiscated by the Nazis. "I want to be Frank Sena's intermediary with Venable and see if I can get him arrested for dealing in stolen art. Then Vito can leverage him for information about the counterfeit watches and the immigrant smuggling."

"Your goal in an undercover operation is to gain the trust of the people you're investigating," Katya said. "And then betray that trust by using what you've learned from them to arrest and incarcerate them."

"You make it sound so attractive," I said. "But it's not really that personal, is it?"

"Of course it is. Imagine one of your friends—your roommate, for example. Suppose you discover that he's doing something illegal. Do you report him?"

"That depends, doesn't it? If he killed somebody, then I don't have much choice. But if I find out he's selling some coke on the side for extra money? I talk to him, convince him to stop before he gets in too deep."

"Sadly, it's not that easy," she said. "What if you end up liking this Venable guy? Say he's had a hard life, he's got a sob story. You understand why he's doing what he does. You have to remember your job isn't to be his friend—your job is to collect enough evidence to arrest him."

I didn't like the idea, but I knew what I had to say. "My first loyalty has to be to the Bureau. Even if what I do hurts someone I like."

I remembered a previous case, where I'd had to arrest two men whose motivation I understood, even sympathized with. It had been a difficult situation, and I still felt bad for both of them, and the way their desperation had driven them to commit dangerous acts.

She finished her drink. "Another round?"

"How about dinner with that?" I asked, and we moved to a booth in the back.

After we'd ordered, she said, "You're going to need some basics before you get started. A cover story, business cards, a website. You want him to be able to find you online if he looks you up to check you out."

"I can put all that together," I said. "I'm thinking that I could say that Frank Sena is one of my accounting clients and he's asked me to help him out with this."

"Why? It's not an accounting problem."

"I thought about combining my background with a bit of my brother's. I can say I'm an art lover, maybe even minored in art history in college. I can get Danny to help me out with any details I need."

"That's good, but again, it's only a start. You must have learned some basic undercover techniques at Quantico – I know I did."

I nodded. "And I used them last week." I told her about Trader Tom's Market. "But this is a longer game."

"It is. You're going to need to know your story inside and out. Let's start with the basics. How long have you been an accountant?"

I thought for a moment. Before I came out, I'd grown accustomed to providing only what my mother and stepfather needed to know, and I'd learned to stick as close to the truth as I could.

"I got my master's in accounting from Penn State four years ago.

Worked for an accounting firm in Philly, where I got my CPA. But I didn't like the corporate world so I decided to strike out on my own. I met a guy online who lived in Wilton Manors, and he offered me the chance to share his house and introduce me to some clients. So I made the move about a year ago."

She nodded. "Good. That's close enough to your real story." She asked me a bunch more questions, including some I hadn't thought about, like how my sexuality had worked into my decisions. "This guy you met online, are you going to say you dated him?"

I shook my head. "But I knew that Wilton Manors would be a comfortable place for an openly gay accountant."

Then our food arrived, and as we ate, she told me how she'd gotten started undercover. "I had to get my real estate license in New York and actually work for a broker in order to make my cover stick," she said. "I stuck as close as possible to my real story – the bachelor's in Russian, then law school. I said that I was struggling to pass the bar and needed to make some money while I studied."

"But you had already passed the bar under your real name, right?"

She nodded. "The Bureau arranged for my mother's maiden name on my license, and gave me all the backup documentation I needed. You're going to need some of that too—a driver's license, a couple of credit cards. Your cover has to be deep enough. Talk to Wagon – he put together some great stuff for me."

I hadn't been aware that in addition to all his other skills, Wagon also manufactured fake IDs, but it made sense that agents would need those in undercover cases.

Katya and I walked through a couple of scenarios. What if Venable offered me marijuana or cocaine? Just say no. If he asked me to do anything illegal? I'd fall back on the need to maintain my CPA. A single client, no matter how lucrative, wasn't worth risking the loss of my professional credentials.

We split a massive ice cream sundae, and I paid the bill. "Thanks so much for meeting me," I said. "I feel a lot more comfortable about this gig now."

"No problem. It was fun. And if you need a beard for any reason, feel free to call on me. I could use a little excitement in my life."

Yeah, that was why I'd joined the Bureau. I'd learned, however, that there was a fine line between a little excitement and way too much.

As I drove home, I thought about how I could put together an identity for Jesse Venable that wouldn't connect me to the Bureau. After dinner, I did a search for myself online. I Googled "Angus Green" and "FBI" and came up with nothing. That was good, not even on a friend's social media account. Then I uploaded a photo of my head to Google's image search feature and looked for matches.

There were a lot of good-looking redheaded guys out there online, but my photo only matched a couple of group shots at Lazy Dick's, the gay bar where I usually hung out. I'd take the chance that Venable wouldn't go so far as to check me out there. I'd had to come out as an FBI agent during a case the year before, but staff and clientele changed pretty quickly, and I'd have to take that risk.

A crook like Venable probably had access to less legitimate means of searching. I often used the first name Andrew because it was close enough to my own for casual use. If I wanted to be thorough I should probably stick to Angus. But my last name could go. Angus Black? Gray? Grant?

I decided to use Angus Gray. It was close enough to my real name that if I fumbled I could recover, and if anyone connected me to Green I could make an excuse and a joke.

Chapter 9
Wipeout

Saturday morning I used a simple website builder to put together a quick site for Angus Gray, CPA. I built a resume for myself that resembled my own in all but last name, starting with my degrees from Penn State. I expanded my public accounting work to cover the years I had spent in Philadelphia, and began my practice in Florida the same time I'd moved to town.

I listed my clients without reference to their names, and embellished a bit of what I had done for them. For the "about me" page I used a photo my brother had taken, and added that I was an art lover who had minored in art history and loved to frequent area museums. With a little fiddling, I was able to make it look like the site had been set up a year ago, which matched my cover story.

I set up a free email account under the name of Angus Gray and then sat back to consider what I'd created. It took me most of the day, and it wasn't perfect, but along with whatever Wagon could create for me, it was something I could sell.

Lester came back from California that night, and I met him at his apartment. We slept in Sunday morning, then went to the gym for a long workout. Over a lazy lunch, I added to what I'd already told him about the stolen painting and he nodded along. I realized I'd never asked him how he knew so much about art, so I did.

"The guy who owned the stables where my father worked commissioned paintings of all the horses who won for him and he showed them off to everyone," Lester said. "I even saw one of the paintings being created at the stable. And then when I was teaching phys ed in Kentucky I dated the art teacher, and we used to go to the Speed Art Museum in Louisville."

I noticed the way he pronounced the name of the city, Lou-a-ville, and it was the first time I ever hear him sound like he was from the south.

"How come you don't have a southern accent?" I asked.

"Because my parents weren't ignorant hillbillies," he said, with what sounded like a bit of resentment. "They were both educated people and they taught me to speak properly. And besides they were both from Ohio and only moved to Kentucky for my father's job."

I held up my hand. "Hey, sorry. I didn't mean to imply that all people with southern accents were ignorant."

"I know you didn't mean that. But it's just like having muscles, you know? People stereotype you a certain way. He has big biceps—he must be stupid."

"I don't see it that way. I figure a guy with big biceps has to be really determined and focused."

"Well, no offense, sweetheart, but you don't have them, so you don't get the attitude I do."

"There is some attitude I'd like to demonstrate to you," I said, smiling, and I snaked my arm around his neck and pulled him close for a kiss.

Lester stayed the night, and we both gave each other as much attitude as we got. In the morning I left him sleeping in my bed and drove to Miramar, where I wound my way through the serpentine hallways to the lab.

Wagon was working at a lab table in a warehouse bay. The floor-to-ceiling shelves were stocked with the tools of his trade, everything from fingerprint powder and brushes to ultraviolet lights.

Wagon was a pretty cool guy, if a bit nerdy, only a few years older than I was. "Katya Gordieva says you can help me with some ID documents," I said, when he was finished with what he was doing.

"What do you need?"

I explained what I was trying to do. "What can you give me?"

"We have the capacity to give you almost anything on paper – birth certificate, diploma, that kind of thing. I can get you a passport under this name as well, but that's going to take some extra time."

When I graduated from Penn State with my master's, I'd been given a laminated wallet-sized copy of my diploma, so I gave that to Wagon to make a copy. He took a couple of head shots to use for a license and other photo ID. "You'll need business cards, too," he said. He handed me a form. "Fill out what you want and I'll have them printed."

I got to choose from a couple of different basic designs, and picked one that I thought looked professional. Wagon gave me a post office box number I could use as my address, and I filled in the name of my website and my personal cell number.

Wagon said he'd have the materials for me the next day and I walked to Vito's office. "I'm putting together an alternate ID as a self-employed accountant," I said. "Angus Gray, CPA. Wagon's helping me with the documentation, and I got a primer on how to act undercover from Agent Gordieva. I want to get Frank Sena, the guy who Venable approached about the painting, to put me in touch."

"On what grounds?"

"My new background includes a minor in art history in college. In the course of helping Frank with his taxes, he mentions the painting and I agree to help him get it back."

"And how about this painting?" Vito asked. "You up to speed with it yet?"

"Working on it. I feel pretty comfortable with the artist, the period and the painting itself. Nowhere near an expert but I can bluff."

"Yeah, I learned that the other day," Vito said. "When are you going to put this in motion?"

"As soon as I get the documentation from Wagon. He says tomorrow."

When I got back to my office I called Tom Laughlin and explained what I planned to do. "You know Frank a lot better than I do," I said. "Do you think he can lie convincingly to Venable about me?"

Tom laughed. "You don't get to be as successful in business as Frank was without some ability to spin a line of bullshit and carry it through," he said. "And he's determined to get this painting back, so I think he'll do whatever he needs."

I worried about the 'line of bullshit' comment. "You think he's being honest with me? Venable lives here in Fort Lauderdale, so I need to be sure that Frank doesn't have some other grudge against him."

"I've spent some quality time with Frank lately—thanks in part to your willingness to help him, which I appreciate, by the way."

I figured 'quality time' was Tom's euphemism for the horizontal mambo, or whatever else two older guys with years of experience behind them could get up to in bed.

"And?"

"And he seems honest and open. So to answer both your questions, I believe he can do what you want him to do, and I also believe his motives are right out there in the open."

"Thanks, Tom. I'm glad things are working out for you with Frank."

"It's early days. One intimate encounter does not make a relationship. But I'm just as determined as Frank is when I see something I want."

I smiled, thanked Tom again, and called Frank. "You have to give him my name as Angus Gray, though, and you can't tell him that I work for the FBI. Just that I've done some accounting work for you, and because I know something about art, you want me to be involved in the transaction."

"I can do that. I'll reach out to Venable and get back to you."

While I waited for Frank and Wagon, I went back to Venable's operation at Trader Tom's. Was there anything else I could find about the booth that might help with the investigation into Venable?

I turned to my computer and combed through reviews on places like Yelp, looking for customers complaining about counterfeit goods, as well as articles in the local press and our own internal reports. Just in case something new had popped up, I went back to Google and searched for Trader Tom's.

The first link that popped up was a headline from the Fort Lauderdale *Sun-Sentinel*. "Margate man dies after motorcycle wipes out on the Sawgrass Expressway."

Why did that come up with a search for Trader Tom's? I clicked through to the article. The dead man was identified as Lawrence Kane, 28. "According to friends, Kane was returning from a part-time job at a call center, where he worked a late-night shift. He previously worked as a barista, a store clerk and at Trader Tom's flea market."

Whoa. Could Lawrence Kane be Larry, the guy I'd spoken to at Venable's booth? I didn't have anything more to go on than a hunch, but my spidey-senses were tingling.

There wasn't much more to the article beyond some statistics about motorcycle deaths. Kane hadn't been wearing a helmet; Florida law didn't require one. I imagined him taking down his man-bun and his long hair flowing behind him as he raced down the highway, and I shivered.

A search on Lawrence Kane through the FBI database came up empty. He'd either been a model citizen, or he'd evaded arrest. I knew one of the bartenders at Lazy Dick's, and that he had not protected his list of Facebook friends. I flipped through page after page of mostly men until I found a contact of his called Larry Kane.

Unfortunately, Larry's profile was pretty flimsy—a photo that focused more on his abs than his face, and a couple of check-ins at random bars. But evidence was building that I had flirted with a man who died soon after.

If I was right, then Kane's death was an additional piece of information in the dossier I was building on Jesse Venable. Maybe an irrelevant one, but I owed it to our brief connection to follow up on Kane's death and make sure it didn't have anything to do with my case.

I called my contact at the Broward County morgue, an assistant medical examiner named Maria Fleitas, and asked her to send me a photo of the dead man. "Not going to be pretty," she said. "His face was messed up. You should come over and see him."

I had been to the morgue too many times already, but I agreed. I hopped into my Mini Cooper: green, like my name, though if I said anything to Venable it would be that I'd chosen the color of money.

I followed a winding local road until I could get onto I-75, which ran beside our office in Miramar. It was a hot, humid July day, with ominous thunderclouds forming out over the Everglades. I got stuck behind a yard company truck zooming down the highway, and leaves and branches and bits of debris kept flying off the back of the truck at me.

I was glad when I could zip past the truck, turn east on I-595, and put my pedal to the metal. It seemed like wherever I wanted to go I had to take one highway or another, but at least it was better than getting stuck in stop and go traffic on local roads.

The Broward County Medical Examiner's office was headquartered in a collection of single-story buildings and trailers next to a sheriff's station, a few miles off the highway beyond the animal shelter and a Tri-Rail station.

Dr. Fleitas was a short Latina with shoulder-length dark hair, bangs, and funky red-framed glasses. She wore light-green scrubs under a lab coat with her name embroidered on the left breast. "Always a pleasure to see you, Agent Green," she said. "Though this time I already have an ID on my client. What's your interest in Mr. Kane?"

I could have said that I'd flirted with him at his job, but I didn't know Dr. Fleitas well enough to joke around with her. "I bought some counterfeit merchandise from a booth at Trader Tom's last week. I have a feeling Mr. Kane was the guy working there."

She didn't ask any further details, and I didn't volunteer any. I followed her to a refrigerated cooler, where she opened the door and bent down to check the ID on one bed-like shelf. Then she slid the shelf out and pulled down the sheet covering the face.

Larry Kane wasn't handsome any more. The right side of his face had been scraped on the pavement and though the bleeding had obviously stopped by then his face looked like it had been run through a meat grinder.

"This the guy?" Dr. Fleitas asked.

I gulped. His wasn't the first dead body I'd seen, but he was the first I'd flirted with. "It is. An accidental death?"

"Not my decision to make. A detective with the BSO's Traffic Homicide Unit is on the case." The Broward Sheriff's Office investigated crimes in unincorporated parts of the county.

She turned to a nearby computer and after tapping for a moment or two looked up at me. "The detective's name is Chancy Pierre. Right now there's no official verdict. But if you know something about Kane that might indicate it's not an accident, you ought to discuss it with Detective Pierre. I'll email you his contact information."

I said that I would, and thanked Dr. Fleitas for her time. When I got out to my car, I pulled up the information she'd sent me, and called Detective Pierre. I introduced myself and said, "What can you tell me about the motorcycle accident on the Sawgrass Expressway that killed Lawrence Kane?"

"What's the Bureau's interest in Kane's death?"

"Can we meet somewhere and I'll explain?"

"Just about to get my lunch," he said. "You know Big Poppa's Subs on Griffin Road west of the Turnpike?"

"I'm at the morgue now, so I'm sure I can find it."
"See you there in fifteen then," he said.

Chapter 10
Daily Entertainment

When I walked into the sub shop, a tall man with ebony skin and a shaved head hailed me. "You must be Agent Green," he said. "Detective Pierre."

He had a light accent and a strong grip. "What's good here?" I asked.

"You can't go wrong with a sub," he said. "They slice the meat for you, and all the toppings are fresh."

My mouth was already watering. "I haven't had a good hoagie since I moved here."

"Hoagie? You must be from Philadelphia."

"Scranton. But I lived in Philly for a couple of years after college." We talked casually as we waited for our sandwiches. He had lived in New York for a while, visited Philadelphia, liked the Liberty Bell.

I paid for both the sandwiches and our drinks and we walked over to a flimsy plastic table by the wall. "So," he said. "Mr. Lawrence Kane, motorcyclist, deceased."

I told him about my experience at Trader Tom's. "There was a fight between a vendor and a customer at a neighboring booth. The customer was angry that he'd been sold fake sneakers, and eventually he punched the vendor."

"Heard about that," Pierre said. "Ended up with an assault charge. Got to be careful where you shop these days."

"Mr. Kane was right there, and he looked pretty unhappy about what had happened. He shut the booth down right after that."

"And?" Pierre asked, between bites of his sub.

"I wondered if Mr. Kane challenged his boss over the counterfeit goods and wanted to quit," I said. "That maybe his accident wasn't an accident, if you know what I mean."

I took advantage of the time he put his thoughts together to bite into the sandwich, which I still insisted on calling a hoagie. Rare roast beef, bright green shreds of lettuce, a juicy slice of beefsteak tomato. A sprinkle of black olive bits and the tang of salt over it all. Heaven on a long roll.

"Sadly, I do," Pierre said. "I don't have much to tell you. It wasn't raining and the highway wasn't slick, so it's unlikely he slid out of control. I tracked the 911 call that reported the crash," Pierre said. "The man who called it in was traveling southbound, in the opposite direction of the motorcycle. He was the only one in his lane, and he saw the single headlight of the bike approaching, and a pair of headlights right behind it."

"He saw the accident?"

"He says that he saw the motorcycle veer off the road and the car behind it continue forward. He couldn't stop because there was no way to get over to the other lane, so he called 911."

"I assume he didn't have any information on the car."

"Can't even say if it was a car or an SUV," he said. "He was going seventy miles an hour and he was past the scene very quickly."

"Was the scene consistent with an accident?"

"I reviewed the skid pattern and checked the tires of the bike. My best educated guess is that a vehicle changed lanes in front of him, sending him into the skid. But without witnesses I can't say whether that was intentional or accidental."

"Have you spoken with any friends or family? Was he a careless rider? He wasn't wearing a helmet, right?"

"Not required in Florida," he said. "I spoke with his parents in a suburb outside Chicago. They were heartbroken, of course. His father said that Kane had an accident when he was much younger and that made him a very careful rider. His roommate agreed with that, said Kane would never ride while intoxicated and so on."

"I'd like to talk to the roommate," I said.

"His name is Paul Snyder, and he works at the same call center, lives off Commercial Boulevard between Sunrise and Tamarac. You can probably catch him now before he leaves for work."

Pierre texted me Snyder's phone number. "The owner of the booth is a guy named Jesse Venable," I said. "He's the subject of an ongoing Bureau investigation, so I'd appreciate it if you didn't approach him until I give you the go-ahead."

"I have no reason to speak with him until you dig up a connection."

We ate our sandwiches and Pierre told me a bit more about how he investigated traffic homicides. Then I walked out to my car and called Paul Snyder. I introduced myself and asked if I could speak with him about Larry Kane.

"I'm really broken up about this," he said. "No way could this be an accident. I'm glad somebody's looking into it."

I arranged to meet him at the condo he'd shared with Kane in a half hour. As I drove there, I wondered what Larry Kane did after he shut the booth down. Did he complain to his boss, maybe ask for extra money because of the hazardous conditions? How could that lead to his death?

How could any of that have led to an intentional attack on him as he rode home from his other job? There was no logic I could follow. I was accustomed to the structure behind a balance sheet. Revenue minus cost plus expenses equals profit or loss. Numbers made sense when you looked at how they related to each other.

You could pull each entry out of a balance sheet and see how it affected the bottom line. This was more like a jigsaw puzzle. All I could do was rely on my instinct to lead me to additional pieces that might help me to figure out what the picture would be when all the pieces were in place.

The address Snyder gave me was in a run-down complex of apartments linked by exterior catwalks, between a car repair shop and a small strip shopping center. It didn't look like the kind of place where a good-looking young gay guy would live.

An ambulance was parked in front of building 12, where Kane and Snyder lived, and my heart seized up. Was I too late to talk to Snyder? Had something happened to him, too?

An elderly woman in a wheelchair sat in the shade on the first-floor walkway and stared at me as I approached the building under a brutally hot sun. Two other elderly women stood on the second-story catwalk chatting. It was marginally cooler in the shade, but the elevator was tied up and I had to climb four flights of exterior stairs.

I was relieved to see the EMTs wheeling a stretcher out of a third-floor apartment. Too bad for whoever was on it, but at least it wasn't Paul Snyder.

The guy who answered my knock was much older than I expected, at least fifty, skinny, with thinning hair.

"Come on in," Snyder said. The apartment was as cold as a meat locker, which was a delightful contrast to the heat outside. "You saw our daily entertainment, I guess."

"The ambulance?"

"It's what they do here. The vultures cluster along the catwalk every time the EMTs show up, wondering whose ticket was up."

I followed him into the living room, where the sofa was covered in plastic. "You lived here long?" I asked, as I sat.

"It was my mother's place, and I inherited it when she died last year," he said. He shrugged. "It's not great, but it's paid off. I thought I could start over again down here, but I never finished college and I can't work outside in this heat, so the best job I could find was this part-time gig at the call center. They only give me twenty-eight hours a week so they don't have to pay benefits. It's lousy money, too, and it means I have to live close to the bone. I met Larry at work and when he needed a place to live, I rented him the second bedroom."

I was trying to use my gaydar to determine Snyder's sexuality, and his relationship to Kane, but all the signs were coming up that they were just roommates.

"What can you tell me about him?" I asked.

"Good guy. Quiet. When he first moved in, I told him I had two rules. If he wanted to do drugs, he had to do it outside. Same with guys. He wanted to get into somebody's pants, he had to do it somewhere else."

"You didn't mind that he was gay?"

"Whatever floats your boat," Snyder said. "I don't swing that way, but then, I haven't swung any way in a couple of decades."

TMI, I thought, but then so was most of what Snyder had said. He seemed like the kind of lonely guy you run into at bars sometimes, who have no one in their lives so they've lost the art of ordinary conversation.

"You said that he was a careful motorcyclist," I said, trying to shift the conversation back to what I needed to know and away from Paul Snyder's nonexistent sex life.

"Absolutely. He was fanatical about it. Hated to ride the bike in the rain. Wouldn't go above the speed limit."

"So you don't think what happened to him was an accident?"

"Not at all."

"Did he have any enemies? Anybody ever threaten him?"

"Not that I know. Like I said, he was quiet. And we didn't talk that much. After an eight-hour shift on the phones, you kind of want to just shut up, you know?"

I didn't know, but I nodded anyway. "What about his other job? At Trader Tom's?"

"Like I said, it's hard to get two nickels to rub together at the call center, so he took this other job on the weekends. He seemed to like it."

"Did he ever say anything about the stuff he sold?"

"What do you mean? Wallets and purses?"

"Mostly knockoffs," I said.

"Yeah, he wasn't happy about that. He'd had some arguments with his boss, and he was ready to quit, and he told me that something happened at the market that made him realize it was time to go."

So the incident I'd witnessed had meant something to Larry Kane. Good. "So he quit?"

Snyder nodded. "His boss wasn't happy about it. He and Larry got into a shouting match on the phone."

His mouth opened wide and he stared at me. "You don't think his boss killed him, do you? So that Larry couldn't rat him out about the fake merchandise?"

That would mean that Venable knew when Larry worked at the call center, and the route he took home. Something he could have learned, had he wanted to. "It's something to consider," I said. "Did you and Larry talk about the conversation?"

"No, I had to work the night shift Sunday, so I left right after they talked. I didn't notice that he hadn't come home until Monday afternoon, when the police called me." He leaned forward. "You don't think I'm in danger, do you? I never even went to the flea market."

"There's no indication at present that Larry's death is anything other than a traffic accident," I said. "But if his boss happens to call you, don't tell him anything, and let me know."

I hesitated for a moment. "Are you going to pack up Larry's things to return to his family?"

"I guess so."

"If you see anything unusual, or anything related to Jesse Venable, will you let me know?"

He agreed, and I gave him my card and walked back outside. It was still hot and humid, but the ambulance had left by then and the vultures, as Snyder had called them, had gone back inside.

Chapter 11

Innocent Victims

It was late Monday by the time I finished with Snyder, so instead of heading all the way back to Miramar I drove home. I met Lester for a workout and dinner. "Where are you off to tonight?" I asked.

"Bar called Saddles in Tamarac," he said. "It's country-western line dancing night and they're making Boulevardiers with two different bourbons I represent."

From my years behind the bar, I knew that a Boulevardier contained bourbon, Campari and sweet vermouth, garnished with either a cherry, an orange slice, or a lemon twist. "Kind of an old guy's drink, isn't it?" I asked.

"That's the crowd they get up there, or so I'm told," Lester said. "You want to come with me? I could use your help with the social media stuff again."

"I was just in that neighborhood this afternoon," I said. As I looked up the address of the bar, I explained about my visit to Paul Snyder. "I wonder if Larry Kane hung out at this place or if anybody there knew him."

"So you kill two birds with one stone," Lester said. "You take some photos and make some posts for me, and you schmooze the clientele in case anyone knows this Kane guy."

We left soon after that. Saddles had a faux-western façade, complete with a hitching post in case any clients arrived by horse. Doubtful on this commercial strip, but in Florida you never know what you're going to find.

When we walked in, they had just started line dancing lessons, and most of the patrons were on the dance floor. While Lester went up to the bar, I joined the crowd. I had done a bit of line dancing when I was in Philadelphia, so I got into the rhythm of steps and kicks and gallops. Most of the dancers, as Lester had said, were older, from their forties to their sixties, but there were a couple of guys my age. Lots of cowboy hats, boots, and jeans.

Hard to believe we were in Florida.

When the lesson ended, I walked over to the bar to get a drink. While I stood there, I talked to a pair of fifty-something men in plaid shirts with pearl buttons. They wore matching wedding rings, white gold with the infinity symbol in tiny diamonds. Would I end up like that? Married to Lester, or someone like him, sharing a passion for art collecting or line dancing or a hobby I hadn't yet discovered?

A man with tattoos lining his arms and a gold ring through his nose pushed his way up to the bar beside us. "Anybody seen that bastard Larry?" he demanded. "He sold me a Breitling turned out to be a fake and I want my money back!"

"You're a damn fool to buy a watch at the flea market," one of the other men said. "You want the real thing you got to go to one of those jewelry stores at the mall."

"He swore to me up and down it was real," the tattooed man said. "That it was gray market, made for sale overseas, which was why it was so cheap. When I get hold of him I'll gray market him."

"You won't have to bother," I said, and all eyes turned to me. "He wiped out his motorcycle on the highway Sunday night."

In the reflected neon from behind the bar, I saw the tattooed man's face go pale. "Seriously?"

"I saw his body at the morgue." I pulled out my Bureau ID. "Special Agent Angus Green from the FBI. Can I talk to you about the watch you bought?"

"There's no way you're an FBI agent," one of the married guys said. "You're too young and too cute."

"He's the real thing," Lester said, from the behind the bar. "Also my boyfriend."

"There you go," I said. "Independent testimonial. I'd like to talk to anybody who knew Larry Kane or bought anything from his booth."

I nodded toward a quiet corner of the bar and the tattooed guy followed me. "What's your name?" I asked.

"Chris Jackson. I'm not gonna get in trouble for buying the watch, am I?"

"Not at all. You're an innocent victim." And a dumb one, I added without saying. "You met Larry here at the bar?"

He walked me through flirting with Larry, admiring the watch he wore, eventually going to the flea market and buying one himself. "From the leather goods stall?" I asked.

"He had some watches behind the counter, only for special customers, he said. Specially stupid, I guess."

"Everybody wants a bargain," I said. "How'd you find out the watch was counterfeit?"

"The battery died and I took it into a watch repair place to get it replaced. The guy there told me it was a fake. A really good one, but still a fake."

"How'd he know?"

"The construction date was missing on the bracelet," he said. "He told me he wasn't surprised I got taken in, because the watch had the right weight to it, metal parts rather than cheap plastic, and even the date window had the right magnification. That it probably came from Turkey, where they do a really good job of making counterfeit watches."

Odds were, the watch he'd bought had come from a previous

shipment sent to Venable. "You like the watch?"

"I loved it. Until I found out I got ripped off."

"So go back to loving it," I said. "Nobody's going to know it's a fake unless you tell them. Your repair guy was right, they make quality replicas in Turkey."

I got his address and phone number in case I had to get back to him. Then I returned to the bar, where a couple of other guys admitted to having bought wallets and belts from Larry Kane at the Trader Tom's booth. None of them were aware that they'd bought counterfeit goods.

"How do you know this isn't real?" one of the men said. He pushed his wallet at me. "Looks pretty authentic to me."

"You really want to know?" I asked.

"Hell, yeah. If I got cheated I want to know."

I took the wallet from him and moved over to where a spotlight shone down over the bar. I looked at it very carefully and finally found the imperfection I was looking for. "This is a really good wallet," I said, as I handed it back to him. "What did you pay for it?"

"A hundred and a quarter."

"You got a good deal. It's a quality piece of work – the Damier Graphite canvas feels authentic." I opened it. "It has the right number of pockets and everything else you'd expect."

"But?" he asked.

"But if you're paying nearly five hundred bucks for a wallet, you have the right to expect perfection, and the Louis V factory would never let something go out with this double stitch down here."

I pointed to the side where the credit cards went. It looked like the stitching machine had made an error, missed a stitch then gone back over it, and the line along the edge was rough.

He looked closely at it. "Fuck me," he said.

"If you paid retail for it, you'd have a right to be pissed. Instead you got a great-looking wallet with a hardly noticeable imperfection for a bargain price."

That got guys lining up to show me their belts, wallets and

jewelry. I asked every one of them about Larry, and if they'd ever met his boss, but no one had anything to offer.

I was finally able to take some drink photos for Lester and post them to social media just before his two-hour stint was over.

"You never cease to impress me," he said, as we walked out.

"Why? I haven't even taken my clothes off yet."

He elbowed me. "How much you knew about that counterfeit stuff. And you didn't make a single one of those guys feel bad about getting cheated."

"I didn't realize you were paying attention."

"Sweetheart, you are always on my radar screen," he said, and smiled.

He dropped me at my place and we made plans to get together later in the week. Before I got out of the car, I leaned over and kissed him, intoxicated by the alcohol I'd had at the bar, the new car smell of Lester's SUV, and the knowledge that even while he was working he'd been watching me and been impressed.

When I got to work the next morning, I stopped at the lab to pick up the documents Wagon had created for me. "Here's your diploma," he said, handing me a duplicate of the one I already had, only with the last name changed. "New driver's license, a prepaid Visa with a thousand dollars on it, a Costco membership card and a Broward County library card, just for verisimilitude."

"Wow. You do good work, Wagon."

"Anybody who digs too deeply will come up with some questions, but that should get you wherever you need to go, for now. I'll have a passport for you in a couple of days."

On my way back to my office, I stopped at Vito's. "Last night I went to a bar where Larry Kane used to hang out, and I spoke to a guy who can connect Venable's booth with a counterfeit Breitling I believe was made in Turkey."

"Does he have a bill of sale for it?" Vito asked.

I shook my head. "He told me he paid cash."

"So it's just his word that he bought the watch from that booth?"

I nodded. "And the guy who sold it to him is dead." I explained about the motorcycle wipeout, and my conversations with Chancy Pierre and Larry Kane's roommate Paul Snyder.

"You followed all these leads on instinct? The morgue, this BSO detective, the roommate?"

I nodded. "That's okay, isn't it?"

"It's better than okay. It's damn good investigation. And if Kane's death wasn't an accident, then it's possible that Venable is beginning to cut off loose ends. Any other employees at the booth? Is it still open with Kane dead?"

"The market is only open from Thursday to Sunday, so I can't tell if the booth will reopen until Thursday with someone else behind the counter. In the meantime I'll focus on getting to know Venable."

When I got back to my office I found an email from Frank Sena. Jesse Venable didn't have the painting in Florida – it was still in Italy. But he'd be happy to meet with me and talk about it. He'd also asked Frank if I was any good as an accountant, because he had a tax filing due August 15 and wanted to find someone cheap to assemble the data his expensive-by-the-hour accountant wanted.

I logged into the Angus Gray email account I'd set up and sent a message to Venable, letting him know I could meet him at his convenience, though I was working for a client out in Miramar and might need some time to get to him. A few minutes later he responded. He'd like me to come to his house the next afternoon, if I could, and he included his street address and phone number.

It was like texting, only less convenient. I responded that I could be there at two, and got a confirmation right back. "Supposed to be a beautiful day," he wrote. "Let's talk out by my pool. Bring your bathing suit – though my pool is very private if you prefer to skinny dip!"

I went back to the email Frank Sena had forwarded to me. He'd noted in it that I was smart, cute—and gay. He must have known Venable would like that.

My first instinct was to write back to Venable and say that I was a professional accountant, and did not meet clients in my weenie bikini. But then I remembered what Katya had said – that it was my goal to get close to Venable, and to gain his trust. Saying no to his first request wasn't going to get me off to a good start.

Because of my fair skin, I try not to spend too much time in the sun, but a few weeks before I'd gone to Fort Lauderdale Beach with Jonas, and he'd snapped a photo of me in a pair of tight-fitting bathing trunks in a tropical pattern. I attached the picture to a message that read, "See you tomorrow!"

Give 'em what they ask for, right?

The next morning I went for a run, then showered and dressed in a pair of navy chinos and a white short-sleeve shirt. I slipped my bathing trunks into the messenger bag I carried to and from work, and made sure to include a couple of my new business cards. I emptied my wallet of everything that identified me as Angus Green, Special Agent with the Federal Bureau of Investigation, including my badge, and put it all in a zippered plastic bag. The Angus Gray material went into my wallet.

My gun stayed in the thumb holster on my hip. When I got to Venable's, I'd lock it in the glove compartment of my car, because I didn't see how I could conceal a weapon in my bathing trunks. At least not a lethal one.

When I got into the office, I looked up Venable's address in Weston, a rich suburb on the edge of the Everglades, just up the highway from my office. He'd purchased the house on the half-acre lot new five years before for $3.2 million; it had four bedrooms, three baths, and a pool/spa.

I wondered how much profit he'd made on the bracelet I had sold to Golden Ticket the week before. You'd have to handle an awful lot of transactions to afford a house like Venable's, which didn't have a mortgage recorded against it. A bit more searching turned up the fact that it was in a gated community called Heron's Nest, which boasted over a hundred acres of lakes and wildlife preserves and a "signature two-story gatehouse entry offering unparalleled security."

Fortunately, Wagon had provided the driver's license under Angus Gray I could show the guard at the gate to Venable's community. And it was a pretty decent picture of me, as those go.

As I drove along the beautifully landscaped streets, I kept coming back to my question. Did Jesse Venable have a motive to kill Kane, or have him killed? Perhaps I'd learn something in my visit to his house.

Chapter 12

Bathing Beauty

As Venable had predicted, the weather was gorgeous as I left the office—sunny in the eighties with scattered clouds, a light breeze swaying the palm trees along the highway. I stopped at the guard house and showed my license. While I waited, I slid my gun and holster into the glove compartment and locked it.

The guard opened the wrought-iron gate, and after a couple of turns and curves, I pulled up in front of a modern single-story house that was miles from the simple place I lived.

A tall entry was flanked by two wings, one with a three-car garage at the end. Venable stood in the doorway. He was about five nine, and must have weighed well over three hundred pounds. If he was going for a slimming look by wearing a black sweatshirt over black jogging pants, it wasn't working for him. And I doubted that he'd been jogging in the past twenty years.

He smiled broadly and reached out to shake my hand. "Great to meet you, Angus. Thank you so much for coming by."

"It's my pleasure," I said. "I'm still building my client base so I'm willing to do whatever it takes to please someone new."

He smiled broadly. "I like that attitude. I understand you're an art scholar?"

"Hardly. Just took a bunch of classes in college because I love looking at paintings."

"Then you won't mind indulging me by letting me show you some of my collection before we get started." He ushered me into a huge living room that looked out at the lushly landscaped pool area. The walls were white, a plain palette to display his artwork.

A huge painting I recognized as a David Hockney hung on the wall to the right, above a white leather sofa. A young man, nude, stood with his back to us, in the shallow end of a pool painted in brilliant shades of blue, aqua and green.

A bronze male nude, about twelve inches high, stood on a side table, beneath a pencil sketch of a nude man who stared confidently at the artist.

Venable was consistent in his collection. Every work, whether a painting, a sketch, a sculpture or a photograph, glorified the male form, and there were enough dicks and asses on display to fill the pages of any of the gay rags that were given out for free at Lazy Dick's, Eclipse and a dozen other bars around town.

Of course, what Venable owned was art, and the queens who turned up their noses at *Hot Spots* would salivate over the men on his walls.

"Who's your favorite artist?" I asked.

'Michelangelo. His David is the finest expression of the male form I've ever seen."

"You've been to see it?"

"In my younger and slimmer days. Florence is a beautiful city, full of amazing art."

"My brother is studying there right now," I said. "A summer program on art history and the Italian language."

"And you're going to visit him, of course?"

I shook my head. "I'd love to, and he'd love me to come. But I don't have the money."

"That's the shame of youth," he said. "The ability to travel but not the cash. Then you get to be my age and you have the money but not the ability."

"Which means you can't travel directly to Italy to get this painting Frank Sena is interested in."

He nodded. "I have a contact there who knows my taste in art and keeps an eye out for me. He offered the painting to me, but the provenance is a little hinky, if you know what I mean. When I heard that Mr. Sena was looking for it, and that he had the paperwork to show it belongs to him, I offered to make the connection."

"You're sure it's the real thing?"

"All the dots connect. And it's not that great a painting that someone would go to the trouble to forge a copy."

Miriam Washington might disagree with him. She seemed to believe the painting was pretty important.

"Do you have any photos of the painting?" I asked. "I might be able to get in touch with one of my professors and have it authenticated."

"I just have one, and it's not very good quality. I can ask my contact to send some better ones and let you know when they come in."

I agreed to that, and then we shifted to the accounting work he needed done. He led me into a large bedroom he'd converted into an office, where a large black and white photo of two naked men swimming underwater hung above his desk.

"As I'm sure you know, employers have to file quarterly returns for employee withholding," he said.

"Form 941, Employer's Quarterly Federal Tax Return," I said. "I've filled out many of them over the years." That was completely true, and a couple of the freelance accounting clients I maintained needed that form as well.

"My accountant has been after me to put in one of those fancy systems where the employees clock in and the software takes care of putting together the data, but it's just too damn expensive. I'd rather pay to have someone assemble the report manually every quarter."

"I can see that."

"Every store manager faxes me the time sheets at the end of the week." He pointed to a stack of pages as thick as an encyclopedia. "There you go. Take a look and tell me when you can get the form finished."

"I'll have to input everything into a spreadsheet." I picked up one of the time sheets. It listed the employee's name, the date, time in, and time out. "You have copies of their W-4s?"

"That folder over there."

Larry Kane's was near the top. At least there weren't that many employees, though a quick glance showed that Venable's businesses weren't strong on employee retention. There seemed to be a lot of turnover.

I flipped through it all and made some quick calculations. "I can have all this done in about ten hours. Say three-fifty for the work?" I wanted to lowball him to be sure he'd hire me, and hey, any extra cash was good for me.

"Sounds great to me. So I'll hear from you later in the week?"

Could I do Venable's work during my FBI hours? Or was that double-dipping? I shoehorned work for my regular clients into my evenings and weekends, but I couldn't very well tell Venable that. "I have some other work I need to finish," I said. "How about Thursday?"

He agreed. "Now, how about a dip in the pool? You brought your suit, didn't you?" He grinned. "Though of course I won't complain if you didn't."

I pulled it out of my messenger bag. "Right here. Somewhere I can change?"

"There's a bathroom right across the hall. I'll see you out at the pool when you're ready."

I went into the bathroom, which was as large as my kitchen, lined with marble and mirrors, and I stripped down, folding my clothes carefully and leaving them on the bathroom counter.

Then I couldn't resist pulling a couple of poses in the mirrors. My dick was stiff and stuck straight out of my reddish pubes. My ass was tight, my biceps nothing like Lester's but still in good shape.

I pulled on the bathing trunks and thought for a moment about Jesse Venable's body. That wilted my erection enough that I could walk out comfortably.

Through the sliding glass doors, I saw Venable on a lounge chair. He was shirtless, in a pair of oversized board shorts in an electric plaid. I walked out and a wave of hot, humid air hit me. Without evening thinking about it, I went to the deep end of the pool and dove in.

The water was tepid but still felt cool and refreshing. I surfaced and shook the water from my hair, then wiped my eyes with the back of my hand. "If I had a pool like this I'd swim every morning," I said.

"And once upon a time, I did," he said. "Now the best I can do is wallow around the shallow end like a hippo."

It was hard to know how to answer that, so I went back under the water and swam a couple of laps, thinking as I did of the refugees on the capsized boat in the Aegean Sea. They didn't have the luxury I did, of swimming for pleasure.

When I finished I climbed up the stairs at the shallow end, the water cascading from my body, my suit glued to me like a second skin. What would I be willing to do to live like this? Become some rich guy's kept boy? Tweak a few laws or accounting rules to make my own fortune?

Sadly, I couldn't see myself doing any of those things. So instead I walked over to where Venable lay, took a towel he offered, and then relaxed on the lounger beside him, feeling the sun bake my pale skin.

His cell phone rang, and he went inside to answer it. I took a bottle of cold water from a cooler and drank, then turned over on my back. Through the glass doors I could see Venable arguing with someone on the phone. Then he disappeared into another part of the house.

I wasn't sure how long I was expected to stick around. I'd gotten my assignment, taken a swim, let Venable ogle me for a while. As I saw him coming back through the living room, I sat up.

He opened the sliding door but didn't step out. "I'm afraid I'm going to have to say goodbye," he said. "I have to get over to my downtown operation to handle something." He motioned to the side of the pool. "There's a shower over there if you want to rinse off the chlorine. I'll be in the office when you're dressed again."

He turned and went back inside, closing the door behind him. I got up and looked at the shower. What the hell, he was gone, and I didn't want to go home with chlorine in my pubes. I dropped my suit and stepped under the shower, rinsing myself well. If Venable was watching from somewhere in the house, so be it.

Did I feel guilty about using my body to hook Venable? Had Larry Kane acted the same way? Look where it had gotten him. So no, I didn't feel a bit of guilt about establishing a friendship with Venable however I could. Not when there was so much at stake, for innocent victims of smuggled goods and for immigrants left to die in the wine-dark sea of the Aegean.

I grabbed a fresh towel from a pile by the loungers, dried myself off and then wrapped it around my waist. Then I padded through the living room to the bathroom and dressed.

I found Venable in his office. He had returned to the outfit he was wearing when I arrived. He was on the phone again, and he motioned toward the pile of paperwork I had to take with me.

I grabbed it and slid it into my messenger bag. Then I put my hand up to my ear, my thumb out, in the universal "I'll call you," gesture.

He waved goodbye, and I walked out. Step one accomplished.

Chapter 13

Sex in the Bushes

It was late afternoon by then, so I drove home and settled in with Jesse Venable's accounting data. I was curious to see if I could find anything there that would tie to watch smuggling or any other information Larry Kane might have had access to.

It took me a while to remember what information to look for on the time sheets and get my spreadsheet set up, and then it was slow, dull work entering the data from the paper sheets for the manager and eight part-time employees at the pawn shop. I couldn't find anything irregular, which was frustrating. Was this going to be a big waste of time?

By six o'clock I was brain-dead and ready for a drink so I drove over to Lazy Dick's to get a beer. With a Magic City Pale Ale in my hand, I circled once around the dance floor, then walked out to the patio. I spotted Tom Laughlin drinking a martini and watching a bunch of twinks in tight shirts and equally tight pants cavort on the dance floor to Calvin Harris and Rihanna telling the boys what they came for.

I was glad to see him because I had a few more questions for him about Frank Sena, and I was curious to see how their relationship was developing. I slid into the table across from him and asked, "Enjoying the view?"

"Of course. You should get out there and dance yourself."

"I'm danced out at present," I said. "Did some country and western line dancing the other night at a bar in Tamarac. But as long I ran into you I wanted to ask you about Frank Sena. You think all he wants is to get this painting?"

"You have to understand something, Angus," Tom said. "Men of my generation were denied so much. Most of us didn't have the chance to be open at work. We couldn't dream of getting married, of having children. We tend to be greedy now—when we see something we want, we're determined not to deny ourselves any longer."

I gave him a capsule version of what I'd learned about the painting, and he stopped me at the phrase *darsi alla macchia*. "Say that again," he said.

I did. "It means to hide in the bushes," I said. "A derogatory way of saying that the Macchiaioli worked outdoors."

"Probably not all they were doing out there," Tom said, and he smirked. "Back in the day, you know, it was hard to find somewhere private to hook up with another man. So we went outdoors. The Back Bay Fens in Boston, the Ramble in New York's Central Park."

I remembered my own encounter with outdoor sex, back when I was an undergrad at Penn State and had gone out hiking in the woods with a friend from the Rainbow Roundtable. It was a hot summer afternoon, and when we found a small secluded lake, we'd shucked our clothes and then.... Well, it was a great memory. For men of Tom's generation, it must have been less fun because it was their only option.

Though I couldn't see that being part of a museum description of the painting, it was yet another reason why the painting was an important part of gay culture and history, and needed to be somewhere people could see it and learn from it. That is, if I could get it back from Italy for Frank while I was trying to rope in Jesse Venable on smuggling charges, and at the same time gather evidence that could save immigrants from death on the sea.

After a solid night's sleep, I went for a morning run, then packed up all Venable's data to take to the office in Miramar with me. I paged through the remaining documents and when I found a time sheet for Larry Kane, I began with him.

He didn't have a supervisor to sign off for him, so I assumed that meant Venable trusted him to show up and leave on time. He worked a regular shift at the flea market, Thursday through Sunday from 9:30 AM to 6:00 PM. But he also worked at various times during the other three days of the week. Some days he noted that he had driven to the airport in Miami, while on others he'd write something like "deliver carton to" followed by a street address.

I could understand going to the airport, if that's where the goods came in. But why make those deliveries? In addition to selling at Trader Tom's, was Venable acting as a wholesaler for counterfeit goods, handing them off to other retailers?

The addresses on the time sheet weren't very helpful. In a couple of cases Larry had only listed a house and street number, and when I checked online that data could map to several different cities in Miami-Dade and Broward counties. A couple also showed up as multi-unit buildings, and without additional information I couldn't tell who he'd been visiting.

I tried everything I could – Google searches, cross-referencing in our own databases, but I couldn't find anything unusual. Maybe he was just delivering belts and wallets to good customers. Only one came up clearly as a business – an art gallery on a side street in downtown Fort Lauderdale. Was Larry picking up items that Jesse had purchased? Or returning art work? Did he know too much about Venable's operations, which had led to his death?

I walked down to Vito's office to brainstorm with him. "Yesterday I met with Venable at his house and agreed to do some accounting work for him. I've gone through the time sheets for the employees at his various businesses and there's no other booth employee besides Larry Kane in the paperwork that Venable gave me."

"The flea market's open today. Go back there and see what the other vendors say," Vito said. "If there's someone else running the booth. Maybe Venable himself."

I couldn't see Venable leveraging his prodigious bulk behind that booth—he seemed like the kind of guy who'd keep it closed until he could find someone else to work there, but I agreed to head over and check.

Vito sat back in his chair. "You used that false ID to get in with Venable? He didn't have any suspicions?"

"Not that he mentioned to me."

"Anything else unusual in what you found?"

"Not so far. I still have a lot of data to go through."

"Keep an eye out for anything regarding smuggled coins through that pawn shop or the gold buyer," he said. "Any unusual prices paid, anything like that."

"You still investigating that theft from the Atocha?" I asked.

"I don't let go of my cases until I close them," Vito said.

"Right now all I have are time sheets. But if I keep working for Venable maybe I can get access to more data."

I went back to my office and spent the next couple of hours entering data for Golden Ticket employees. I had grossly underestimated how much time it would take me to compile all the data, and I was glad that I didn't need whatever I could collect from Venable to pay my bills.

Trader Tom's was open on Thursdays until six in the evening, so I drove up there from Miramar and retraced my steps to Venable's booth. It was closed, and when I chatted with the neighboring vendors they told me it had been shuttered since Kane left on Saturday.

I managed to work my way around to the incident the previous weekend where the booth owner had been knocked out, and asked if there'd been any similar incidents at Venable's booth. "People always complain," one woman told me.

She leaned in close. "I didn't trust that boy Larry. Every so often I'd notice him putting cash in his pocket instead of into the register."

"You ever say anything to the guy who owns the booth?"

"Never saw him. I figured if he was stupid enough to trust the kid, it was his own fault."

Was that what had gotten Larry Kane murdered? Dipping into Venable's cash flow?

Chapter 14
Dirty Job

As I was driving to work the next morning I got a text from Vito, summoning me to his office as soon as I got in.

"New developments in the immigrant smuggling case," he said. "The Turkish police intercepted a truck on the road from Istanbul to the coast filled with Syrian refugees and a couple of cases of counterfeit watches."

"Were the watches intended for Jesse Venable?"

"No one is talking, and we can't figure out who the go-between is who could connect the watches to Venable. If we can't do that, then our investigation is dead in the water. No pun intended."

"What can I do to help?"

"Keep pushing Venable. You've got to get something on him so we can pressure him to give up his contacts in Turkey. Then the powers that be will can try to shut down these operations."

"I've been reading up on immigrant smuggling," I said. "Honestly? If we shut down one operation, another one pops up, doesn't it?"

"You could use that argument on any operation we bust," Vito said. "Look, I sympathize with these people. My grandparents were immigrants to this country, and if they hadn't risked their lives I wouldn't be here today. But there are laws in place to govern immigration, and it's our job to enforce them."

"I know that this is my job, and I don't get to pick and choose which laws we want to enforce. But what if we don't believe in one of them?"

"That's a question way above my pay grade," Vito said. "It's our job to take the micro view, not the macro. You and I can't solve the world's problems, but we can help take down people doing bad things. Capisce?"

I nodded. "I get it. Focus on the individuals, like Jesse Venable." I hesitated for a moment, then added, "Agent Gordieva told me that the purpose of going undercover is to get someone to trust you, then to betray that trust."

"You're thinking deep this morning, Angus. You want me to pull you from this investigation? I'd hate to do it because you're making good progress, but if you're uncomfortable, I can switch you back to the college information detail."

Not that. I'd spent a month after getting shot going around to local colleges, showing them a video and talking about how students and faculty could be victimized by foreign governments. It was a poorly organized operation and I'd felt like I was being punished by being sent there, even though it was reasonable to put me on a low-stress detail while I was recovering from my injuries.

"No, I'm good," I said. "These kinds of doubts are valid, right? Shows that we're paying attention to what we do and why it matters."

"You got it. Did you get to the flea market yesterday?"

"I did. Venable's booth was closed and I talked to a bunch of the other vendors, but I didn't get much."

"When do you see Venable next?"

"Tomorrow. I'm delivering the spreadsheets I created for him."

"See if you can get him to talk about his business. Maybe he'll be willing to brag about how smart he is. And what's the scoop with this painting?"

"He says he's acting as an intermediary for my friend. He's going to get some better quality photos and if they look good, we'll move forward with the deal."

"If your friend is the legitimate owner, then it's hard to make a case that Venable is dealing with a stolen work of art," Vito said. "I'm tempted to tell you to forget about it, but the longer you stay in touch with Venable to more chance you'll have to find something we can make stick."

As I walked back to my office, I was depressed. Venable was too slippery. Once he admitted that he knew the painting was stolen, and focusing on getting it back to its rightful owner, I'd lost the ability to use the connection against him. I'd only been able to come up with the most tenuous connection between him and fake watches smuggled from Turkey, and the only person who could have strengthened that tie, Larry Kane, was dead.

Lester had flown to Pennsylvania for the weekend, to tour a single-batch whiskey distillery and go out on bar visits with the regional rep up there. After the week I'd had, I didn't feel like going out, so I went home after work, where I spent some more time staring at the data I'd collected and got nowhere.

Saturday morning Jonas and I went for a long run, and I showered, then spent another couple of hours making sure everything was complete with the work I'd promised Venable. Early in the afternoon I drove out to Weston. I had to drop off the paperwork, and at Vito's direction, I had to keep playing the man until I found something we could use against him.

It was yet another sunny day, and I shivered as I thought about the dark dealings that had bought Venable this expensive house. He met me at his front door, dressed in what I took to be his usual attire, the black top and track suit bottoms. "You're a breath of fresh air," he said, as I walked in. "I've been stuck in my office all morning. Let's go out to the pool."

I agreed, but before I could move forward, he said, "Can I ask you a favor, Angus?"

Crap. Was this where he was going to ask me to blow him—or let him blow me? I hadn't even had the chance to get friendly with him. And I sure as hell wasn't going to have sex with him. That was one of those very basic Bureau taboos that had been hammered into us at the Academy, and I valued my career way too much to take the chance.

"You can ask."

"Would you mind getting into your bathing suit before we go out there?"

"It's not exactly the way I do accounting work," I said.

"I know. But..." He hesitated. "I'd really appreciate it."

What the hell. I was going to get into the suit eventually so I could go in the pool. Why not sooner rather than later? And my goal was to get close to him, get him to trust me, so that I could betray him.

I agreed, and he smiled broadly. "Terrific. I'll meet you out there."

He went down the hall toward his bedroom, and I went into the guest bath to change. This time I didn't bother posing for the mirrors. I worried about how Venable would show up poolside—naked? What would I do? It wasn't a question I'd gone over specifically with Katya, but from what she'd told me about her Russian sting operation I had the feeling she'd stretched the boundaries herself.

It was a great relief to see Venable in another huge pair of neon bathing trunks. I carried my laptop out and set it up on a table in the shade. He joined me there, and I showed him the work I'd completed. "This is terrific," he said. He handed me a letter-sized envelope, and I looked inside to see a bunch of small bills, singles, fives, and tens, with the occasional twenty. "You can count it if you want, but it's what we agreed on."

"I trust you." I figured the collection of small bills had come from either his take at the flea market or the pawn shop. I slid the envelope beneath the laptop and started the shutdown process.

As I did that, he asked, "You know anything about prostate cancer?"

I was thrown off by that question, and all I could do was say no.

"They say it's no big deal," Venable said. "It's a slow-growing cancer, it's usually localized in the prostate. And who needs the prostate anyway? All it does is create the fluid that carries the sperm, and if you're not going to have kids, it's about as useful as tits on a bull."

"I never really gave it much thought," I said. "Don't they call the prostate the male G-spot?"

I kicked myself mentally. What was I doing bringing up sex, when that was the last thing I wanted to talk to Jesse Venable about?

"Yeah, but I was never much of a bottom," he said. "So when the doc told me that my prostate had swelled up to the size of ripe mango, and it was the reason why I had to take a piss every hour, I was fine with getting rid of it. Kick the fucker out, I said."

He looked at me. "I used to have a figure, you know," he said. "I was never as slim or as muscular as you, but I swam every day, watched what I ate, all that crap. I was so fucking glad I never got AIDS, all the sex I had, that I swore I was going to treat my body like a temple."

Jesse Venable wanted to talk, so I was going to listen. Maybe I'd be able to swing the conversation to Larry Kane at some point.

"As you can see, I ended up more like a Buddha than a temple," he said. "One thing the doc neglected to tell me before he cut me was that there are these nerves wrapped around the prostate." He held up his hands as if he was cupping something. "These nerves, they're what control your ability to get a hard-on. Bet you didn't know that, did you?"

I shook my head.

"I didn't either, back when I was young and I could get hard just looking at a cute guy. Tell me the truth, that's the way it is with you, isn't it?"

"It can get embarrassing sometimes," I admitted.

He roared with laughter. "Tell me about it. And you know, I'm no slouch in the size department, so when I got excited the world knew about it."

His laughter ended up with a hiccup, and it took him a moment to get his breath back. "So after a week or so, they took the tube out of my dick and I could piss again, the stitches healed up and the pain went away. I ask the doc, when can I get laid again? And he gives me this bullshit about every man is different, yada yada yada."

I reached over to the cooler and grabbed a bottle of cold water. "You want one?" I asked him, and when he said yes I tossed one over to him.

He took a long swig from the bottle, and then leaned forward. "But I don't get hard, so three months later, I'm back in the office and he explains this shit about the nerves. The cancer had gotten into the area by them, he had to take them all out, and that's that. He can give me a pump, I can get injections, he'll get my sex drive back for me, no problem."

I drank some of my water. While I was sorry to hear about his problems, I really wanted to find a way to ask him about Larry Kane.

"It was like pissing money away," he continued. "Nothing worked. I started eating like nobody's business, put on all this weight. And the only thing that gives me any pleasure is looking at guys." He took another long swig. "Paintings, photos on the Internet, the real thing when I can convince a good looking guy like you to come out here and play around."

He must have seen something on my face then because he said, "Not sexually. Like I said, I can't get it up, and to be honest with you, I never got much pleasure from dicks in my mouth. Call me a selfish pig, call me a complete top or a complete asshole, doesn't change the truth. All I got left to me is watching."

I couldn't help my curiosity. "So you never get off?" It seemed like a gay man's worst nightmare.

"I do, but I gotta handle it myself, if you know what I mean. Takes a long time to get where I'm going, and other guys, even if you pay 'em, they don't have the patience. And I can see it in their faces when they look at me. Big fat sloppy pig. Can they even find my dick under all those layers of lard?"

"Ouch," I said. "That must hurt."

"Yeah. But if you don't expect anything from people, you don't get disappointed, you don't get hurt," he said.

He was a crook, but my heart still broke for Jesse Venable. I tried not to take my looks for granted, but I'd never considered what would happen if I lost them completely. What if I ended up fat and sad, with a limp dick like his? I'd hate to be the object of anyone's pity.

"So I gotta surround myself with people I trust," Venable said after a while. "The managers at all my locations, I pay them well so I know they've got my back."

Finally, my opportunity. "The guy from your flea market booth, too," I said. "I noticed on his time sheet he was running a lot of errands for you. You must trust him."

"I did," Venable said. "You know that bastard was homeless when I met him?"

"Really?"

He nodded. "His father caught him giving a neighbor boy a blow job, kicked him out of the nest at fifteen. He made his way down here and he was living on the street, giving blow jobs and taking it up the ass for anybody who'd pay. I found him in the alley behind the pawn shop, miserable little rat in the pouring rain."

He shook his head. "You ask anybody I do business with, they'll laugh if you say I have a heart. But I took the kid in that night, dried him off, gave him clean clothes. Hooked him up with a job at the pawn shop. Treated him like my own kid."

"But there are no more time sheets from him after last Saturday," I said. I realized that connected with what Paul Snyder had said, that Venable had fired Larry on Saturday, right after I'd bought the fake belt at the booth and witnessed the incident with the other vendor. Why? "He's not still working for you?"

"Had to fire him last week. He'd been stealing from me but I didn't know it until I showed up there on Saturday evening—I was gonna take Larry out to dinner, celebrate another successful season. But he'd already shut the booth down and booked, which wasn't like him at all. Then the nosy broad at the next booth told me to check my accounts, that she saw him pocketing way more cash than he should have been."

That was probably the woman I'd spoken to myself when I went back to the market.

I remembered that Larry hadn't written down anything about the sale of the belt, at least not while I was watching. Was that how he'd been stealing? Writing down one price on the inventory documents and pocketing the difference between what the customer paid?

"I tracked him down on his phone and challenged him, and he admitted it right up front. Talking about all the risks I made him take, how he needed to be better compensated. Little turd. I shit-canned him right then and there."

Did Jesse Venable know that Larry Kane was dead? Had he been responsible for it? I wasn't ready to confront him. My business, after all, wasn't Kane's death. I had bigger fish to fry and I needed to keep Venable on sizzle for a while. So I stood up. "Hot out here," I said. "You mind if I take a dip in the pool?"

"My pleasure," he said.

I repeated my process of the other day—a jump into the deep end, a number of laps, then pulled myself out, cascading water. Did I notice Venable's hand move quickly away from his groin? Was I creeped out to be putting myself on display for him?

Or was I just doing my job, getting his trust? Either way, I felt dirty, and the shower I took before I left the pool area didn't do much to make me feel cleaner.

Chapter 15

Surprising Offer

When I returned from changing back into my clothes, Venable was waiting for me in the living room. "I trust you, Angus. You've got one of those faces, you know? Like a Renaissance angel."

I could feel myself blushing, and not just because of the artistic reference. I was exactly the guy he shouldn't be trusting right then.

He offered me a glass of wine, and I accepted. I sat on his oversized sofa until he returned with two balloon glasses of white wine. "An Italian pinot grigio," he said. "In honor of our mutual interest in Italy."

It took me a moment to remember that I'd talked to him about Danny's studies in Florence. I sipped the wine, which was cold and fruity and quite good. "I got those photos you asked for," he said. "Of the painting in Italy."

He picked up a manila folder from the table next to him. "This is a photograph of the painting, front and back," he said, as he handed a sheet to me, with two color photos.

The picture looked even more vibrant and alive than it had when I'd seen it online, or in the movie Frank Sena had shown me, and I felt again that curious sense of connection to it. The water in the background reminded me of bathing in the Lackawanna River at Nay Aug Park with Danny when we were both kids.

Because I didn't want to reveal too much knowledge, I asked Venable about the markings on the back of the painting, the ones that indicated it had been stolen from a Jew in Venice, and he either didn't know what they meant, or wasn't telling. He said they were simply some kind of code from a dealer who'd sold the painting at some point.

"The man with the painting is ready to sell. He's willing to ship the painting to me, or to Mr. Sena, but I don't know this guy from Adam, and I'm not about to send a stranger fifty thousand dollars without knowing what I'm getting."

He sat back in his chair, one hand around the stem of his wineglass. "I spoke to Mr. Sena about this idea, and he agreed it's a good one. He's willing to pay you to go to Venice and pick up the painting."

"Me? Why?" I was stunned, yet in a way not so surprised. I'd been trying to position myself both as an intermediary between Frank Sena and Jesse Venable, and also as someone Venable could trust. But send me to Italy?

"Because you have the art smarts. I can't make the trip myself. If I sit for too long, even in a first-class seat, I'm subject to deep vein thrombosis in my legs. You're young and healthy. Mr. Sena thinks it would be too emotional for him to go back to this place where his family lived for generations. We both agree that we can trust you."

I experienced a momentary pang of guilt. Though Frank could trust me, Venable certainly shouldn't.

"You could take a few days' vacation, couldn't you?" he asked. "As a freelancer, you set your own work hours. You could even visit your brother while you're there. And your friend Mr. Sena has offered to cover the cost of your flight, your hotel, even your meals while you're in Venice."

The offer was very tempting. I really did want to see Danny and see Italy, too. But what would Miriam say? Was this a legitimate extension of my undercover work?"

"I can't say yes right now. I have to speak with Frank, of course. Then check my schedule, see when I could free up a couple of days. When did you want me to go?"

"As soon as possible. Mr. Sena doesn't want to let this painting slip away, and like I said, we have no reason to trust this guy in Italy."

I left Venable's house a few minutes later, with a promise to get back to him quickly. I called Miriam's cell phone, but got her voice mail, and asked if I could meet with her first thing Monday morning to go over a new development.

The other person with a vested interest in the painting was Frank Sena and on my way home, I called and asked if I could stop by and chat with him more about Venable's request. He agreed, and I fought my way through Saturday afternoon traffic to the Intracoastal. At the top of the bridge, I caught a glimpse of bright blue water sparkling in the late afternoon sunshine, and not for the first time realized how lucky I was to have landed in South Florida.

Frank opened the door to his apartment for me, looking very formal – black slacks, white shirt, a bright blue silk square in his pocket. All that was missing was a pipe and he'd have looked like a detective in one of those PBS shows.

He went into the kitchen to get me a glass of ice water, and I walked over to the cabinet I'd noticed before, the one full of collectables, in porcelain and silver. I recognized the figurine of a tall, slim boy with a skullcap as Lladro – my mother had a couple of those pieces.

"Are you interested in Judaica?" Frank asked, as he returned with water for both of us and a pair of wood coasters.

"That's what this is?" I asked.

He nodded. "For the most part, they're Jewish ritual items. My father had a small collection and I've expanded on it, focusing primarily on antiques from the Italian Jewish community." He pointed to an ornately engraved silver and brass cylinder, about eight inches long. "That's an antique *megillah* holder," he said. "It has a parchment scroll inside, the Book of Esther, which we read at Purim."

"You can read from that?"

"Well, I can't. And that scroll is purely decorative. But the rabbis read from that book at the holiday. Beside it, that's a *hamsa*, the hand of God."

The stylized hand he pointed at was decorated with Hebrew letters, curlicues and other designs. "It's all beautiful," I said.

I drank some water, then sat in one of Frank's wing chairs. I placed the water glass on the coaster on the coffee table, then said, "I understand you spoke with Jesse Venable and he suggested I ought to fly to Venice and pick up the painting for you."

"I agreed with him. I don't want to make the trip myself." He frowned. "I went to Venice maybe twenty years ago, on a tour, and it upset me a great deal to be there and think about generations of my family living there, how with one swoop the Nazis destroyed a whole community."

He took a deep breath. "But I do want to get the painting back. This is about more than just my uncle's painting, at least to me," Frank said. "What do you know about the Italian Jews and the Holocaust?"

"Not much. The Fascists under Mussolini were allies of the Germans. So I assume they had the same anti-Jewish policies, right?"

"To a degree. Many of the Jews in Italy were secularized, often intermarrying with Italians. My family can trace its history back to 1492, when the Sephardim, the Spanish Jews, were expelled under the Inquisition. They lived in Italy for centuries after that, so they felt Italian, and when Mussolini enacted laws regulating Jews in 1938 they were completely surprised."

He sipped his water. "They were called the *leggi razziali* or racial laws. They restricted civil rights of Jews, banned Jewish books, and excluded Jews from public office and higher education."

I couldn't imagine living in my own native country and suddenly being subjected to rules that governed what I could and could not do.

"Your father was in the United States, so how come your uncle didn't join him?"

"By the time Ugo decided to leave, more laws had been enacted that stripped Jews of their assets and restricted their travel. In his last letters my uncle was very worried, but he still believed that he was Italian before he was Jewish, and that would save him. And he thought that the Pope would intervene, and the Italians, who were fervent Catholics, would obey him rather than the government."

I could imagine that kind of hubris because I'd seen it in criminals. Laws didn't matter to them. Even if the laws were wrong.

"The Pope never spoke up," Frank said. "When Mussolini fell in 1943 and the Nazis occupied the country, they began to round up the Jews for deportation to the camps. From what I can trace, my uncle went into hiding, but eventually he was caught and sent to an internment camp at Fossoli di Carpi near Modena. From there he went to Auschwitz, where he was murdered."

We were both silent for a moment. Frank's last word echoed in my ears. I'd been accustomed to thinking of the Holocaust as genocide—a fancier word that hid the true meaning of all those deaths. Murdered was a harsher word—and a true one.

"I have the money," Frank said, his voice low and sad. "Tom's spoken highly of you as a man I can trust, and I'd greatly appreciate this if you could do this favor for me. And for my uncle."

Ugo Sena had lived in another time, another place, but he was a gay man imprisoned and murdered for the crime of being who he was. It felt like the universe was telling me this was something I had to do.

Chapter 16

The Art is in the Selling

As I drove home, I became more and more excited about the chance to go to Italy and see Danny. I just had to get Miriam to sign off on the plan. I couldn't wait to get to work on Monday morning and spell it all out for her. I thought about emailing Danny or trying to set up a Skype call with him, but I didn't want to get his hopes up until it was definite. I was enthusiastic enough for both of us.

When I got home, I opened the envelope Jesse Venable had given me. We'd agreed on three-fifty for the work, but once I separated the bills into piles and totaled them up, I counted four hundred bucks. I guessed the fifty-buck bonus was either for a quick turnaround or the chance to see me in my wet bathing suit.

I was scrupulous about recording all my freelance income. I certainly didn't want to get tripped up by the IRS for neglecting to report what I earned. The mix of small bills was interesting, and I remembered the case I'd helped Katya with earlier that year, the one involving money laundering. Businesses that dealt in cash, like Venable's pawn shop, were prime opportunities for laundering money.

Had those bills in the envelope come to Venable through illegal means? Maybe he was laundering cash for a drug dealer. I reminded myself that where the cash came from was outside the limits of the investigation into the illegal sale of *Ragazzi al Mare*, though I made a note to include all that information in the FD302 I'd prepare Monday morning about my interactions with Venable.

That night I went out to Lazy Dick's with Jonas, but only stayed for a single drink. I missed Lester, and was glad when he texted me Sunday afternoon that he'd landed at the airport. I offered to pick him up, and on our way back to Wilton Manors I heard all about the distillery he'd visited, how little differences like the source or the age of the oak barrels could have such an effect on the taste of the whiskey.

At least that's what I think he said. I was too caught up in my own thoughts about Jesse Venable and the potential trip to Italy, which I finally had the chance to spill out as we pulled up at Lester's apartment building.

"Your bosses will let you do that?" he asked.

"I hope so. My assignment is to get Jesse Venable to trust me, and hope that leads him to open up about illegal activities. This is all part of building trust."

"Uh-huh," Lester said, as he crossed his arms over his big chest.

"What? You're not jealous, are you? You've been flying all over the place while I've been tied to my desk."

"I thought the FBI only investigated US crimes. That the CIA did anything overseas."

"Actually, the CIA doesn't have any law enforcement function. They just collect and analyze intelligence information. And they're only authorized to investigate foreign countries and their citizens, not anyone who could be considered a U.S. Person – citizens, resident aliens, legal immigrants."

I got out of the car and popped the trunk to retrieve Lester's bag. "I can't arrest anybody in another country except under very specific circumstances, but there's nothing to prevent me from following the lead of an investigation to Italy."

"Hey, don't get huffy," Lester said. "I just asked. Because I don't trust this Venable guy. What if he's setting you up for receiving stolen goods or something?"

"I couldn't get arrested for doing something within the scope of my job. And besides, I have to confirm with Miriam Washington before I can do anything," I said, handing him his bag. "And if all the documentation I've seen is real, then there's nothing illegal about a government agent retrieving stolen goods on behalf of the legitimate owner."

Lester still wasn't happy, but I coaxed him into going to the gym with me, where we worked out together, focusing on cardio, and as usual he pushed me farther than I'd have gone on my own. By the time we were exhausted we were both in better spirits, and after some languorous love-making I went home for a well-deserved sleep.

Monday morning, I got to the office at eight-thirty and spent the next two hours putting everything I'd learned that weekend into a series of FD302s. Then Miriam called me and said she could see me. I hurried down to her office, and told her about my conversations with Jesse Venable and Frank Sena.

"Are there any problems with my traveling to Italy to retrieve the painting?" I asked. "Even if the painting is listed as stolen, Frank has the paperwork to show that he's the legal owner."

"It's interesting that the legitimate owner of the painting is willing to purchase it, rather than chase it through the courts. It makes our job a lot easier. That is, if he has the provenance you say he does. I'd like to see what he has and talk with him myself before I sign off on this."

She sat back in her chair. "The art in art theft comes in the selling, not the stealing," she said. "Despite best intentions, most of the world's art is vulnerable to theft. Private homes, small galleries and museums, churches and archaeological sites are prime targets. Any reasonably competent thief can steal a work of art, but what do you do with it once you have it?"

"Sell it on the black market?" I asked.

"Easier said than done. Most thieves aren't sophisticated enough to access the market for stolen art, so they end up trying to sell what they've stolen at pawn shops or else they're stuck with something they can't sell."

"Pawn shops like the one Jesse Venable runs," I said.

"Exactly. So it's not surprising that he had the connections to learn about this painting. The more well-known the artist or the work, the more valuable it is— but the counter to that is the more well-known it is, the harder it is to sell legitimately. On the black market, stolen art usually sells for ten percent of its market value."

In familiarizing myself with the work of the Art Crime Task Force, I'd learned that criminals used paintings, sculptures and statues as collateral to finance arms, drug and money-laundering deals. Small pieces of art that can be carried in a suitcase are easier to carry across borders than cash or drugs, and it's hard for customs agents to spot the value. Half the art and antiquities that we and other law enforcement agencies recover is found in a different country from the one where it was stolen.

She sat back in her chair. "You'll need to clear the trip with Vito Mastroianni, because he's your supervisor. Assuming he has no problems letting you go, how soon do you think you could leave for Italy?"

"This is all I'm working on right now. So I could leave whenever necessary."

"Check with Vito and see what kind of arrangements you can make. I'll contact someone I know in the Italian *Carabinieri* who works on art theft."

I was so excited I could barely put my thoughts together as I walked to Vito's office. I had gotten a passport right after I graduated from Penn State, with grand plans to travel the world as soon as I built up some savings. But life and bills had gotten in the way. I'd be getting my first foreign country stamp in it. How cool!

"Miriam Washington says I can go to Italy to pick up this stolen painting," I said, as I hovered anxiously in the doorway to his office. "As long as you say it's okay, that you don't need me for a couple of days."

"Slow down, rookie," Vito said. "Sit." He pointed me to the chair across from him. "This is the painting Venable had a line on?"

I explained all that had transpired. "Venable has made the contact with the seller in Italy, but he doesn't want to send the money without seeing the painting, and he can't go."

"I'm not understanding something," Vito said. "It's a big jump from doing some research on a stolen painting to traveling to Italy as an agent of the FBI to retrieve it. And that usually requires a much more seasoned operative. *Non si parla Italiano, si fa?* You don't speak Italian, do you?"

"No. But I'm hoping to meet up with my brother, who's studying there this summer. He speaks the language."

Vito ignored that. "You don't know anything about the man you're going to meet. You won't be able to have a weapon with you in Italy. You're a smart guy, Angus, and you have good instincts. But you've been a sworn agent for a little less than a year, right? Not a good idea to send you on your own on a mission to a foreign country."

I was stunned. The idea of traveling to Europe and seeing my brother had been so exciting, and now it was all swirling down the drain. "But..."

He held up his hand. "I can't make the final decision," he said. "But you asked, so I'm telling you what I think."

It took me a moment to marshal my thoughts. "Agent Washington said she could hook me up with someone in the Italian police who handles art theft," I said. "I wouldn't be on my own, and I'd have someone to interpret who knows all the ropes."

He pursed his lips together, then finally sighed. "I'll call Miriam and talk to her. If she thinks you'll be all right, then I won't stand in your way. But trust me, you don't want me to say I told you so if you mess up."

I stumbled back to my office. I hadn't realized how much I wanted to go to Italy until Vito had pointed out all the problems and seemed to snatch the opportunity away from me. By the time I was seated in front of my computer, I had made up my mind. I wasn't going to sit by and let Miriam and Vito make the decision whether I could go or not without doing everything I could to prove that I was capable of taking on the assignment.

Chapter 17
Navigation

First, I had to see if Danny could meet me in Venice. Despite my bravado with Vito, I knew I'd need my brother's help to navigate a foreign language and culture.

I looked at the clock and did some quick calculations. If it was two o'clock in Florida, then it was seven in the evening in Florence. I emailed Danny and told him I might have a chance to come to Venice in the next couple of days. I explained about meeting the person who had the painting.

Would Danny be able to meet me, translate for me, if the person with the painting didn't speak English? I told him I'd be at my computer at work at least for another three hours, and asked him to Skype me when he could—even later that night, once I was home.

I initiated the Skype program on my laptop and left it running in the background. What else could I do to prove that I was competent? Investigate travel arrangements. If I could show Miriam and Vito that I had flights on hold, that I knew where I would be staying and how I'd get around Venice, that might sway their opinion.

Air Berlin had a flight from Miami leaving the next afternoon, changing planes in Dusseldorf, and then arriving in Venice on

Wednesday morning. With that on a temporary hold I called Frank Sena. "It looks like I might be able to fly over and pick up the painting for you," I said. "I just want to make sure you still want me to." I swallowed hard. "And that you can cover my expenses. I won't take advantage of you, but I can't afford the airfare and the hotel out of my own pocket."

"I'm so pleased you can do this, Angus. And of course I'll pay your expenses. Do you think five thousand dollars would cover you?"

I was stunned that he could throw around that kind of money so easily. "Honestly, Frank, I have no idea. I've never been out of the United States before. And the flight alone is over a thousand dollars."

"I know, I already checked myself, before I figured out that it would be too emotional for me. Don't worry, I'll cover whatever it costs," Frank said. "And I don't expect you to skimp on meals or sleep on a floor somewhere."

"I just have to make sure my bosses agree, and that Venable can arrange for me to meet with whoever has the painting. I'll let you know when it's confirmed."

"He'll make it work. I'm paying him a commission for his services. Once you know for certain, I'll have my travel agent book a flight and a hotel for you."

Jesse Venable was next on my agenda. "It's possible I'll be able to go to Venice in the next couple of days to pick up the painting," I said. "I'm juggling a couple of clients and waiting to make sure it's okay with them. Can you verify with this guy that he'd be able to meet with me and deliver the painting? Find out as much information as you can about him. Where in the city he is, how I'll recognize him."

"I'll get right on it," Venable said.

I wondered how much of a commission Frank Sena was paying him. Venable had mentioned a purchase price of fifty thousand bucks – there had to be at least ten or fifteen percent on top of that for him.

From there, I went online and found a travel guide to Venice and an Italian language translation app for my phone. I discovered that when I landed in Italy I could buy a SIM card for my iPhone that would give me a local number and enable me to make calls in the country.

Then my computer beeped with an incoming Skype call from my brother, and I pulled on the headset and microphone.

There was a time lag so I heard his voice before I saw his lips move. "You're coming to Italy!" he crowed, and then his face appeared on my screen. It was so great to see him, and more than ever I wanted to be able to be with him in person.

"I hope so," I said. "It's not definite yet. Can you meet me?"

"Absolutely. I've been wanting to go to Venice since I got here. It's only about two hours on the train, and if I go second class it's not that expensive."

"And do you think you could translate for me if you had to? I got this app for my phone, too."

"I use an app like that all the time and I get along fine," Danny said. "*Io parlo italiano molto bene.*" My brother's face was glowing with pride.

"I'll take your word for it. If I get the authorization, I'll be in Venice on Wednesday morning."

"That's awesome! How long can you stay?"

"I won't know until I find out when I can meet this guy and pick up the painting. But I'll email you later tonight with the details."

"*Ciao, mio fratello!*"

I repeated the words to him and added, "Love you, bro."

"Back at you, Angus."

I ended the call and looked up to see Miriam Washington and Vito Mastroianni in the doorway to my office.

"I was just on a Skype call with my brother in Florence," I said. "He can meet me in Venice and translate. I got this translation app for my phone, and I have maps and a guide to the city, and Frank Sena will cover my expenses."

Vito laughed. "Hold your horses, rookie." He turned to Miriam.

"I managed to get hold of a man I met at a conference," she said.

"His name is Leonardo Foa, and he's willing to help with whatever you need."

"That's awesome! So does that mean I can go?"

"You can go," Miriam said. "Hopefully your transaction will enable him to make an arrest on his end. Then he can lean on whoever he arrests to give up information on Venable."

"Which in turn could give us what we need to catch the people smuggling immigrants and counterfeit watches out of Turkey," Vito said.

Miriam agreed to email me Foa's contact information, and then they both left.

I sat back in my chair. The trip was really going to happen – that is, if Jesse Venable was able to make the arrangements.

I fidgeted for the rest of the afternoon, waiting to hear back from Venable. I was tempted to call him again, but I knew he was as eager as I was to get the painting, and that he'd call me as soon as he could. I also didn't want to let any sudden enthusiasm for the trip make Venable suspicious of my motives.

Would I be able to get that flight I hoped to take? What if it filled up? It was the height of summer. Suppose I couldn't get a hotel room in Venice? What if I got lost on the way to the meeting and couldn't do what I was supposed to do?

I took a couple of deep breaths. Everything would work out, and if something went wrong, I'd roll with it, make adjustments. I was a full-fledged special agent with the Federal Bureau of Investigation. I knew how to handle a gun, interrogate suspects, and navigate in unfamiliar environments. And after years behind a bar, I knew how to read people and situations.

Lester came over to the house that evening with grilled salmon and take-out salads from Whole Foods. As we sat at the kitchen table and ate, I told him about the trip. After we finished eating, I opened my laptop and pulled up the photo of the painting.

"The more I look at that painting, the more it reminds me of something," he said, staring at the screen. "I have an idea. Let me see the laptop for a minute."

He typed for a moment or two, then turned the screen toward me. "See this painting? It's called 'Swimming,' and it's by a painter from Philadelphia named Thomas Eakins."

The subject matter was very similar to the Fabre painting. A naked young man stood on top of a rock by a lake, with his back to the viewer. The pose was similar to what I'd seen in the classical nude statues I'd researched.

Another naked guy reclined on top of the rock in a pose that reminded me of the some of the female nudes I'd studied in art history. A third dove into the water and two more were in various positions on the rock. "That's Eakins himself there," Lester said, pointing at a man neck-deep in the water, watching the boys.

The description under the painting read that it had been painted between 1883 and 1885, around the same time that Fabre had been working in Italy. The technique was similar, too, though the men's anatomy was much more carefully done than Fabre's.

We looked at the painting of the swimmers again, and I began to understand more clearly how Fabre's work fit into artistic traditions. His art needed to be shown to the world.

Then my cell phone rang and I saw from the display that it was Jesse Venable. "This is the guy," I said to Lester.

"My contact just emailed me," Venable said. "He wants to meet with you at eleven o'clock on Thursday morning at an internet café near the church where the painting was taken from. I'll email you the details."

"How will I recognize him? Did he give you a name?"

"His name is Remigio Grassini. I told him to look for a young American man with red hair. He'll find you."

"How am I going to pay him?"

"He emailed me his bank information. I'm sending him a token down payment to make sure the transaction goes through and to demonstrate my intent. Once you verify that you have the painting in your possession, I'll send him the remaining balance."

"Then I guess I'm going to Venice," I said. After I hung up, I called Frank and let him know I was good to go. He had gotten me a prepaid credit card with a thousand dollars on it, and all I had to do was stop by his apartment the next morning and pick it up. That was good, because it meant I wouldn't have to use my own card, or the prepaid one that Wagon had given me.

I hung up, and Lester and I went into my room and began looking through my closet for clothes I could take with me. A short time later, Jonas joined Lester and me in my bedroom. Jonas looked at the shirts, slacks and boxers that covered my bed. "You're not doing another strip trivia contest, are you?" he asked.

I realized that the last time I'd had so much clothing out was when I was about to enter a contest a few months before, to earn some money for Danny's trip. How much had happened since then.

"No, dude, I'm going to Italy." I explained about the stolen painting and the plan to retrieve it.

Jonas gave a low whistle. "Nice to have rich friends," he said. "I wish somebody wanted to send me to Italy for the weekend."

Because I didn't want him to be jealous, I tried to point out some of the negatives. "I'm sure it won't be that great," I said. "Hours on the plane, jet lag, time difference, and then turning around and coming back right away."

"Yeah, tell yourself that," Jonas said, but he laughed. "Have a good time."

"But not too good," Lester said. "No handsome Italians getting into your pants."

"Not as long as I have you to come home too, sweetheart," I said.

Jonas made a gagging noise, and we all laughed. I wasn't worried about running into handsome Italians—I wanted to retrieve the painting for Frank, get evidence to use against Venable, and see my brother. With luck and strategic thinking, I hoped I could do all three.

Chapter 18

Business Class

Jonas left us to call his boyfriend, and Lester checked the weather forecast for Venice. Temperatures were going to be in the seventies and eighties, with high humidity, so he helped me pick out shorts and lightweight shirts, with one pair of slacks and a small umbrella.

Frank's travel agent sent me confirmations of my ticket on the Air Berlin flight the next afternoon and my reservation at a hotel called Locanda del Ghetto in Venice. She noted in the email that it was a five-minute walk from the second stop on the boat from the airport, and included walking directions from the hotel's website.

Venable had emailed, too. Frank Sena would go to Venable's house on Thursday, and I'd Skype them on my laptop before Grassini arrived. The Italian would show us the painting, and if it was all kosher, Frank would initiate the wire transfer to Grassini's account.

By the time Lester and I were finished I was even more excited—which led to great fun together before we fell asleep.

We went for a run together the next morning, and after I showered, dressed, and checked my luggage twice to make sure I had everything, I drove to Frank's condo. "I'm so pleased that you're doing this for me, Angus," he said as he handed me the credit card. "Your flight and your hotel will be charged directly to me. Feel free to use all this for your expenses, and if you run over, just let me know when you get back."

"Thank you for the chance to go to Italy," I said. "I can't tell you how thrilled I am to be able to travel, and to meet up with my brother."

"Tell me, is your brother as handsome as you are?"

"Even better-looking. And straight."

Frank laughed. "Then you two should have a great time in Italy. Remember, you're part of a great gay fraternity. All you have to do is turn on your gaydar and you'll be able to find men to give you directions, point out the best restaurants and bars." He smiled. "And whatever else your heart desires."

"I'm looking forward to spending the weekend with my brother," I said. "And I have a boyfriend back here who's more than enough for me."

Frank leaned forward and kissed me lightly on the left cheek, then again on the right. "Just so you're prepared for Europe."

I slid the charge card into my wallet and drove to the office in Miramar with my suitcase and my backpack in the trunk. When I got to my desk I saw that Miriam had emailed me the work and personal cell phone numbers for Leonardo Foa, the Carabinieri officer I was to liaise with, as well as his email address. I sent him a message with my arrival time and said that I'd call him once I was able to get a local SIM card for my phone.

Then I went to see Miriam. "I have a name and address for the guy who says he has the painting," I said. "And I was thinking, someone who has one piece of stolen art might have more. Do you know how to see if this man has been involved in other transactions in the past?"

"I can check the Interpol database," she said.

I spelled the name for her, and she typed. After a moment or two had passed, she shook her head. "He doesn't come up. That doesn't mean he hasn't sold stolen art before, just that he hasn't been caught. You should be careful with him."

"How do you recommend I bring this painting home?" I asked. "According to what I've been told, it was painted in oil on wood, and it's about two feet tall and three feet wide."

"Your best choice is to find a shipping outfit and have them pack the painting for you, then carry it on board on your return flight."

"That sounds like a plan," I said. "I'm picking it up on Thursday so I should have plenty of time to get it wrapped."

I didn't have any more work to do after I'd finished with Miriam, and I figured I was better off fidgeting at the airport than in my office. Before I left I went over to the quartermaster to check in my Glock, because I couldn't carry it on the plane, and I didn't want to leave it in my office or my car. I felt almost naked as I walked back to my office—I'd grown so accustomed to having it with me that I missed it.

It was a brutally hot day, and I was hoping that Venice might be a little more pleasant, especially if I'd be sightseeing with Danny. But no matter the weather, I'd be with my little brother, and that was all that mattered.

I drove to the Miami airport, parked in a long term lot, and rode a bus to the terminal. It was exciting to be surrounded by all kinds of people on their way somewhere, from grungy-looking backpackers to Latin businessmen speaking rapid Spanish on their cell phones.

I was stunned to discover that Frank's travel agent had booked me into Air Berlin's business class, which had a separate check in line. I learned that I could carry on a second item on my return flight and that my bags would be unloaded first on arrival in Venice. After waiting in the TSA line, I made my way to the gate, where I sent Lester a text to let him know that I was on my way, and almost immediately got one back from him, full of airplane and smile emoticons, telling me to have a great time.

The flight attendant, a trim gay man in his early forties with

Hans on his name tag, came by after I'd settled in. "Is this your first flight on Air Berlin?" he asked.

I smiled at him. "Yes. It's also my first international flight."

"We'll, if there's anything I can help you with just let me know," Hans said. "Let me show you how to recline your seat."

He leaned over me to demonstrate that I could change my seat to fully horizontal once we were in flight, and I smelled his spicy cologne. Maybe Frank was right after all and the great gay fraternity would help me on my travels.

There was plenty of leg room, a table where I could work, and a USB plug to charge my laptop if I needed. It made me feel almost guilty, but I kept making Facebook posts so that my friends could see the luxury.

Once the crew lowered the lights, I stretched my chair out and settled in. I was afraid I was too excited to sleep, but I went out right away and woke the next morning as the lights came up and the pilot announced we were beginning our descent into Dusseldorf.

The ground staff were very helpful getting me to my flight to Venice. The airport reminded me of others that I'd passed through, with a high lattice of beams above and a constant movement of people towing luggage. I was in a foreign country, even if I was only seeing the airport and staying in Germany for a few hours. I was living the life my father had dreamed of. I changed money into euros while I waited for the next flight.

The short-haul plane wasn't as fancy as the international one, but I was still in business class and had room to stretch my legs. Frank's travel agent had gotten me a window seat, and as the plane lined up for landing at Marco Polo airport, I got my first glimpse of Venice. I was able to easily make out the bell tower and elaborate domes of St. Mark's and the open square in front of it, and get an idea of the way the island city was laid out, all the canals snaking through the city, the long causeway to the mainland, the outlying islands and a strand of beach along the Mediterranean.

The water was a rich blue-green, the islands a mass of tightly packed terra cotta roofs. We came in low over a corner of the city and I saw four- and five-story buildings butted next to each other and facing on a canal, with gondolas and power boats moored at docks.

We landed smoothly, and I could barely contain my eagerness as I waited for the cabin door to open so I could burst out into the jet way. Venice, here I come!

Chapter 19

Brotherly Love

I hurried out of the gate and into the mass of people crowding into Marco Polo airport. On my way to baggage claim, I bought a SIM card from a kiosk, and the clerk showed me how to swap it out for the one in my iPhone. It came with a new phone number, and the first call I made was to the number my brother was using while he was in Italy.

"Danny? I'm at the airport in Venice!"

"That's awesome, bro," he said, and he sounded like he was calling from right next door. "I'm on the train now. I get into Venice in about half an hour. I'll meet you at the hotel."

"Can't wait."

I had worried that I'd be intimidated by all the foreign language around me, but living in South Florida had prepared me for that. All the signs in the airport were in English as well as Italian, and I made it to the boat dock easily. The air smelled like salt water and exhaust fumes but it could have been the richest perfume.

My phone had automatically updated to Italian time. It was almost noon, which gave me a little over twenty-four hours to have some fun in Venice before I had to meet Remigio Grassini and pick up the painting. I sent Lester another text, letting him know I'd arrived safely, with a couple of kiss emoticons of my own.

A low, yellow-hulled water taxi pulled up a few minutes later. It rocked slightly beneath me as I stepped on board. I'd had little experience of boats growing up, and even in South Florida I rarely had the chance to get out on the water. Despite some queasiness I was determined to enjoy every new experience. Tugging my suitcase behind me, I moved forward until I could find a seat by the window.

The water taxi took off and we motored along a narrow channel that paralleled the runway. Then it picked up speed as we entered open water, and I grabbed the railing next to me. There was a brief recorded message in several languages as we rode. I learned that the lagoon was an enclosed bay of the Adriatic Sea, with a surface area of over two hundred square miles. There were 117 islands, separated by canals and linked by bridges. The area had been inhabited since the tenth century BC, and today over sixty thousand people lived within the commune of Venice.

We passed the island of Murano, where decorative glass was made, and as the second stop approached, I began to make my way toward the exit. When we pulled up to the dock I noticed a dark-skinned man standing in front of a cloth spread on the street beside a building. The cloth was piled with a collection of wallets, purses and handbags.

They had to be counterfeit, I thought, without even looking closely. Had these fakes come from the same places as the ones I'd seen at Trader Tom's? I'd read an article on the plane about Venice that mentioned these traders, the *vu compra*, who were mostly refugees and immigrants from Senegal or Bangladesh.

Would they soon be replaced by Syrians like the ones on the boat that had capsized in the Aegean?

I shook my head. This wasn't my problem. I was here at Frank Sena's expense to pick up the painting for him. And I hoped that transaction would lead to information that would incriminate Jesse Venable. Immigrant traders in Venice were well beyond my scope.

From the boat stop, I walked along the canal past colorful red, blue and orange houses. Fishing boats festooned with small flags were docked beside me, and the air smelled like raw fish and salt water, with a hint of sewage I chose to ignore.

I turned left onto the Calle del Forno. I knew enough Italian, from eating out, to know that *forno* meant oven, and it was pretty uncomfortable that a street by that name led to the Jewish quarter—and that from there, Italian Jews like Frank's uncle had been sent to the ovens of the concentration camps.

It was hot and humid, my backpack weighed me down, and my rolling bag bucked on the rough sidewalk. When I reached the Calle Ghetto Vecchio I spotted the café where I was to meet Remigio Grassini the next day.

Fortunately, it was only another few minutes until I came into a broad square and saw the sign for the Locanda del Ghetto ahead of me. The lobby was at least a few degrees cooler and drier than the air outside, and I was happy to shuck my backpack and show my passport to the woman behind the desk.

She spoke a little English, and after she had taken a photocopy of my passport she handed me a key to a room. "*Due, per favore,*" I said.

She shook her head. Eventually I figured out that to get a key for my brother, he'd have to check in too. I accepted that, and took the stairs to the third floor, where I found a room with two double beds and a tiny balcony that looked out onto the square.

I hurried over and opened the doors and stepped outside. More of the hot, humid air rushed in, but I didn't care. I lived in Florida, after all.

Then I saw my brother approaching through the square the same way I'd come. "Danny!" I yelled, conscious that I was behaving just like an American.

He looked up and waved at me, and I rushed downstairs to greet him. We met in the lobby, hugging and laughing. Danny looked older than the last time I'd seen him. His skin was tanned and his brown hair was longer and shaggy, and there was something more mature about him.

"I can't believe you're really here," Danny said as I led him to the desk.

"I can't believe it either."

I was impressed at how fluently he spoke to the woman behind the desk, the way she smiled in what I was sure was a response to his flattery.

It was so strange watching him. Did I behave that way with guys? Would I be like him with women if I was straight?

Danny followed me up the stairs to our room. "How come you brought so much luggage, bro?" Danny asked when he saw my suitcase and my backpack. "I thought you were only going to be here for a few days."

I shrugged. "Didn't know what I'd need so I took whatever." I sat down on one of the beds. "So, what do we do? You want to see Venice?"

"I thought we could go to the Peggy Guggenheim Museum this afternoon," Danny said. "I checked and they have a couple of paintings by the Macchiaioli in a special exhibition. I'd really love to see their regular collection, and it would be good for you to see one of the paintings in person before you meet this guy."

"Of course," I said. "You can be my tour guide."

"Hardly. I've been in Venice less time than you have."

"But you can speak Italian. You were awesome with the woman at the front desk."

He waved his hand. "That's nothing. You should hear me in Italian class."

We took a vaporetto a couple of stops and then walked to the museum, housed in an old palazzo on a canal. I paid for our admissions with Frank's credit card and Danny and I walked inside. We stopped in front of a painting called "Empire of Light" by Rene Magritte.

"Look at the way he directs your eye," he said. "You can't resist looking at the street lamp in front of the little house, right? And then your eye naturally travels up to that big tree pointing to the sky."

"Okay," I said.

"What else strikes you about the painting?"

I shrugged. "I don't know. It's pretty?"

"Come on, Angus. Think. Use that analytical brain of yours."

I stared at the painting, trying to figure out what Danny wanted me to see. It looked like an ordinary scene, a house with a street light in front of it. Then I forced myself to stop thinking and just look at the painting. I'd read that the Macchiaioli did sketches for their paintings outdoors, then did the oil work in their studios, and I tried to imagine Magritte at his easel in front of the scene. How could he see to paint in the dark?

Then I realized what Danny was trying to show me. "There's a contrast," I said. "The bottom of the painting is dark but the sky above is light, like daytime."

He slapped me on the back. "Exactly! So you see that there's more going on than just a pretty picture. The artist is trying to tell you something, to get you thinking. Now let's go see these Macchiaioli paintings."

We followed the signs to the special exhibit, which was called *En Plein Air*. "You know what that means, right?" Danny asked.

"Paintings done outside," I said. "The way the Macchiaioli worked."

"Yup. But more than that, it also means painting exactly what's in front of you, as opposed to in a studio, where you could stage a still life, for example."

"That was part of what the Macchiaioli were after, wasn't it?" I asked. "Trying to show the world as it was. To shake off the shackles of the old traditions of painting."

"You did your homework," Danny said. We talked about the way many of the Macchiaioli had fought in the Risorgimento. "See, it's all tied together. Their view of their country and its art traditions."

The first painting in the exhibit was called *A riposo a Riomag-*

giore by Telemaco Signorini, one of the best-known of the Macchiaioli. "I see the same thing here as in the Magritte," I said. "The way he's directing your eye from the cobblestones up to the sky."

"Good. Now step up close. You see these splotches of paint? Those are the *'macchia.'* From this perspective they don't look like much. But now step back."

I followed him. "From farther away you get a sense of how the light and shadow work," he said.

"You studied all this in your classes?"

"Yeah. And once you told me you were coming, I read some stuff and talked to my professor."

"Thanks, bro. I appreciate all the help."

We walked through the rest of the museum, and I was happy that Danny was so excited to see these works of art he'd only studied in textbooks. By the time we finished at the museum, both our stomachs were growling. "A friend of mine told me about a cheap restaurant with great food," Danny said.

"We don't have to eat on the cheap," I said. "I have Frank's credit card."

"Still. He said this was popular with students and travelers, and I thought it would be fun. Show you a little of what my life is like in Florence."

We took another vaporetto, then walked a lot, following directions on Danny's phone. Though it was still daylight, the shadows cast by the close buildings made the narrow streets seem dark, and a couple of times I felt uneasy being jammed in with so many other people, a mix of tourists, locals and more of those African street vendors. I missed the comfort of having my gun by my side.

The restaurant was a boisterous one, filled with students in their early twenties with Canadian and Australian flags sewn onto backpacks. I felt almost ancient, though I was only five years older than Danny. We slid into two seats across from each other at a crowded table, and Danny ordered for us in Italian.

Then he turned to the girl beside him, who had exuberant

auburn curls. She and her sister, beside me, were traveling through Europe. Alexandra was a sophomore at Auburn and Beth a junior at Brown. We had a lively conversation with them as we ate our way through courses of tortellini in chicken broth, fried artichokes, and chicken sautéed with lemon and mushrooms.

Accompanied by a bottle of white wine, which we shared with the girls, it was an awesome meal. Danny was such a flirt and it was funny to see him operate, and wonder if I was the same way at Lazy Dick's.

"My brother's here on business," Danny said. "He's a special agent with the FBI. Tracking down a stolen painting."

The pride in his voice made me smile. "It's not a big deal," I said. But they demanded to know what my job was like, and I told them a couple of stories about cases I had investigated.

"You got shot!" Alexandra said. "Oh my God."

Though the experience had been pretty upsetting for me, I wasn't interested in sharing my feelings about it with total strangers. "The bullet bounced off my vest. It wasn't a big deal."

"Of course it was," Danny said. "My brother, the hero."

I blushed and changed the subject.

By the time we finished it was dark out. "Would you mind walking us back to our hotel?" Alexandra asked. "On the way here these creepy African guys followed us for a couple of blocks, trying to sell us drugs and asking for money."

"It freaked us both out," Beth said.

I could imagine how they must have felt, based on my own experience walking through those shaded streets with Danny, and of course we agreed.

It was even creepier walking back to the girls' *pensione* in the dark. The streets were no longer so crowded, but some of the cobblestones were slippery and we had to watch our steps. We crossed a lot of bridges and made a lot of turns, and I regretted having had to leave my gun behind in Miramar.

That was ridiculous. There was no way I was going to shoot

anyone in Venice. But I had become accustomed to its bulk against my waist, to how comforting it was knowing I could defend myself and those I was with if I had to. I reminded myself that I'd learned a lot of self-defense skills at the Academy, and with all the workouts I did with Lester I was in the best shape of my life.

A couple of times I sensed men hovering on the edges of the street, but no one approached us. In the end, it wasn't that far from where we dropped the girls to our own hotel, and we made it back there without incident.

"I had a lot of fun today," Danny said, once we were in our room. "I'm still having trouble believing that we're together. In Venice, of all places!"

"Me too. And tomorrow, after I pick up the painting, we can do some more sightseeing. Maybe hang out with the girls again, if you want."

"You think it will be dangerous?" Danny asked. "Meeting with this guy?"

"Not at all," I said, though I had my doubts. "It's a straightforward business transaction. He has the painting, and as long as you and I agree it's the right one, he gets his money. What could go wrong?"

Chapter 20

Rendezvous

The jet lag must have caught up with me because I slept late, waking after nine to see Danny sitting on the balcony with a porcelain cup of coffee. I sat up and yawned. "I never thought I'd see the day that I'd sleep later than you," I said. Danny had always been tough to wake as a kid, and working nights at the restaurant had only reinforced his late-sleeping habits.

"Gotta seize the day, bro," he said, smiling. "I figure I can sleep when I get back to State College. I've been up with the birds every day. I usually go for a walk around Florence, to stretch my legs and absorb the culture. And to pick up a pastry for breakfast, of course."

My brother sounded more and more like me, I thought, as I used the bathroom. Was it genetics, or upbringing, or was he trying to be like me? When he was younger he'd wanted to do everything I did, have sneakers like mine, eat the same cereal I did.

"Any more of that coffee?" I asked, when I finished my shower.

"Breakfast downstairs only ran until nine," he said. "But Enrichetta told me there's a great café down the *calle* where we can get coffee and pastry."

"Enrichetta?"

"The girl at the desk. You know, the one I was talking to yesterday."

Once again I marveled at my brother's touch with women.

"She also told me some sights to check out as we walk around the neighborhood. So come on, let's get moving."

I put on a lightweight shirt and a pair of cargo shorts with big pockets to hold my wallet and passport secure. Once again I missed the feel of my Glock against my waist.

Danny was a walking guidebook as we strolled over to the café. We passed a set of seven bronze plaques with scenes from the Holocaust, including a crowd lined up to board railroad cars and one that showed three soldiers aiming rifles at a woman, while a man and child looked on. It chilled me despite the hot morning air. This was what Ugo Sena had faced, all because he was gay and Jewish.

I learned that breakfast was called *prima colazione* in Italian, and Danny ordered us steaming mugs of cappuccino and a platter of cornettos, rolls that looked like French croissants but were sweeter. Some were filled with cream, others with jam. I was surprised to see that the café served kosher meals, but then figured that they must get a big clientele of Jewish tourists.

The food was great, and we laughed and talked, continuing to catch each other up on the small things hadn't been worth putting into an email or using up time on Skype. We walked around the neighborhood for a while, and I noted a yellow haze in the air. I couldn't tell if the nasty odor was from that pollution or the murky green water in the canal, but I didn't like it.

At ten-thirty we made our way through crowds of tourists to the Caffe del Campo, a small storefront jammed with backpackers using the internet, laptops displayed on tables, charging on long snaking cords. We waited until a table became available, and while Danny turned on my laptop I got us a pair of cappuccinos. "How will you know who's coming?" he asked, when I returned with the coffees.

"It'll be the guy with the big painting under his arm," I said. "And he's been told to look for an American with red hair."

While we waited, I sent Lester a long, enthusiastic email, about how great it was to see my brother again, describing the buildings and canals but leaving out the yellow haze and the nasty smell. A few minutes after I finished and sent it, a skinny man with a rectangular parcel nestled in his tattooed arms walked in the café, took one look around, and headed for us. "Guess I'm easy to spot," I said to Danny as I waved at the man.

"Hello, I am Remi," he said, as he eagerly shook our hands. His accent was heavy but understandable.

"I'm Angus, and this is my brother Danny," I said. "And that's the painting?"

"*Si*," he said.

I moved my laptop so there was room on the table to lay out the package, and he unwrapped the single layer of brown paper.

"Wow," I said. There was a layer of dust on the painting, but it looked vibrant. It was the closest I'd ever been to a painting and I didn't know what to do.

Danny was prepared, though. He used my phone to pull up the information Frank had given me, and we compared the painting and the frame to that, and to what I'd seen in the 8-millimeter movie. Fabre's signature, with a big ornamental F, matched other paintings he had done.

"You like?" Remi said, after we looked back at him.

"It's beautiful."

"Can we see the back?" Danny asked.

"Of course." Grassini carefully lifted the painting up and flipped it over, then rested it once more on the brown paper. The frame was deep enough that the paint didn't touch the paper.

Danny pointed to a piece of wood on the bottom of the frame that looked different from the rest. "What happened here?" he asked.

Grassini shrugged. "Was like that when I find painting. Is old, after all. Maybe frame break years before and was repaired."

I looked at my brother. "What do you think?"

"He has a point," Danny said. "As long as the picture's the same, who cares if there's a little problem with the back of the frame?"

"Let me get Mr. Venable on the computer." I initiated the call and plugged in the headset and microphone I used when I spoke with Danny. A couple of moments later Jesse Venable's face appeared on the screen. I held the painting up to the screen, and his voice was excited. "That's it! You've got it!"

"Looks like it," I said.

He shifted places and Frank Sena popped in. He'd already put through the transaction, and all he had to do was enter an authorization code to release the funds. "That should only take a little while," he said.

I told Grassini what Venable had said, and he agreed. "But I don't give you the painting until I see the money."

"That's all right. We have all afternoon, if you need."

Frank let me know that the money had been released. "There's no reason for me to stay on the line," he said. "Just email us when you're all finished."

I agreed, and ended the call. I remembered my conversation with Miriam, that if Grassini had one stolen painting he might have more. And other paintings would add to our evidence against Venable.

"Do you have any other art like this?" I asked Grassini. "Mr. Venable might be interested in buying something else."

"I have, at my apartment." Grassini looked at his watch. "I have other appointment there, but not for some time."

"Then let's go," I said. "You can check your bank on your phone, right?"

"Yes. I will check soon."

Danny and I drained our cappuccinos as Grassini taped the paper over the painting again. Then we followed him outside, into the hot sun of the *calle*. "Is just up there, around corner," he said.

I had a momentary pang of doubt. We were going off script here, and who knew what could happen? But Vito had told me to trust my instincts, so I did.

Survival is a Dying Art

"How did you find this painting?" I asked, as we walked.

"My family, they live a long time in same apartment," he said. "From before my grandfather, even. He die a few years after the war is over, when my father is still boy. Then as he grow up, my father store things in shed on roof of building. I never go up there—who needs old stuff, right? But then my father die last year, and I have to clean up."

He stopped in front of a narrow, four-story building beside a church, and I realized from the name plate that this was Beata Vergine della Laguna, the church where the Nazis had stored some of the art works they confiscated from the Jews of the Ghetto.

No wonder Remigio Grassini had ended up with the painting. Had he stolen it himself? But then I remembered it had disappeared a few years after the end of the war. Had his grandfather been the one who "liberated" it from the church?

His phone trilled, and he pulled it out his phone. "*Eccellente!* Money has arrived." With a sketchy bow, he handed me the painting. "Is all yours now."

I took it, and then we walked into a dim lobby and began climbing the stairs. Grassini "You grew up here?" I asked.

"Yes. My father, he never make much money. But he is determined I have better life, so he push me to go to school, to get my technical certification."

Leonardo Foa had told me that Grassini had been arrested a few times for theft, and so I was curious to hear what he said when I asked him what he did for a living.

"I am entrepreneur," he said. "Little business here and there. You want to buy cell phone, I am man to see. Now, I fix up apartment to sell for big profit. Selling painting will be important money for me."

The stairwell smelled of stale food and mold and I was glad when we reached the top floor. Grassini opened a door and ushered us into an empty apartment. The wallpaper was peeling and the linoleum on the floor had yellowed. He led us into the kitchen, where he reached up and unlatched a panel in the ceiling, and pulled down a ladder.

"Now we climb," he said. "I go first, so I open door. Then you follow, yes?"

"Yes," I said, though the ladder didn't look very strong, and I wasn't sure how I could manage it while holding the painting under my arm. I thought about leaving it in the kitchen, but what if Grassini had an associate waiting who would come in and steal it? And for that reason, I couldn't leave Danny with it either.

I'd have to manage.

Grassini climbed up quickly and then opened a door so that sunlight flooded down in to the kitchen. I looked at Danny, who said, "After you, bro."

I rested my backpack with the laptop inside against the wall, then gripped the painting under my left arm. My right was my dominant one, so I used that to balance my body as I climbed the dozen rungs.

As I reached the light, I stuck my head out onto the roof to see a small square platform between canted roofs of coral tile, much like those back in Florida. Across from me was a small wooden shed.

I clambered off and rested the painting against the wall, glad to be able to put it down. Danny followed me up. "It's beautiful up here," I said as I looked around at the panoply of pale pink and orange walls, barrel tile roofs, and lines of laundry stretched from windows to balconies. We were right in the middle of the city, yet the sky was expansive.

A low metal railing that looked as rickety as the ladder was all that stood between us and the street below. Beyond it, I could see the murky blue green of one of the many canals that snaked through the city.

"There, that is San Marco," Grassini said, pointing through the maze of buildings to where the bell tower and domes stretched toward heaven. "You have been there?"

"Not yet. Maybe tomorrow," I said.

"You must go! Is very beautiful."

Danny and I turned three hundred sixty degrees, admiring the landscape, as Grassini opened the padlock on the storage shed.

The inside looked like Aladdin's cave. Paintings were lined up against the walls, and paper shopping bags filled to the brim were piled in the middle of the floor. A couple of small sculptures sat beside them, including one I recognized as the male nude I'd seen in the film of Frank's uncle's apartment. An antique sword rested on top of one of the bags, beside what looked like a brass Russian samovar.

"Your father collected all this?" I asked.

"Was maybe my grandfather." As I admired the stash, another man suddenly appeared at the top of the ladder to the roof. My first reaction was that Grassini had engineered some kind of double cross, that this man would take the painting away. How stupid of me to have followed Grassini here.

The new man looked older than Grassini, maybe early fifties, but that could have been because his skin was wrinkled and the color of old leather. Angry black and white pandas fought on his green T-shirt.

Instead of going for the painting, though, he began to yell at Grassini in Italian. I stepped back, keeping Danny behind me. Should I grab the painting and hurry back down the stairs? "Get ready to run for the ladder, bro," I said.

I moved slowly toward where I'd left the painting, as Grassini argued back at the man, spitting once on the tar roof. Then the man lunged at Grassini and grabbed him by the throat, and I knew that I couldn't just run away.

"Stay here!" I said to Danny. Then I rushed across the roof and got my arm around the newcomer's throat in a move I'd learned at the academy. By putting pressure on his throat, I forced him to release his grasp on Grassini, who slumped back, gasping for breath.

The man I held onto struggled against me, and I had to let him go. By then Grassini was back on his feet, yelling something. He grabbed the antique sword from the pile of rubbish in the shed and rushed at the man.

I had only a moment to yell, "No!" before Grassini had pierced the man in the chest with the sword. I stared in horror as Grassini used his grip on the sword to push the man toward that low railing. He gave the man, who stared open-eyed ahead, a final push, and he went backward, over the railing and down, down, to the street below.

I realized I'd been holding my breath. "What the hell!" I rushed over to the edge of the roof and looked down. The man was on his back on the pavement, four stories below, the sword sticking out of his chest.

"Who was that?" I asked Grassini, as I turned back to him.

Sweat was running down his face. "Bad man," he said. "Thank you for help me."

"You going to call the police?" I nodded to the phone in his hand.

"No police!"

"Remi. You just killed a man. Of course you have to call the police. You want me to do it?"

He shook his head. Then in the distance I heard the familiar high and low sound of a European police siren. "Looks like someone already took care of it," I said.

Grassini wanted to get away, but I grabbed his arm and told him that I couldn't let him go. "Remi, it's your house. Your shed. Of course the police will find you. And besides, Danny and I are here to tell them that you stabbed the man in self-defense. It wasn't your fault that he fell off the roof."

"The police will not trust me. Or you."

"I'm afraid it's out of our hands now."

Chapter 21

Deferred Plans

I looked down at the ground again. The man was resting face up on the cobblestones, half in sun and half in shadow, the sword still stuck out of his chest. A crowd had gathered around him—a couple of men, an old woman towing a shopping cart, a younger woman with a small white dog on a leash.

"You see yellow cloud in the sky?" Grassini asked, as if he hadn't just killed a man in front of us. "Is from chemical complex in Marghera, on the mainland. This gas, it stains the air. It will kill all of us one day."

If the sword doesn't get you first, I thought. But then I remembered the news I'd seen before leaving Florida, about a toxic algae bloom that had swept down from Lake Okeechobee, poisoning the water north of Fort Lauderdale.

"It's everywhere." I hesitated. "Who was that man?"

"Very bad person. A southerner. You cannot trust them at all." He shrugged, then pulled out his phone. "I call police."

As Remi did that, I walked over to my brother. "You all right, Danny?"

"I'm okay," he said, though he was shivering, and I heard a catch in his voice. "Is this what you do, Angus?"

"Not usually," I said.

He nodded toward the railing, and I noticed he was staying well back from it. "Do you think that guy is really dead?"

"Hard to imagine that he isn't, after getting speared like that and then toppling down four floors."

"This isn't the first dead guy you've seen, is it?" he asked.

"No, it's not. It's easier, I guess, because I didn't know him."

"How do you do it?"

"I don't know, bro. I just do." I thought about Larry, the clerk at the booth who'd wiped out on his bike. I still didn't know if he'd been murdered, or if his death had been an accident. And then I remembered the other dead bodies I'd seen on my visits to the morgue and I shivered like Danny had, even in the heat of the rooftop.

Remi was still on his phone as the sound of the siren grew closer. I wondered how they were able to get police cars through those narrow streets, but when I saw the flashing lights bouncing off of a neighboring building I realized the police had arrived not in a car but in a low-slung blue and white boat with POLIZIA on the side. A red, green and white Italian flag flew from the stern, flapping in the breeze.

I kept an eye on Remi as the boat pulled up along the sidewalk. I didn't want him to run off and leave Danny and me to face the police alone.

Down at the water's edge, a man in a blue polo shirt and blue slacks with a red stripe jumped out. Another man on the boat, similarly dressed, threw him a rope, which the first man looped around a tall wooden pole.

Both men wore navy blue ball caps, and even from the roof I could see the badges on their shirts. I watched as the officers approached the dead man on the street. One moved the crowd of onlookers away while the other leaned down to the man and took his pulse.

He looked back up and shook his head at his partner. Then they spoke to the old woman with the shopping cart, who pointed up to the roof. When the officer looked up, I waved at him, and then sent Danny down to show him and his partner up the ladder.

I stood there with Grassini, who looked morose. "That man," I began.

Grassini shook his head. "Is better not to say."

Another police launch pulled up beside the first, and a blonde woman in a navy business suit stepped out. Was she the detective?

Through the opening in the roof, I heard my brother's voice, speaking in Italian to the officer. As soon as the officer arrived, Remi launched into a long diatribe in Italian, of which I understood nothing. I glanced at Danny, and though he was concentrating, I could see he was getting little more than I had.

The officer listened for a moment and then must have asked Grassini who we were. Grassini pointed at us and said our names.

"American?" the officer asked.

"Yes. Do you speak English?" I asked.

He shook his head. "Commissario comes. Speak English."

It got crowded up there quickly, with the officer and then the female detective, who introduced herself as Commissario Nerina Affogato. Up close she was older than I'd thought originally, probably in her early fifties. She looked like she ate nails for breakfast.

I asked her to step aside so that Grassini couldn't hear us. Then I showed her my FBI badge and my passport. I told her that Danny was my brother, and she nodded, as if it was standard for her to find an American law enforcement officer at the site of a grisly death in Venice.

She told us to go back down the ladder to the apartment, and when I picked up the painting she said, "No, no, you must not remove evidence."

I shook my head. "I bought this painting from Grassini earlier today, so it's mine, and not part of the evidence here."

"Fine. We will sort everything later."

I once again stuck the painting under my left arm and went down the ladder. Danny and I sat on hard chairs in the kitchen with a different officer, who didn't appear to speak English. Danny tried to speak to him in Italian, but the man shook his head and refused to answer.

From above us we could hear the sound of agitated conversation between Commissario Affogato and Remigio Grassini, but Danny couldn't tell what they were saying. After about fifteen minutes, the Commissario, the other officer, and Grassini all came down the ladder.

The officer followed Grassini out of the apartment, and then closed the door behind him. "So, Mr. Green," the Commissario said in English. "Can you tell me please why you are here today?"

I explained about the painting, and the chain of events that had brought Danny and me there. "I don't know who that man was, but he attacked Signor Grassini right in front of us," I said. "Grassini was defending himself."

"That is not what Signor Grassini says," she said. She tipped her finger against Grassini's kitchen table, and I noticed that she wore no jewelry, not even a watch. "He says you killed the man, not him."

My mouth dropped open. "All I did was pull the man off him. Grassini stabbed him. You'll find his fingerprints on the sword, not mine."

She said, "You will come with me to the *Questura*, the police station, please. We will speak there."

"You can't believe him. I don't even know who that man was. I had no reason to want to hurt him." I motioned to Danny. "My brother will tell you the same story."

"Yes, you say he is your brother. Is he FBI, too? Maybe he is CIA? Or you would like me to believe he is from some other agency? Maybe KGB?"

I was smart enough to shut my mouth at that point. When we got to the police station, I would ask to speak to someone at the American embassy. Then we would get all this sorted out.

Commissario Affogato turned to speak with another officer. While her back was turned, I sent a text to Leonardo Foa. From what I'd looked up before I left, I knew that the Carabinieri were a division of the military, and that Foa held the rank of *Colonelo*. I hoped that was enough to help us out.

Being taken to Questura for questioning after the man we got painting from killed another man in an argument, I texted him. *Can you help?*

"What's going to happen, Angus?" Danny asked me, when I put my phone back in my pocket.

"We'll have to rethink our sight-seeing plans for this afternoon," I said. "Sorry, bro. But I have a feeling we'll be tied up for a few hours."

I didn't want to tell Danny that I was worried that somehow Grassini had set us up, though I couldn't see how yet. And even if he hadn't, this could turn into an international incident that might cost me my job at the Bureau.

Chapter 22

The Criminal Gene

I shouldered my backpack, and Affogato allowed me to carry the painting with me as we accompanied her back to the boat that had brought her to the scene. She walked with a slight hitch in her step, as if she'd hurt one leg somehow, and I remembered the way I had been shot myself. If that bullet had hit a few inches lower, I might be walking with the same kind of limp.

She stepped onto the launch and immediately went to the bow to make a phone call. The pilot offered Danny and me a hand to get on the boat, which rocked gently in the current. There was enough room for both of us to stand in the stern comfortably.

The pilot went up to the console and expertly backed the boat out and made a sweeping turn in the canal. We went forward, then he turned right onto another, narrower canal, which eventually led us out to the Grand Canal. I couldn't concentrate on the scenery, because I was worried about what would happen. How long would it take the police to figure out the true story? Who was that man, and did he have anything to do with the painting?

Would Danny and I end up in jail on some trumped-up charge?

I stole a glance at Danny, who leaned against the gunwale and looked out at the small boats and gondolas we passed. This wasn't the kind of experience I'd hoped to share with him in Venice, and my anger toward Grassini began to rise. Why had he involved us in this drama? Why bother to blame the man's death on me, when it would be so easy to prove otherwise?

What if the Venice police weren't careful, though, and they weren't able to pick up Grassini's prints from the sword? Then it would be his word against mine and Danny's. A local resident versus two foreigners – though Grassini already had a criminal record, which ought to count against him. A lot was going to hinge on who the victim was, too.

The pilot zoomed expertly down the Grand Canal, then docked in front of a long three-story building, in the middle of a row of similar boats. The Questura was a three-story building of stone and coral-colored stucco, with the tired look I had come to associate with government buildings in the US. Affogato shouldered her way past Danny and me to get off the boat first, and then we followed her through a white stone arch into the building.

We climbed stairs to a hallway lit by broad windows that looked out the side of the building. "You will wait here," she said to Danny as she opened the door to what looked like a small interrogation room.

"I'll stay with my brother," I said.

"You will be right next door," she said, motioning to the adjacent room. "If he cries, you will hear him."

What a bitch. I would see her cry long before she did anything to hurt my brother.

She closed the door behind me. I was alone, but she hadn't taken the painting, my backpack and laptop, or my cell phone. I used my cell to find the number for the U.S. Consular Agent at Marco Polo Airport in Venice. I dialed the number, but before the call connected I had to hang up and answer an incoming call.

Fortunately, it was from Leonardo Foa. "Tell me what has happened," he said.

I explained quickly about meeting Grassini, transferring the money and getting the painting, then the approach of the other man, the argument, and his death.

"This is very interesting," Foa said.

Interesting to him, perhaps. But he wasn't the one in custody.

"This man Grassini is known to us, but he is very smart and it has been difficult to gather enough evidence for an arrest."

"You've got it now," I said. "I saw him kill that man. The Commissario told me that Grassini says I killed him, but that's ridiculous. His fingerprints will be on the sword."

"It can take some time for the fingerprint match," Leo said. "Affogato, you say? I have heard of her. I will come to her office."

"Should I call the U.S. consulate?"

"Wait, please, until I arrive. Perhaps we can keep this from becoming an international incident. When you involve the politicians things often get worse before they get better."

Then he hung up. An international incident? That would not look good to my bosses back in Florida. It was hot in the small room and I was sweating. I could imagine the way the press would see the story. A gay FBI agent sent to buy back a family painting confiscated by the Nazis from a gay Jewish art lover who was later killed at Auschwitz.

I was glad that I'd worn shorts and a short-sleeve shirt, though I knew that outfit didn't make me seem all that professional. But hey, I wasn't in Venice as an agent of the FBI. I was a tourist, carrying out an errand for a friend. I could wear whatever I damn pleased.

What if the police wanted to keep the painting as evidence in a case against Grassini? I didn't want to have to go back to Fort Lauderdale and face Frank Sena without it. And what if he blamed me for losing it, and wanted me to reimburse him for all the money he'd put out to send me to Venice, not to mention the fifty grand he'd paid Grassini?

I wished I could let Danny know that Foa was on his way, but we'd never practiced Morse code as kids, and I had no way to speak with him beyond going next door—and I had a feeling there was an officer stationed outside to prevent that.

I stewed for a half hour before Affogato returned and sat down across the scarred table from me. She had taken off her suit jacket, and spots of perspiration showed on her white cotton blouse. "Tell me again how you know Signor Grassini," she said.

"I don't know him. I only met him an hour ago." I explained how Danny and I had met him at the café, then accompanied him back to his apartment, and what I had seen on the roof. "I don't speak Italian so I don't know what they were saying. But it was clear the dead man was angry. When he grabbed Mr. Grassini by the neck and began to strangle him, I felt obliged to help."

"By stabbing this man with a sword?"

"No! All I did was pull the man off Grassini!"

"Tell me again what happened on the roof. Slowly."

I went back through a step-by-step explanation. How after the man stumbled away from Grassini, Danny and I had watched as Grassini grabbed the sword and plunged it into the man's chest.

Finally it seemed like she understood. I took a deep breath.

"So, Mr. Green. You say you are with the American FBI. But you have no authority here in Venice. Why should you be investigating Signor Grassini?"

It felt like I had said the same thing over and over again. "I'm not investigating him. I'm just picking up this painting for a friend."

I didn't feel the need to tell her about the investigation into Jesse Venable and immigrant smuggling. That would only muddy the water—which already had begun to smell.

"You have proof of this?" she asked.

I opened my laptop and showed her the material that Frank had sent me – the copy of the bill of sale and so on. "Mr. Sena is the legal owner of the painting, and the cash transaction was between him and Mr. Grassini. I'd have to contact Mr. Sena to get his record of payment to Mr. Grassini."

We went back and forth a few more times, until she finally gave up. She pushed her chair back with a loud scrape and then walked out the door, closing it sharply behind her before I could challenge her on how much longer Danny and I would have to stay there.

Her attitude had become more than just irritating – it was threatening. I could not understand why she would listen to Grassini, even if he had implicated me. What possible reason did I have to stab a stranger? With a sword I'd only seen for the first time moments before?

I heard the door in the room next to me open and then close, and I tried to listen through the wall but I couldn't make anything out. If she hurt my brother....

I got up and paced around the small room. Every moment Affogato kept us apart was a moment I couldn't spend with Danny before I had to fly back home, and he returned to Florence.

Another half hour passed before the door opened once again. This time, Affogato was accompanied by a thirty-something man in white tennis shoes, jeans, and a bright blue World Cup jersey with ITALIA printed sideways, surmounted by the Italian flag. Was he some neighbor of Grassini's? Would he pretend to have seen the incident on the roof, and implicate me?

"This is *Colonelo* Foa," she said. "With the Carabinieri."

There was an antagonistic undercurrent in her voice, and when I turned to see Leo Foa, I worried. He was younger than I'd expected, and he looked like we had interrupted him on a day off. He didn't seem like the kind of cop who had enough pull to rescue me and Danny from the clutches of Commissario Affogato, who for some reason had decided to suspect everything I said.

The two of them spoke quickly in Italian, and though I didn't understand the words, I got the subtext. They were arguing in a turf battle. Had I fallen into some larger investigation? Was Foa trying to exert his own authority, or help out my brother and me?

"*Acceto*," Commissario Affogato said finally. Then she turned and stalked away.

Foa turned to me. "Miriam Washington speaks very well of you," he said, with only a light accent. "She says you are very smart and very courageous. From what I understand, you acted well today, even if you were protecting a bad guy."

I was curious to know what kind of "bad guy" Grassini was, but Leo said, "Now we get your brother and I take you away from here."

He led me into the hallway and opened the door to the room next door. I was worried that Danny would be upset, nearly in tears, but instead he said, "Oh, good. Angus. Can we leave now?"

"Yes." I introduced him to Leonardo Foa, and as we walked downstairs I asked, "If Grassini is a known criminal, as Miriam said you told her, then why was Affogato so quick to suspect us?"

"I do not know, but I do not trust her."

We walked outside into the sunshine, which sparkled on the canal that ran alongside the front of the Questura. It seemed a lot brighter and cleaner than it had earlier that day.

As I chewed on the idea that Foa didn't trust Affogato, he said, "I saw the name of Signor Sena in the papers Miriam sent me. You believe he is the rightful owner of the painting?"

"I do. He showed me a home movie his uncle Ugo took, of the painting in Ugo's apartment, and a copy of the bill of sale."

"His family is from the Ghetto?"

"His father was born here, and his uncle lived here until the war." I gave him the information I'd gotten from Frank, and he nodded.

"I think I know the family," he said. "I am Jewish myself, and my family has lived in Venice for many generations."

"Through the war?"

"My grandparents were fortunate. Neighbors hid them until it was safe for them to come out. Do you know the history of the Ghetto?"

I shook my head as we continued walking along the canal, my backpack over my shoulder and the painting under my other arm. The pavement was barely wide enough that Danny could walk on the other side of me from Foa.

Foa said, "In 1516, the Venetian Republic created an area to segregate and protect the Jews, and to appease the Catholic Church, which had already forced Jews to leave many parts of western Europe."

"Like the concentration camps of the Nazis?" I asked.

"No, not at all. The Jews could leave during the day to work or travel throughout the city. By the 17th century, Jews controlled much of Venice's foreign trade, and there were Jewish physicians, lawyers, and scholars. The gates to the Ghetto were locked at nightfall and guarded by watchmen paid by the Jewish community, but it was more for their protection than incarceration."

And wasn't that what the Nazis had said as well? But I didn't say anything.

"Eventually the neighborhood of the Ghetto Vecchio, or 'Old Foundry' was annexed, because there were so many Jews arriving. They did not always get along—there were Jews from the Levant, from Spain and North Africa and parts of the Ottoman Empire. When Napoleon invaded and destroyed the Venetian Republic, he had the walls torn down, and the Jews could live wherever they chose. But of course, most remained in the area where their families lived. Like my own. But non-Jews moved into the area as well, like the family of Signor Grassini. He comes from a family of petty criminals, going back to his grandfather and before."

"The grandfather who probably stole all that art work from the church next door?"

"Yes, that one. Nunzio Grassini. A collaborator with the Nazis, or so I have heard. He died a few years after the war. Then his son, this Grassini's father, picked up from him. He made sure Remigio went to school and then college."

I nodded. It was what my father had wanted for me and Danny.

"But Remigio has the criminal gene, and he becomes a high level crook. He is the leader of a local gang involved in money-laundering, drugs trafficking and illegal arms dealing in the Veneto. We have been unable to arrest him for anything, because he is very smart. And some say because he has connections within the police."

"Affogato?"

"I cannot say. But I will be watching her very carefully."

We reached a pair of bridges that led in opposite directions, and Foa halted. "The Commissario says there is additional art work at the home of Grassini," he said. "You saw?"

"Yes. I think I recognized a few other pieces that belonged to Ugo Sena. On my laptop, I have a digital copy of a movie he sent to his brother in America, showing off his apartment and his artworks."

"Interesting," he said. "You are how long in Venice?"

"We both leave Sunday morning."

"Then you will be able to go with me to Grassini's apartment? Show me this artwork, and the movie you have? Maybe there are other artworks that your Mr. Venable wished to purchase."

"Right now?" Now that the tension had begun to drain from me, I felt exhausted.

"No, my family waits for me at dinner. Tomorrow? You can come to my office at ten?"

We agreed, and he gave me the address. It wasn't too far from our hotel, which meant that it was close to Grassini's apartment as well. Then he turned to Danny. "You are a student of art," he said. "You will follow your brother to the FBI?"

"I don't think so," I said. "Danny's still figuring out what he wants to do with his life."

"You never know," Danny said with a smile. "I could do what Leo does, and the woman you're working with in Florida. Hunt down stolen artwork."

"That is just a small part of what we do," Leo said. "But yes, someone with your background could be quite successful."

That is, I thought, if his big brother would ever let him take a dangerous job. Which wasn't likely as long as I was that big brother. It was OK for me to get shot at – but not Danny.

Chapter 23

Quite a Collection

In addition to carrying the painting, I felt the weight of my laptop on my shoulder and figured that I ought to send a couple of emails while the details of the day were still fresh. I suggested we stop at one of the internet cafés and Danny agreed. He used his phone to check his own emails, while I sent a message to Miriam Washington about what I'd seen, and copied Vito. I also emailed Frank that I had the painting and would be bringing it back to Florida.

I sent a much less detailed message to Lester, leaving out the parts where a man was killed in front of us, and where we were taken in for questioning. No need to worry him; I'd tell him all about it in person when I saw him.

For a moment, when he was busy with his phone, I looked at my brother. He had stopped shivering, but there was something hunched and closed-in about his posture that told me was upset. "How are you doing, bro?" I asked.

"Not really sure," he said, looking up at me. "I didn't know the man who was killed, but it freaks me out that one minute he was breathing and yelling and the next... I mean, you see that kind of stuff all the time in the movies and on TV shows, but you know that it's all an act, probably a stunt man, and everybody walked away at the end."

"The first time I saw a dead body I was pretty upset," I said. "He was a busboy at a gay bar where I hang out sometimes, and though I didn't know him, by the time I saw him at the morgue I had talked to a lot of his friends and co-workers, and he'd become a real person to me."

"What did you do?"

"I focused on finding out who killed him," I said. "But this guy, I don't even know his name, and even though I was a witness it's not my case or my responsibility."

"You haven't killed anybody yourself, have you, Angus?" Danny asked, in a small voice.

I shook my head. "I've shot at people, and hit them, but none of them died. And I hope that never happens, but I recognize it's part of my job."

"Maybe I ought to stick to art history, then," Danny said.

"Good plan." Danny's stomach grumbled, and we both giggled. "Some things never change, bro. You still have the appetite of a horse, even though you spent the afternoon in police custody."

"Were we in custody? I thought we were just there to answer questions."

"We couldn't get up and leave. That's my definition of custody."

"Hey, I'm a Green," he said. "We're tougher than we look. And besides, I knew you'd be able to work things out." He elbowed me. "You're my big brother."

I put my arm around his shoulder and pulled him close, and kissed the top of his head. "What do you want to do for dinner? Frank Sena told me not to skimp on food, so let's pick some place nice."

Danny shook his head. "That feels too much like celebrating, and I'm not quite ready for that. Alexandra and Beth told me about a great student place near the train station, real Italian food but big American-style portions."

We went back to the *pensione* first, to drop off the painting and my backpack, and I then I let Danny lead me onto a stone bridge over the Grand Canal. We stopped at the top and leaned across the balustrades, looking out at the water. It was early evening, and lights had begun to come on along in hotels and restaurants along the water's edge. The city looked magically beautiful, with gondolas on the water and a steady stream of tourists and locals around us.

The restaurant was cavernous, with long shared tables like where we'd eaten the night before, but the atmosphere was different. Almost like we were cattle lined up at a trough, the way the waiter tossed menus at us, then demanded to know what we wanted.

Danny handled the ordering, impressing me with the fluency in his voice, and I could tell the waiter treated him with more respect because he spoke the language. We were surrounded by families, some tourist, some local. The noise level was high, lots of talking and laughing in loud voices to be understood over the Italian pop music blasting in the background. It was the right kind of place to let the events of the day wash away from us.

Danny and I shared a bottle of wine, a huge platter of flat noodles in a meat sauce and then what looked like chicken parmigiana. It wasn't delicious but it was comforting and filling, and that's what we both needed. We didn't talk much except to agree we'd go for dessert to a gelato place the girls had also recommended.

It was strange to be with my brother again, outside of the restrictions of work and family. He'd grown up since the last time I'd spent much time with him. He wasn't a kid anymore, but a handsome, self-confident man. I was impressed at how easily he navigated the intricacies of language and geography. Not bad for a boy from Scranton.

We walked back over the bridge, through narrow alleys and church squares, to reach a long promenade that faced another island, where the white dome of a church glowed in the setting sun. The water was rough and only a few launches were out.

"I wouldn't mind living in Italy for a while after I graduate," Danny said, as we waited for our gelato. "Despite what happened this morning, I really love the country and the people and the sense that history is all around us."

"What would you do?"

"I could look for an internship with a museum or foundation," he said. "Or I could teach English. I met an Australian girl who's doing that in Florence."

I wondered if it was the girl or the idea of teaching that appealed to Danny, but I didn't say anything. He was young, and I hoped that by the time he graduated he wouldn't be burdened by student loans, so he could do as he pleased.

We laughed, talked and ate our gelato, and I was able to push away all the fear I'd felt that day, about being arrested for murder, causing an international incident, losing the painting that meant so much to Frank Sena. I'd followed my instincts and my training, and it had all worked out for the best. Now I could just enjoy hanging out with my brother. The little kid who'd hung on me had blossomed into a smart guy with a great sense of humor, and I could see a lot of myself in him.

We took a vaporetto back to the Ghetto, and collapsed into bed soon after getting back to the hotel. It had been a long day, and I was sure that it would take me a while to fully get over what I'd seen that morning.

The next morning I was up in time to have the coffee and pastry that Enrichetta served in the lobby of the hotel. "You don't have to come with me today," I said to Danny, as we sipped our cappuccinos. Both of us wore T-shirts and shorts, though mine featured a rainbow of surfboards, and his was a mashup of a giant kitten pushing against the Leaning Tower of Pisa.

"You probably have a museum you want to go to, don't you?" I asked.

"My tutor told me I shouldn't miss the Ca'Rezzonico," he said. "It's another one of those old palaces along the Grand Canal, stuffed with 18th century art," he said. "I could go there this morning, and then maybe in the afternoon we could go to St. Mark's and the Doge's Palace together."

"Sounds like a plan. You think you could get the painting wrapped up for me before that? I'm not sure how long I'll be tied up with Leo."

Danny agreed readily, and I used the map on my phone to follow a series of narrow *calles*, broad plazas and arched bridges to the Carabinieri headquarters. Even though it was early in the morning, the streets were crowded with locals on their way to work and backpack-laden tourists determined to see everything Venice had to offer. I wished Danny and I could join them, and that I didn't have to spend my morning with Leonardo Foa. I was supposed to be on vacation, wasn't I?

The clerk on the ground floor of the Carabinieri building directed me to Leo's office, a small room on the third floor overlooking the façade of a church under renovation. He looked much more professional there, in a starched white shirt and dress slacks. We shook hands, and I thanked him for rescuing us the day before.

"It was very strange," I said. "I couldn't believe that the Commissario thought I stabbed that man."

"The Polizia have identified the man Grassini killed. He is a Sicilian, a man with ties to the Mafia there. Gianluca Bianchi. From Agrigento, on the southern shore of Sicily. A history of small crimes like robbery and assault. Our intelligence says that he has been in Venice for nearly a year, though we don't know what connection he had with Grassini."

"Was he trying to steal the painting?" I asked.

"I don't know. Maybe yes, maybe something else from the rooftop. Or maybe some other deal gone bad. Hard to say with a man like Grassini."

He shook his head. "Affogato, too, is a Sicilian. It makes me wonder what her motives were."

"You think she belongs to the Mafia, too?"

"We do not joke about the Mafia," Leo said. "And I would never accuse a fellow police officer of anything without definite proof. But I am a northerner, you know, and distrust of southerners is engrained in us."

"But you're all Italian."

"So they say. But just like in your United States, we are a mix of peoples and cultures. Italy was not even a single country until the Risorgimento in the 19th century. Less than two centuries is a short time in the life of a people."

"When I researched the painting, I learned that Mauricio Fabre fought in the Risorgimento, like many of the Macchiaioli. Was that what he was fighting for – to unify the country?"

"More for freedom from Austria and better lives for the people," Leo said. "Then after the Hapsburgs were gone, Garibaldi came in to unify the country." He smiled. "There are some who say that was a terrible mistake, that we should have remained a loose federation of nation-states. Especially in Venice, one of the strongest, the Pearl of the Adriatic."

I set up my laptop on Leo's desk and initiated the digital copy of the movie Ugo Sena had taken so many decades before. Leo and I watched all the way through once, then went back over it, freezing the frame periodically to look at specific artwork. Ugo had owned several sketches which Leo explained were probably the *en plein air* work done by the Macchiaioli before they painted the final work in their studios.

"Are you an art historian like Miriam?" I asked, when we'd watched at least four times.

He laughed. "No, I am just a policeman. But I have learned much in my work."

I started a spreadsheet on my laptop for the art work we'd seen in the movie. "We will fill in details as we find the items," Leo said. He recognized some genres, such as those sketches by the Macchiaioli, and then had me enter things like "in the style of..."

Before we left his office, I checked my email. Miriam Washington had responded to the message I sent her, telling me that I'd done a good job. "You'll have to write up a very detailed FD302," she wrote. "This could be useful information for further investigation and possible prosecution." I groaned at the thought of filling out all that paperwork. But at least I'd have my own email for reference.

There was also a brief message from Lester. He'd been working hard, managing a special promotion for his whiskey brand at a bar in downtown Fort Lauderdale. "All in all, I'd rather have been on the door," he wrote. "Very stressful watching people try the whiskey, worrying how they would respond."

Yeah, almost as stressful as watching a man die in front of you, I thought, but of course I hadn't told Lester that part, so I couldn't complain.

After I finished, Leo said, "Grassini is still in police custody. But Commissario Affogato has made a copy of his keys for me."

The way he said it made me think she'd only done that under protest, but I didn't press him. He had a hand truck and several flattened boxes in his office, and I helped him carry everything down to the ground level, where he recruited a pilot and a boat to take us to Grassini's apartment.

As we motored along a canal, Leo pointed to where a bright blue boat was docked, with a large silver-colored canister on it. A long hose snaked from the boat into a restaurant with a stylish glass front. "See, everything in Venice must come and go by boat. Even our sewage. You have only to smell the water to realize that much of our waste still goes directly into the canals, as it has for over a thousand years. The tides come and go twice a day, and they take the waste out to the lagoon, and ultimately to the sea."

"I've noticed."

"That restaurant is newer. It has a *pozzi nero*, a black well, to collect the waste, and then the boat comes and removes it."

Since arriving in Venice, I'd seen a man killed, so a sewage boat shouldn't have made much of an impression, but Venice was beginning to look a lot less romantic. Though I'd be sorry to say goodbye to my brother, I'd be glad to get back to Florida.

When we reached the closest spot to Grassini's building, the pilot docked the launch. Leo left the hand truck on the boat and we carried the flattened boxes past the church, to Grassini's building. A steady line of tourists were going in and out of Beata Vergine della Laguna, and I wondered if any of them knew its history during the Holocaust, or were there just to admire the frescoes above the altar that the guidebook had mentioned.

Leo unlocked the front door of Grassini's building we climbed to the apartment. Whoever had locked the place up had closed the windows, and it was hot and stuffy inside. Leo opened the windows and turned on an electric fan, trying to cool the place down a little. I showed him the access panel to the roof, and we climbed up there. It was a lot easier without having to manage *Ragazzi al Mare* under my arm.

The yellow cloud Grassini had pointed out the day before still hung in the air, and there was little breeze. Leo unlocked the padlock on the shed and opened the door. "Now, we will see what we have," he said.

He whistled as he surveyed the pile of artwork. He picked up a framed sketch from the side of the shed and turned it over. "See this?" he asked, and pointed at the code on the back of the frame.

It was the same as the one on the back of the Fabre painting, though a few numbers different. "Signor Grassini has quite a collection here," he said. "Fortunately Commissario Affogato was happy to turn the investigation of stolen property over to me, and I have the authority to remove everything from the premises while I investigate each piece's provenance."

I thought I recognized several other pieces from the home movie of Ugo Sena's apartment. "How do you figure out who owns all this stuff?"

"It will be a big project," he said. "I hope it is all in that database of artwork stolen from the church. If so, I can begin to trace the owners."

We began ferrying the paintings and other items down the ladder and into Grassini's kitchen, where we stacked the art works against the wall, and placed the smaller items on the table.

The police had confiscated the sword used to kill Gianluca Bianchi, but we emptied the shed of everything that remained that looked valuable. By the time we were finished all that remained were some rusty hand tools and boat parts. Leo clasped the padlock and we went back down the ladder into Grassini's sweltering kitchen. Both of us were drenched in sweat and the fan did little but move the hot air around lazily.

We began opening the shipping boxes we had brought, taping them together, then packing the art work carefully inside. Fortunately Grassini wasn't much of a housekeeper, and we found a stack of newspapers called *Il Gazzettino* we used to cushion the items. We stopped periodically to dampen paper towels with cold water and wipe them across our brows. We had to be careful not to get the paintings wet.

By the time the last box was packed, my shoulders ached and I felt like I'd gone for a swim in one of the fetid canals. This was certainly not how I had hoped to spend my brief time in Venice, but I had a responsibility, both to the Bureau and to Frank Sena, who might end up with more art than he had anticipated.

Leo radioed the launch pilot, who met us on the ground floor with the hand truck, and we took turns carrying boxes down the stairs. It was another half hour before we had the boat loaded up.

It was doubtful that there was anything in one of those boxes that would help nail Jesse Venable, but I had done well in beginning the process of returning these stolen works to their rightful owners. I didn't want to get Frank's hopes up about some of the other works; I'd tell him about them when I saw him back in Fort Lauderdale.

I stood at the prow of the narrow boat with Leo as we knifed through the canal, and the cool breeze off the water was rejuvenating. When we got to Carabinieri headquarters, he delegated two of the officers to unload the boat and carry everything to his office.

By then it was well past lunchtime, and Leo took me to a small café nearby that was blessedly air conditioned. I sat on a hard wooden chair and fanned myself with the menu. "It is not hot like this in Miami?" Leo asked.

"It is. But in Miami I go from my air conditioned car to offices and stores with air conditioning. I only go running in the morning just after sunrise, and then I jump in the shower as soon as I get home."

Leo ordered us a platter of *tramezzini*, triangular sandwiches on soft white bread with the crusts cut off. We had several filled with olive and prosciutto, and bottles of cold Italian lemon soda. My body finally began to cool down, and I texted Danny to let him know I was still working with Leo.

"Tell me about your Mr. Venable," Leo asked. "How do you think he is involved with smuggling?"

We talked for a while about the counterfeit goods sold by the *vu compra* and the flood of immigrants from war-torn parts of Africa and the Middle East, and I was thoroughly discouraged by the time we finished. Leo didn't have any idea how what I had learned of Grassini could help in nailing Venable, and I worried that my whole trip had been a failure.

Then I remembered I was taking Frank Sena the picture that had been stolen from his uncle. At least that.

The sky had turned cloudy by the time we walked back to his office, and though it wasn't as hot, there was no breeze and the air stunk of pollution and dirty canal water.

The Carabinieri headquarters were another of those venerable buildings without air conditioning, but Leo had a strong fan in the window which kept the room relatively cool. We began to unpack and categorize the items, and I was able to identify six other pieces, from a small statue of a male nude to sketches and another painting, that had clearly come from Ugo Sena's apartment. I was sure Frank would be happy about that.

It was late afternoon by then, and Leo said, "I can finish this work. You must wish to go spend time with your brother. See some of Venice."

"He was hoping we could go to St. Mark's and the Doge's Palace before they close for the day."

"Excellent. You will enjoy them both." I emailed him the spreadsheet program from my laptop so that he could continue to work on it, and then realized that Leo might be able to use the bank information Grassini had sent to Jesse Venable. I showed him Grassini's address, the information for his bank, its SWIFT code, and Grassini's account number.

"This is excellent," Leo said. "I can use this to get Grassini's bank records. If we can prove he was selling stolen artwork, then my office will have a case against him."

"If you find more connections to Jesse Venable, you'll let me know?"

He agreed, and I called Danny and arranged to meet him at St. Mark's. A breeze had picked up that blew the rain clouds inland and cooled down the air. Following Leo's directions, I headed down a series of narrow alleys that seemed to bulge inwards, past an ancient, urn-shaped Venetian well. I crossed a bridge and then walked through a pink loggia, across a deserted courtyard past a church, where a Franciscan friar hurried past me, humming along to the soft organ music that seeped out of the stone walls.

As I walked I thought of how helpful Leo had been in clearing things up with Commissario Affogato. I remembered how Frank had told me I could get help from the fraternity of gay men—and yet my colleagues in law enforcement, with the exception of Commissario Affogato, had been equally helpful.

Chapter 24

Art Lovers

St. Mark's Square was crowded with tourists eager to get into the historic buildings before they closed for the day. Danny had managed to book us last-minute tickets for a guided tour, and I met him at the side of the church, where the tour was about to depart.

"Everything all right?" he asked.

"Interesting day," I said. "Though I feel like I spent it in a sauna." While we waited for our guide, I told him about meeting Foa and cataloging the art work.

Our guide was a charming older woman, and she led us into the church past a long line of tourists waiting for admission. The interior was truly awe-inspiring, and we sat in the middle of the central nave, listening to a story of the church's construction and how it became the Cathedral of Venice.

I thought how much my father would have enjoyed being there with us. I hoped that wherever he was, it would give him some comfort to know we were living the dreams he'd had for himself, and for us.

After the tour ended, we walked back out into the square. While we were inside, the wind had shifted direction and brought those dark-bellied rain clouds back over the city. The sky turned an eerie dark blue and the first drops of rain hit. I cursed myself for having left my umbrella back at the hotel. We raced across the square and into a *pasticceria*, where Danny ordered us cappuccino and *zaletti* – soft biscuits studded with raisins.

Through the big window, we saw people huddled under the narrow eaves of shop fronts, crowded into porticoes, and squashed up under arches, as rain bucketed down. By the time we were finished, the rain had passed. We stepped outside into a total silence, which was slowly filled by voices, the odd door slamming, edgy TV chattering.

Danny pointed up. "Look there," he said. "You can see the mountains." We saw the snowy peaks of the southern Alps and the golden light that made the buildings around us shimmer. "That's what the light looks like in Canaletto's paintings."

As we walked away, a small boat passed us, bright blue like the one with the sewage tank I'd seen earlier that day. This one, though, held a coffin topped by wreaths of pink and white flowers. The two men with it were dressed all in black, and I remembered what Leo had said, that in Venice, everything traveled by boat.

Even the dead.

Was that the body of Gianluca Bianchi? Or someone who'd died a peaceful death, surrounded by friends and family? Perhaps an accident or a violent death, like that of Lawrence Kane?

I shivered and shook out my still-damp shirt. I wondered why I hadn't heard anything more from Commissario Affogato. Had she given up on the idea that somehow I was responsible for Bianchi's death? Or would she come after me and Danny again?

At least I'd be back in the States. Danny would return to Florence. Would he be safe there? Suppose Affogato spread the word to the Mafia that I had killed Bianchi, and they came after my brother in retribution?

I took a deep breath. I'd spent most of the day with Leo Foa, and surely if there was something to worry about, he'd have spoken to me. I'd take comfort that he was looking out for us.

When we got back to the Locanda, I saw that Danny had been able to get Frank's painting wrapped carefully so that I could carry it on board my flight. "Thanks for taking care of this," I said to Danny as I examined the packaging.

"No problem, bro." He flopped down on his bed. "Your flight isn't until Sunday morning, right? So we still have tomorrow to spend in Venice?"

I agreed, and we plotted out an agenda for the next day. A gondola ride down the Grand Canal, a walk through some of the historic neighborhoods, and then, when we were tired, a hydrofoil trip around the outer islands.

We had a great time sightseeing Saturday, though I kept checking my phone for messages from either Foa or Affogato, worrying that I wasn't hearing from either of them. But maybe law enforcement in Venice took the weekend off.

My happiness at spending time with my brother was also tinged by what waited for me back in Miami. I hadn't been able to collect any evidence that connected Venable to watch or immigrant smuggling, and I doubted that Chancy Pierre had been able to nail Venable for the death of Larry Kane.

That night at dinner I said, "It's been great to hang out with you, bro. I'm really happy I could get over here, even if it's only been a few days and we had a bunch of interruptions."

"We take what we can get," Danny said. "I didn't want to tell you, because I didn't think I'd get it, but I applied for this internship at a museum in Miami for the month of August. I was hoping I could spend some time with you, but it didn't come through. So maybe instead I could come to Miami over Christmas instead of going back to Scranton."

"That would be awesome."

Sunday morning Danny and I both woke early, had breakfast at the hotel, and went for a last walk together around Venice before I had to leave for the airport. Kiosk owners unpacked the day's papers, men pushed handcarts laden with restaurant supplies, and well-dressed people stopped for a quick gossip on the way to church.

I wished I'd had more time to see Venice, to hang out with my brother. But I'd done what I came there to do, and it was time to go home. We checked out of the Locanda, and then stood in the lobby to say goodbye. "Love you, bro," I said, as we hugged. "Have a great time for the rest of your stay in Florence."

"I will," he said. "Travel safe, Angus."

I promised that I would.

I slung my backpack on my back, tucked the painting under my shoulder, and trundled my suitcase down to the dock. Once I got on the boat to the airport, I stood at the prow watching the city rush by, relishing my last moments in Venice, thinking of all that I had missed, and vowed that I'd come back again someday, maybe with Lester.

Thinking of my boyfriend put a smile on my face. I hoped that I'd get home in time to see him that night, though of course if he was working we might have to postpone our reunion.

At the airport, I hurried through security, and because Leonardo Foa had called in on my behalf I was able to skip a lot of the scanning and get right out to the gate. I didn't mention that someone else had packed the painting for me—it was my brother, after all. What could he have wanted to stick in the package? It wasn't like he was an international terrorist who planned to take down my plane with a bomb.

The flight was on American Airlines through Philadelphia, and the plane wasn't as lavish as the Air Berlin one, the flight attendants not nearly as accommodating. But everything I'd been through over the past few days caught up with me, and I zonked out as soon as we reached cruising altitude.

During a long layover in Philly, I found a café in the airport where I could get internet access, and checked my Bureau email. I read through all the messages with little relevance to me that I'd skipped over the last time I checked my mail, from Leo's office.

I also checked my personal email, and the Angus Gray account. A new message from Jesse Venable had come in there, asking me to stop by his house with the painting before I took it to Frank, so that he could see it and make sure that Frank hadn't been cheated. I could do that. It would give me another chance to speak with Venable and see if he had any other dealings with Grassini. I still held the faint hope that there would be something in this operation that the Bureau could use to leverage Venable about the immigrant smuggling.

I emailed Venable that I was back on U.S. soil with the painting, but would be getting in too late to stop by that night. I said I'd be in touch the next day. I swapped out the Italian SIM card in my phone for the US one and sent a text to Lester letting him know when I'd be back.

Sadly, he was in Vero Beach that night on another promotion, and wouldn't be back until Monday night. He'd managed to dig up a variety of penis emoticons which accompanied the message, and I'm sure someone around me noticed that I was blushing.

It was after nine at night when we landed at Miami International Airport. I was relieved to be back on American soil, happy that I'd been able to carry the painting through without incident.

I drove home to Wilton Manors, where Jonas's car was in the driveway and his door was closed, so I figured he was already asleep. My body was still on Venetian time, though, and after my long nap on the plane, I couldn't get to sleep. I threw my dirty clothes in the washer and then sent Danny an email to say that I'd arrived home, and hoped he'd had a safe trip back to Florence.

I sat up in bed for a while, thinking of all I'd been through in the past couple of days. I thought my way through the wash cycle and put my clothes in the dryer. Then sleep finally caught up with me, but I was up at my regular time Wednesday morning. Folded my laundry, went for a run, sat down for breakfast with Jonas and filled him in on my travels.

"Can I see the painting?" he asked.

"I guess I ought to open it up and make sure it didn't get banged up in transit," I said. After we cleaned up the breakfast dishes I laid the package on the kitchen table and slit open the wrapping tape. Then I carefully pulled the painting from the packaging.

"Wow," Jonas said. "It's gorgeous."

It was even more beautiful in person than it had been in the pictures I'd seen. In Venice, I'd been so concerned with getting the painting and getting home that I hadn't taken much time to look at it, but there in my kitchen it shone like a jewel in a tarnished setting. The colors were so much more vivid, and the water looked like I could jump right into it.

"He's got a really small dick," Jonas said, pointing to one of the bathers and spoiling the artistic moment. "And this guy over here looks like he's got a boner."

"Trust you to get right to the point," I said to Jonas.

"Hey, I never said I was an art lover. A dick lover, yes."

I laughed. It didn't look like the painting had been damaged in transit, though there were a couple of nicks in the frame that looked like they'd been there for a long time. Jonas helped me slide the painting back into the wrapping. Then I carried it carefully to my car. I knew that I had a long morning of paperwork ahead of me, but I was also satisfied that I'd been able to carry out the mission I'd agreed to.

Now all I had to do was figure out how to use what I'd learned to nab Jesse Venable.

Chapter 25

Motorcycle Accidents

I was on the highway when a call came through on my cell from an unfamiliar area code. "Good morning, this is Angus," I said.

"Agent Green? It's Paul Snyder. Larry Kane's roommate? I hope it's not too early to call."

"No problem. What can I do for you?"

"You asked me to let you know if I found anything unusual in Larry's things. I found this notebook Larry kept of ideas for making money. I skimmed through it and he wrote a lot of stuff down that seems dangerous to me. I thought you ought to look at it. I know you think I'm crazy, and that I ought to accept that Larry's death was an accident, but I just can't."

"I don't think you're crazy at all." I arranged to head right over to his condo, and was relieved when I arrived to see no ambulances or ghoulish spectators on the catwalks.

"I'm glad you called me," I said, as Snyder answered the door. He wore a sweat-stained T-shirt and baggy shorts, and wiped his hand on the shorts before he shook mine.

The apartment still had the same sad air of a room in a museum, the plastic slipcovers on the sofa and the cluster of old photos in dusty frames on the etagere against the wall. "Larry was involved at least peripherally in some very dangerous stuff, so it's not a big leap to assume there's more to his death than we know."

"You don't think I'm in danger, do you? That someone might want to come after what Larry left behind?"

"Let's not worry about that until we see what we've got, okay?"

He led me down the hall and into Larry's bedroom, where he had piled boxes on the bed and the floor. I saw he'd been diligent about folding clothes and packing carefully.

He handed me a slim spiral-bound notebook about the size of a paperback novel, with a clear plastic cover stamped with the name of a pharmaceutical company. I sat on the bare mattress and skimmed through the pages until I found a strange name – Evren Kuroglu. I'd been reading so much about the refugee smuggling out of Turkey that I was able to recognize it as a Turkish name.

I showed the page to Snyder and asked, "Larry say anything to you about this guy?"

Snyder peered at the page. "Not a guy, a woman," he said. "I remember once Larry's boss was sick—some kind of leg pains or something – and Larry had to deliver a package to a client in Boca. He was pissed because it was a rainy day and the only way he had to get there was his bike."

He looked up. "He told me that when he got to this woman's house, in a really fancy development, the bitch made him wait in the foyer, dripping wet, didn't even offer him a towel. But while he waited he snooped around and he saw a bunch of watch boxes. He said that this woman had to be supplying watches for the booth at Trader Tom's."

I looked at the page, where Kane had scribbled an address on a street called La Sabana Verde. You could always tell those high-end communities because they liked to use fake Spanish names.

Beneath it Kane had written the name of a corporation, and then a big arrow that pointed to Kuroglu's name. "Thanks for calling me about this," I said. "It could turn out to be very important."

I left him to finish his packing and drove to work. As soon as I got there, I called Miriam Washington. She had a meeting, though, and told me to work on my FD302 reports.

So it was back to paperwork. Fortunately I had kept notes of everything I did in Venice, everyone I met with who had a relationship to the case, and I was able to begin transcribing them, writing in the more formal voice used in official documents.

Every now and then I'd look over at the painting, still in its brown paper wrapping. I knew Frank Sena was eager to see it, and I was looking forward to seeing his face when he opened up the wrapping. But my duty was also to the Bureau, and I wanted to show the painting to Venable first and see how he reacted.

The paperwork took all morning, as I kept stopping to remember details and look up information on line, including the exact addresses of the Questura, the Carabineri headquarters, the café where I met Grassini, and his apartment. It was nearly noon by the time I was finished. I saved the document, then emailed a copy to Miriam Washington.

I was still waiting for her to meet with me, so I turned to Larry Kane's notebook. I read every entry, from opportunities to work with someone flipping houses to pyramid schemes and Internet opportunities that promised six-figure incomes with minimal work.

Sometimes he'd included follow up notes, where he'd contacted someone and discovered that the opportunity wasn't all it was cracked up to be. In many cases he had drawn big red Xs through URLs and phone numbers. Though Larry Kane was turning out to be more of a jerk or a potential criminal than I'd originally thought, I still believed he didn't deserve to die, and I was intent on finding justice for him.

The information on Kuroglu came late in the notebook. Larry had looked up the address on La Sabana Verde and discovered it was owned by a corporation, Turkish Time LTD. He had apparently searched for information on the company and found indications that the company manufactured watches in Turkey. That tied in to what

Vito had discovered from the crash of the refugee boat in the Aegean Sea.

I flipped the page. It looked like Larry had hand-written the draft of a letter to Kuroglu, addressed to her at the house in Boca. He said that he knew she was supplying fake watches to the booth at Trader Tom's, and threatened to tell the police about her unless she paid him to keep quiet.

He had written $100,000 and then crossed it out, then $50,000 and struck through that, too, finally ending with a demand for $25,000.

I had no way of knowing if he had ever sent the letter, but it drew a clear connection between Kane and Kuroglu, and provided Kuroglu with a motive for Kane's murder.

I went into the FBI database and found a single reference to Kuroglu in a dossier from a Turkish informant on another case. The informant indicated that Evren Kuroglu was known to own several factories that manufactured counterfeit watches, but was shielded by several levels of corporate structure. She was a prominent figure in Turkish society, alleged to have political influence, so the informant couldn't find anything specifically incriminating.

Then I shifted to Google and found an article by a blogger about counterfeit watch manufacturing in Turkey that mentioned Kuroglu and Turkish Time. The article had been reprinted on a website out of Switzerland, but when I clicked on the link for the original posting I got a web error. I tried heading to the blog's main page, but it was also a no-go.

One more search told me that Luca Albrecht, the blogger who had researched Turkish Time and written the article, had died about three months after its publication.

In a motorcycle accident.

The only article I found was in German, and I had to use Google to translate it. As best I could tell, Albrecht had gone off a narrow road near his home in La Chaux-de-Fonds, a small town in the Jura mountains that was also home to the workshops of Rolex and Patek Philippe, among other fancy watch brands.

Was it a coincidence that both Albrecht and Kane had died in motorcycle accidents? That both of them were connected at least peripherally to Evren Kuroglu?

I took the information down to Vito's office. "I found something weird," I said, as I slid into the chair across from him. I explained about the connection both dead men had to Kuroglu.

Vito turned to his computer and started typing. After a while he turned back to me. "I can't find anything about this Albrecht guy's death. So either it's not connected to Kuroglu or nobody has figured that out yet."

I showed him the handwritten letter in Kane's notebook. "I think it's possible that Kane sent this letter, and that Kuroglu had Larry Kane killed."

"This is a good start, but you need more than the draft of this letter. Keep digging."

I agreed that I would, and walked back to my office, jumping to catch the phone as it rang. "Give me about fifteen minutes to go through the material you just sent, and then come to my office," Miriam said.

Frank Sena had emailed me, asking when he could see the painting. I responded that I had to hold onto it for a day or two as evidence against Jesse Venable, but I'd get it to him as soon as I could. "You won't be disappointed when you see it," I added. "It's beautiful and certainly worth everything we've gone through to get it back."

I caught up on a few other work-related emails, then walked to Miriam's office, carrying the painting in its wrapping. "Let's see what this painting looks like," she said, and I laid it on her desk. She helped me slide it out of the wrapping carefully.

"Beautiful," she said, after a moment. "You can really see the immediacy of the brushstrokes, and Fabre's classical training comes through in the positioning of the figures."

She didn't have a word to say about the dicks.

Chapter 26

Spintria

I pointed to the back of the frame. "My brother Danny noticed that this looks like much newer wood," I said. "And when you hold it up, the frame seems heavier on that side. Could there be something inside there?"

Miriam picked up the picture and hefted it in her hands. "You're right, it does seem a lot heavier in this corner where the wood was replaced. The wood could be newer, or a different species that's harder and heavier." She looked at me. "Or there could be something inside there."

"Can we take a look?"

Miriam hesitated. "Technically, we don't have any authority to pry into this painting. It belongs to your friend Mr. Sena, and we don't have an open case against either Jesse Venable or Remigio Grassini that would give us authority to potentially damage the work."

"What if I call Frank and get his permission?"

"If you can do that."

I had to go back to my office to get my cell phone with Frank's number, and I made the call from there. "I'm glad I got hold of you, Frank," I said.

"Are you ready to bring me the painting?"

"Not quite. There's something unusual about the frame, and I'd like your permission to open it up."

"You aren't going to damage the picture, are you?"

"Not at all. Just the frame."

"I don't like that frame anyway—I was planning to have it reframed. So do what you need to do." He hesitated a moment. "But I really want to see it, Angus."

"I know, Frank, and I'll get it to you as soon as I can."

I returned to Miriam's office, and told her we had Frank's permission to pry open the frame. She opened her desk drawer and pulled out one of those all-in-one handyman tools. "I'll try to do as little damage as possible," she said.

Very carefully, she inserted one of the tool's many blades into the border between the different colored woods, and sliced along the edge. Then she chose a different blade, put it under one edge, and began to pry.

With a pop, the different piece of wood came lose. I could see where someone had tried to paint over the new wood to match the old—it was a different, lighter color underneath.

With the piece of wood out, we saw what had been concealed within: sixteen small rounds wrapped in cotton. Miriam went back into her drawer for a pair of the blue latex gloves we used to handle evidence.

I watched in fascination as she lifted one of the rounds out and placed it on her desk. She unwrapped the cotton swathing and the first thing I noticed was the glint of gold. Wow. Did each one of those packages contain a gold coin?

Then I noticed the image on the front – a naked man on a table, face down, another reared up behind him ready to enter his butt.

Miriam gave a low whistle. "This is a *spintria*," she said, lifting the coin. "Plural *spintriae*. The museum where I worked in Boston had a display of them, so my knowledge is limited to what I learned there."

She flipped the coin over. The Roman numeral X was engraved on the rear, with what appeared to be a date below it.

"The Greek historian Suetonius used the word spintria for a young male prostitute—same root as the word sphincter, so you can figure out why. These coins are alleged to have been used as tokens in Roman brothels, though none of the literature actually supports this."

She hefted it in her hand. "I understood that they were usually found in bronze or brass, and I can tell you without even getting it assayed that this is gold. The date here is from the first century AD, which makes this about twenty-three karat."

"How much is it worth?" I asked.

"The gold coin used by the Romans at this time was called a solidus, and depending on condition, a solidus can be worth anywhere from its value based on the amount of gold, up to thousands of dollars."

She placed the coin down on the cotton cloth and began to open the second round, then continued, "But if these are what I think they are, they're much more valuable to a collector or a museum because they're so unusual."

She got a magnifying glass from her drawer as well as a pair of gloves for me, and I helped her unwrap each coin and lay it out on her desk. I peered closely at the collection. Each featured scenes of sexual intercourse between two people. Some showed two women, some two men, others a man and a woman.

"These are amazing," Miriam said. "Nearly perfect condition—no wear on the face or the edges, as we usually see with very old coins that have been in use for centuries."

"Could they have come from a collection at a museum?" I asked. "Or maybe some grave robber dug them up at an archaeological dig?"

"If they were stolen, Interpol might have a file on them." She moved around behind her desk, took off the gloves and began to type. As she worked, I picked up the first coin, of the naked man about to be entered. The magnifying glass revealed remarkable detail, obviously the work of a fine craftsman. Because of the lack of body hair, and the slimness of the figure, I could tell the man on the table was younger, perhaps a teenager, while the other man's body was larger, fleshier and hairier.

The second coin featured a man and a woman, with the same level of detail, from the woman's stiff nipples to the suggestion of hair at her crotch. The naked man beside her flaunted a prodigious penis. They made them big back then, I thought.

"You're right," Miriam said, and for a moment I worried I'd said that out loud.

"Interpol lists a set of these as stolen from an architectural site in Sicily. I'll email you the details."

"Jesse Venable has called me three times since I landed," I said. "He wants me to bring the picture over to him, and then he'll deliver it to Frank Sena. He says Frank owes him a commission for helping locate the painting. Maybe he knows about these brothel tokens. He has a pretty extensive collection of male nude art, and I could see him wanting a couple of these. And since he's also a gold dealer and a pawnbroker, he'd have the contacts to dispose of the rest of the tokens."

"That is assuming that he himself is the private buyer for the coins that Grassini wanted to sell," Miriam said. "Let's not jump to any conclusions right now. I want you to learn everything you can about these – where they came from, how they got into this painting, and who they were intended for."

"I'll do my best." I left Miriam's office, and suddenly made the connection that had been at the back of my mind. Son of a bitch. Had Vito been holding out on me? He had been investigating Venable for the theft of those gold coins from the Atocha, and maybe he knew that Venable was still in that business. Had Vito set me up to bring stolen goods into the country without my knowledge, just to trap Venable?

I was in a fit of righteous anger by the time I reached Vito's office, but before I knocked on his door I forced myself to stop and calm down. There was no way Vito could have known that Grassini was smuggling coins in the picture frame—hell, I had brought the case to him.

He should have warned me, though. He was my boss and it was his responsibility to tell me everything I needed to know about an operation. Suppose I had been stopped at Customs with that painting, if someone there had been savvy enough to feel the weight of the frame and require it to be X-rayed.

I knocked on Vito's door. "Come," he called.

Vito was as surprised as I was to learn that there were gold coins in the picture frame. "Be careful with this, Angus," he said. "If Venable knows about those coins, then he's going to be determined to get them before you can pass the picture on to your friend."

"He asked me to bring the painting to him first," I said. "That must mean he knows about the tokens."

"Don't get ahead of yourself, rookie. What did Miriam tell you to do?"

I repeated that she'd asked me to research the tokens. "Then you go back to your office and do that," he said. "I'll talk to Miriam."

I felt left out of the loop yet again, but I was pretty sure that whatever happened, I was going to be the one to deliver the painting to Venable, so I'd have to learn what was going on between Vito and Miriam eventually.

I comforted myself with that knowledge as I jumped into my research. According to the Interpol case notes, the tokens had been discovered at an archaeological dig at a villa in eastern Sicily, and gone missing soon after being put on display at a local museum. The archaeologists had speculated that the tokens had been commissioned by the wealthy landowner as gifts to his favorite mistress, who lived on the property.

They were unique because while most such tokens were made of bronze, brass or gold plate on pewter, these were solid gold, and rather than being pressed at a mint, they'd been created by a talented goldsmith, and were particularly valuable because of the high quality of the workmanship.

I did a quick Google search and found an article, written in Italian but translated for me by Google, which detailed the theft. The villa, built in the fourth century AD, was known for its well-preserved mosaics, particularly one of women athletes competing in bikinis.

The article quoted a dealer in antiquities who put a value of a hundred thousand euros on the collection. I whistled. That was an awful lot of money for some very old porn.

I started to put the timetable together in my head. The tokens were stolen in Sicily, and Interpol police suspected Mafia involvement. The man Remigio Grassini had killed, Gianluca Bianchi, was a Mafioso from Sicily. Did Bianchi know about the tokens? Was he the one who had provided them to Grassini to smuggle into the United States? Or had Grassini stolen them from Bianchi, who wanted them back? If that was the case, then it was a good thing Bianchi hadn't known the coins were in the frame of the painting.

I checked the clock. It was six hours later in Venice, so I hoped that Leonardo Foa would still be at work. I sent an email to him asked him to see if Grassini knew anything about the stolen tokens.

About a half hour later, I heard back from him. "I give great credit to Commissario Affogato," he wrote. "She has pursued the death of Gianluca Bianchi like a dog on a scent, and has uncovered much of interest. I spoke with her as soon as I received your message and she agreed to ask Grassini about the coins you mentioned. She has just responded to me that this information helped her break through to Grassini."

Well, that was great. But would she be able to supply anything that would help us arrest Jesse Venable?

He went on to explain that Grassini had encountered Bianchi during a business deal, and, learning of Grassini's cache of art, had approached him for help facilitating the sale of the brothel tokens on behalf of a capo in the Sicilian Mafia. Grassini had cheated

Bianchi out of payment, claiming that the tokens were fakes and that he had discarded them. The day of Bianchi's death, the Sicilian had come to Grassini's apartment to challenge him. My brother and I were accidental witnesses to their confrontation, and to Bianchi's death.

Grassini had admitted that in the course of his negotiations with Jesse Venable over the sale of *Ragazzi al Mare*, he had made arrangements with Venable to sell the coins to a private buyer in the U.S., one whom Venable would not name. Frank Sena's interest in the painting had provided a safe vehicle for transport. Venable had assured him that the courier for the painting was beyond reproach, and should have no problem bringing it, with the coins in the frame, into the country.

Did that mean Venable had broken through my cover to know I was an FBI agent? That implied Frank Sena had told him. Or he could have mentioned a gay red-headed accountant to someone at a bar, who might have fingered me.

Or maybe I had done a really good job of appearing honest and trustworthy?

It made me wonder exactly what Frank Sena had said about me. If Frank was a party to this illicit deal—perhaps getting a cheaper price on the painting for his cooperation—he could have told Venable that I worked for the Bureau and would be a perfect patsy as a courier.

My blood began to boil as it had when I thought Vito was holding out on me, but once again, I forced myself to calm down. I'd have to see what Vito and Miriam cooked up and whether they suspected Frank Sena of being involved.

Foa asked that I arrange to photograph the brothel tokens and send him the pictures. Miriam and I were to hold onto the coins as evidence in the case against Grassini, and whoever had stolen the coins from the villa.

I returned to Miriam's office and told her what I'd learned from Foa. "An FBI agent would certainly get less scrutiny at Customs than an ordinary citizen," Miriam said. "Especially if you identified yourself and said that you were recovering stolen property."

"I didn't say that."

"But if anyone questioned you, you would have," Miriam said. "A perfect cover. And you say that the only party to this deal who knew you are an agent is Mr. Sena?"

I nodded, though it made my heart hurt. "There is also the possibility that Jesse Venable broke my cover and didn't confront me," I said. "It wasn't very deep to start with."

"Either way, you're going to have to take the painting to Jesse Venable as you promised. You'll have to get him to pry off the back panel. If he indicates the tokens are missing, then he admits knowledge of the transport of stolen goods, and we nail him."

Miriam and I replaced the discolored back panel, using the same nails to secure it in place. Then we wrapped the painting back up exactly as the Venetian shipping company had. I returned to my office, where I emailed Jesse Venable and made arrangements to take the painting over to his house that afternoon. About an hour later I walked down to the lab, where Wagon hooked me up with a recording device under my shirt. Good thing I wasn't planning on going swimming with Jesse Venable that day.

Then I drove to Venable's house. I felt a weird mixture of emotions. I was excited that my efforts might save refugees a world away. But I had gotten Venable to trust me, and now I was going to betray him and send him to jail.

I drove more and more slowly once I was in his community, reluctant to face him and my betrayal. But I pulled up in front of his house, grabbed the painting and locked my car.

Once again, he was waiting at the front door for me,. I handed him the wrapped package, and closed the front door behind me, careful to leave it slightly ajar so that Miriam and the other agents she would undoubtedly bring with her would be able to get in easily. Then I followed him into his dining room, where he placed the package carefully on the table.

He got a switchblade knife from a drawer in the armoire and carefully sliced away the wrapping paper so he could pull it off the painting. "You can just call Frank Sena and verify that it's the right painting, and he'll transfer the commission to you, can't you?" I asked. "And then I'll take the painting over to him this evening."

"I'll take care of getting the painting to him," Jesse said. "You can go now, Angus. Thanks."

"I told Frank I'd bring the painting over to him after I showed it to you," I said. "So I'll just take it with me now."

He turned on me, and I could see the venom in his eyes. "I said I'll take care of that."

I couldn't walk out without getting something from Venable on the tape. "There's something about the painting you should know," I said. "There's a damage to the back of the frame."

He flipped the painting over, and I could tell by the way he tried to glance at the frame without letting me see that he knew those brothel tokens had been placed in the frame by Remigio Grassini. How could I get him to admit it, though? "When my brother and I saw the painting in Venice, we were worried about that, so we had Mr. Grassini pry the back panel off. You know, just to make sure there was no damage to the painting itself when the frame was repaired."

He glared at me again, and I thought Larry Kane had been pretty stupid to challenge a man as dangerous as Venable – something I'd just done myself.

"You took the frame apart?"

"Just that loose piece on the back. You can pry it off yourself."

He flipped the knife in his hand to a different, deadlier blade, and used its edge to remove the loose piece. "Son of a bitch!" he exploded, when he saw that the cavity inside the frame was empty. "Did you steal those coins from me, Angus? I swear to God I'll kill you if you did."

He rushed at me, moving surprisingly quickly for such a big man.

I jumped back, pulling my Glock from its holster and aiming it at him. "Back off! I am a Federal agent and I am armed!"

A boom at the front door startled both of us, and we turned to see Miriam Washington striding in, with two burly guys from the SWAT team behind her. "Jesse Venable, you are under arrest for trafficking in stolen property," she said.

He brandished the knife. "Who the fuck are you?"

"Special Agent Miriam Washington from the FBI," she said. "Put down the weapon, Mr. Venable. This will go much easier if you cooperate."

Venable turned to me. "You fucked me over, Angus. I won't forget this."

He let the knife clatter to the table, and I was grateful that his contact in Italy, Remigio Grassini, was in police custody. At least I hoped Grassini was his only contact.

Chapter 27

A Bitter Pill

Miriam read Venable his rights, then led him out to the Bureau SUV she'd arrived in. I packed up the painting once more and followed them back to the office. By the time I parked and walked in, I had a text from Miriam. "Venable invoked his right to an attorney. Meet me in my office."

When I got there, she was on the phone, but as soon as she hung up she said, "Venable's attorney should be here within the hour. In the meantime, he can cool his heels in the interview room."

"What about Frank Sena? Should I let him know what's going on?"

"Do you believe that he was part of this operation?"

I shook my head. "I don't think he had any idea about the coins in the frame. But it's his painting, after all, and I promised to bring it to him as soon as I could."

"Call him and let him know you're going to be delayed. But don't tell him why."

I stepped out of Miriam's office to call Frank. "You're on your way over with the painting?" he asked.

"Not quite yet. I got hung up on something at work. But I'll get it to you as soon as I can."

He sighed. "I waited this long to see it, I'm sure I can wait another few hours."

When I went back to Miriam's office, we were joined by an Assistant District Attorney named Caleb Lewin. He was a couple of years younger than I was, probably fresh out of law school, and he looked about as comfortable in his suit and tie as I usually felt. I went through everything I had learned about Venable, including our suspicion that he was connected to the smuggling of watches and refugees out of Turkey.

"All we have is a shipping manifest addressed to a private mailbox leased by the LLC that operates Venable's booth at Trader Tom's market," I said. "Not enough to bring charges. But if we can get him to flip on whoever he buys the watches from, we have a chance to track down not only the manufacturer of the counterfeit watches, but whoever is shipping them out of Turkey and at the same time putting refugees in mortal danger."

"I'll see what I can do," Lewin said. "It looks like we have a strong case against Venable for the smuggling of the gold coins. It's going to be tough to trade that for anything less than solid evidence against this smuggler."

"Larry Kane, who worked for Venable, died about a week ago, and in his effects I found the name Evren Kuroglu, who has some connection to watch manufacturing in Turkey. That might be your key."

I hurried back to my office, and emailed the material I had on Kuroglu to both Miriam Washington and Caleb Lewin. By the time I got back to Miriam's office, she walked me down the hall to a door beside one of our interview rooms. Inside it, a mirrored window looked into the room, and I could hear everything that was said.

Venable sat facing me at a wooden table. His attorney, Alfredo Sandler, a brusque middle-aged man with a strong Spanish accent, sat beside him. I watched as Miriam went through the basics of why Venable had been arrested. "We know about the gold brothel tokens, Mr. Venable. A conviction for trafficking in stolen artifacts could land you in federal prison for a long time."

"My client had no knowledge of any gold in the frame of the painting. He was simply brokering a deal between Mr. Frank Sena and Mr. Remigio Grassini."

"We have your client on tape admitting to knowledge of the coins," Miriam said. "And Grassini has already admitted to making a side deal with your client about these tokens, Counselor. He has supplied the Italian police with an email chain confirming the deal."

Venable's face paled, and he leaned over to confer with Sandler.

After a moment's conversation, Sandler said, "Mr. Venable can admit to knowledge of the gold tokens in the picture's frame. But once again, he was simply brokering a deal for someone else. He did not know the history of the tokens or where they came from. Mr. Grassini knew of Mr. Venable's work as a dealer in gold, and approached him during the negotiations for the Italian painting. He indicated that a contact had some gold coins to sell and asked if Mr. Venable could assist in the transaction."

Lewin nodded. "Go on."

"Mr. Venable approached several past customers and found someone who was interested."

"Name?" Lewin asked.

Venable looked at Sandler, who nodded. "Evren Kuroglu," Venable said.

I pumped my fist and mouthed a quiet "Yes!"

"If this was a legitimate transaction why smuggle the coins in the picture frame?" Miriam asked.

"Mr. Venable's customer preferred to keep the transaction *sub rosa*," Sandler said. "Mr. Venable's understanding was that Ms. Kuroglu wanted to avoid calling attention to the purchase."

"And paying the appropriate import duties?" Lewin asked.

Sandler pursed his lips together. "My client has no knowledge of Ms. Kuroglu's financial situation."

"Other than that she can afford a hundred thousand dollars for a purchase of stolen antiquities," Miriam said. "Or was the price lower because of the illicit nature of the transaction?"

Venable simply shrugged, and Sandler stared ahead.

I sent Miriam a text asking if Venable had bought his counterfeit watches from Kuroglu. I saw her look down at her phone, then show it to Lewin.

Then she looked at Venable. "Your relationship with Ms. Kuroglu was more a mutual buyer-seller relationship, wasn't it? Ms. Kuroglu bought gold from you. And you bought counterfeit watches from her to sell at your booth at Trader Tom's."

Venable's mouth dropped open. "Don't say anything," Sandler said to him. He turned to Miriam and Lewin. "Can we call a brief recess to these negotiations so I can speak with my client?"

They agreed, and I met Miriam and Lewin in the hallway. "Venable's got to be very careful because he doesn't want to get implicated in the death of Larry Kane," I said.

"There's no way I'm giving immunity for murder in exchange for art theft," he said. "Just so you know."

"But if Venable can implicate Kuroglu in smuggling those watches, she in turn could lead us to the immigrant smugglers," I said. "People die in those boats every day."

"Kuroglu's name is not unfamiliar to me, Agent Green," he said. "But is she responsible for the immigrant smuggling? And can Venable give her to us if she is? That's a lot of ifs in a row, and more than any judge is going to want to see."

"We don't know even that Venable was responsible for Mr. Kane's death," Miriam said. "And unless he or an accomplice confesses, we have no evidence against him. So I doubt it's going to get that far."

Which meant that there would never be justice for Larry Kane. I had to remind myself that there was still a possibility, however slim, that his death had been accidental, and that it wasn't my job to lock down the circumstances.

It was a bitter pill to swallow, but one I knew I had to.

Chapter 28

The Glitter of Gold

Sandler came to the door of the interview room and invited Miriam and Lewin back in, and I returned to the other side of the one-way mirror. When they were all seated again, Sandler said, "My client invokes his fifth amendment rights against self-incrimination."

"Then he has nothing to deal with," Lewin said. "Here's what we have so far. Your client agreed in writing to facilitated the smuggling of stolen artifacts into this country. That's a felony. And there are sixteen of these tokens, which means sixteen felony counts. That's going to add up to serious jail time."

Lewin sat back in his chair. "Now, there are ways to reduce that."

Sandler looked at Venable, who nodded slightly. "We're listening."

"In the grand scheme of things, Mr. Venable is a bottom feeder. He sells counterfeit watches at the flea market. Who suffers from that? A bunch of big corporations who make the legitimate watches, and a bunch of fools who think they're getting a bargain. Not a big deal to me."

He banged his hand on the table, startling all of us. "But there is a much bigger fish out there. In addition to manufacturing these watches and arranging to get them to the United States, Evren Kuroglu has picked up a side trade in smuggling refugees into the European Union. People who die because they trust one of her minions to get them to safety, and often get stuck on flimsy boats or sent crashing into the shore because the pilots don't want to get caught."

Venable would not look up so I couldn't see his face, but I'd read body language enough during my years behind the bar to know he knew he was done.

Lewin took a deep breath. "And those deaths are a big deal to me. If you can give us Ms. Kuroglu, then all the charges against Mr. Venable are open for negotiation."

Sandler leaned in to speak with Venable again. While they did, I looked at Lewin, who had just proved the old saw about appearances being deceiving. I liked him for it.

Venable and Sandler appeared to be arguing, but eventually Venable won. He turned back to us. "I don't know anything about smuggling people. I see that kind of shit in the newspaper and it makes me sick. If what I tell you helps some of those refugees, then I'm ready to talk."

"In exchange for consideration in charging Mr. Venable with any crimes," Sandler added.

"Definitely on the table," Lewin said.

Venable described meeting Kuroglu a few years before, building a relationship that involved buying cartons of fake watches and reselling them through his pawn shops and his booth at Trader Tom's.

"She bought gold from me now and then," Venable continued. "Anything antique that came in, I called her, and if she was in town she came over and looked at it. If she wasn't, I put it away until she could see it. She was a good customer. When Grassini told me he had this collection of gold coins I was interested right away, and I thought of Evren."

He took a swig from the water bottle in front of him.

"I didn't know where the gold coins came from and I never had any concrete evidence that they were stolen. You know, don't ask, don't tell."

"That's not a legal defense," Lewin said drily. "But continue."

Venable didn't have much more to offer. But we did have what I'd been looking for since I began this investigation – a link to the woman who ran the smuggling operations. Evren Kuroglu.

Through the window I watched as Lewin led Venable out of the room, followed by Sandler. I walked out into the hallway as Venable was passing.

"I trusted you, Angus," he said.

"Because you knew I was an FBI agent, didn't you?"

"Don't say anything," Sandler said, but I could tell from the slight nod of Jesse's head that he had known.

Venable was a crook, and he should have known better than to trust a Federal agent to keep his secrets. That made me feel better – but only a little.

I watched as Venable and Sandler followed Lewin down the hall. I'd worked hard to get Venable to like me, and as Katya had prophesied, I had betrayed his trust. I had to remind myself that he must have betrayed or hurt a lot of people on his journey to that fancy house in Weston with its glittering pool.

Karma was a bitch, and all I could do was hope to stay on her good side.

"I appreciate all your work on this, Angus," Miriam said, as she walked out of the interview room. "I'll have to liaise with Agent Mastroianni because the immigrant smuggling case is his. You should check in with him tomorrow and see what he wants to assign you to now that I won't need your help anymore."

And just like that, I was out of the picture.

It wasn't the first time it had happened to me on an investigation, and I was sure it wouldn't be the last. "One thing, though," I said. "I really want to hand over the painting to Frank Sena. It belongs to him, and I promised him I would retrieve it." I took a deep breath.

"But I understand if it's evidence in the case and you need to hold onto it."

She considered for a moment. "The brothel tokens are what matters. Just ask him not to leave town with the painting in case we need to examine it again."

I walked back to my office, called Frank, and agreed to bring it by his condo on my way home. He thanked me effusively. I wrapped up the painting again and left the office a few minutes later. At least this part of the operation would be a positive one.

Then my cell phone rang with a Skype call from my brother.

I figured something was wrong because calls to a phone number cost more than calling another Skype customer, as we'd been doing. Had the Italian police come after him? Was Affogato still trying to get at me, going through my brother?

"Hey, Danny, what's up?"

"Awesome news, bro. Remember I told you I applied for that museum internship in Miami?"

So much had happened that it took me a minute to remember. "Yeah, you said you didn't get it."

"They called me today. The girl who was supposed to do it got sick at the last minute, so I'm next in line. I can have it if I want, but I have to be there Monday morning."

"Wow. That's fast."

"Yeah, I know. Fortunately I can wrap up the rest of my course work on line. Can I stay with you?"

"Of course you can. When do you think you'll come in?"

"I checked the flights, and for a change fee I can get a flight out of Rome Thursday morning, and get into Miami at 3:45 in the afternoon. I know you're probably busy so I can just hang at the airport until you can get there, or maybe if there's a bus or something…"

I interrupted him. "That's great, Danny. I can pick you up. Email me your flight number so I can check the status, and then I'll wait for you in the cell phone lot."

My emotions were all over the place as I left the FBI building, through all the elaborate security that made me feel like a knight leaving a moated castle. I was happy to get Frank the painting, but sad for Jesse Venable, whose life as he knew it was over. Excited to be able to see Danny, bummed that I was being shut out of the rest of the case.

Rush hour had already come and gone, so I made good time on the highway. The setting sun glared off the rear window of the car ahead of me on Oakland Park Boulevard, and I felt a headache coming on. But once I handed the painting over to Frank, my personal involvement would be over. My trip to Italy would turn into a pleasant memory – especially if I could forget about the deaths of Larry Kane and Gianluca Bianchi.

I parked at Frank's condo and rode the elevator to his apartment. After an awkward greeting I handed the paper-wrapped parcel to him. He stood there with it in his hands for a moment.

"Aren't you going to open it?" I asked.

When he spoke there was a hitch in his voice. "It's just..." he began, then he stopped.

He put the package down on his dining room table. "It's hard to explain," he said. "I always felt a sort of connection to Zio Ugo, even though I never met him. If homosexuality has a genetic component, as some say, then we shared that, right?"

I nodded.

"And look at the advantages I've had, growing up in the United States. When my uncle was forty-one, he died in a concentration camp. When I was that age, I was a success on Wall Street, making more money in one year than my father had in his whole life."

"Were you happy?"

He cocked his head, as if that question hadn't occurred to him. "What do you mean?"

"From what you've said, your uncle had a great life in Venice before the Nazis came. He made money, he had friends, and he bought art that brought him pleasure. Yes, it's terrible that he was killed, and his collection stolen. But it sounds like he had a good life, the years he had."

"You're right. I didn't really start living until a few years ago. Maybe I'm picking up where Zio Ugo left off." He smiled. "Let's see what this painting looks like."

He got a pair of scissors from the kitchen and carefully cut away all the brown paper and the packing material. When Frank removed the last layer of paper, the painting glowed beneath us.

"Oh, my," he said. "It's beautiful."

Though I'd already looked at the painting several times by then, I had to agree. "It is, isn't it?"

Frank turned and embraced me, and there were tears in his eyes. "Thank you so much, Angus," he said. "From me, and from my uncle."

I was embarrassed at the show of emotion. "I'm glad I was able to help," I said, when he released me. I explained about the brothel tokens that had been smuggled in the frame, and pointed to the place where they'd come from.

He looked shocked, but then he pursed his lips and thought for a moment. "I don't care," he said. "Whatever happened is over. I have this memory of my uncle to hold onto."

I told him about Miriam's request, and he said, "Don't worry. These boys aren't going anywhere except up on my wall."

"And you may have more of your uncle's art soon, too," I said. We sat in the living room and I told him about the other artwork we'd found in the shed on Grassini's roof, and that I'd been able to identify another half-dozen pieces from the video.

His eyes opened wide. "That's amazing," he said. "I never considered I'd be able to get anything else back. You think the video will be evidence enough?"

"I think so, especially since they all have the same marks, indicating that they were confiscated from Jews in Venice."

"This certainly calls for a celebration," he said. "A glass of my homemade limoncello?"

"Sure. You make it yourself? An old family recipe?"

He laughed. "No, one from the *New York Times*. You just mix lemons, sugar and vodka together and let it marinate. It reminds me of what my father made. Yet another tie to my childhood and my family."

He poured a couple of ounces into a pair of crystal shot glasses, and we toasted, to art and Zio Ugo. The gold liquid glittered in the light.

Chapter 29

The Sun Metal

As I rode the elevator down from Frank's apartment, I got a text from Lester. The bar where he was doing a demo that night had cancelled, and he was unexpectedly free. Did I want to get together?

You bet I did. He said he'd pick up dinner for us and come over to my place, then stay over. He included a couple of Italian eggplant emoticons with his text, the ones that are supposed to represent the penis. I replied with a pair of lips.

Jonas was home when I got there, though he was on his way out to see his new boyfriend. "Hey, before you go, I need a little favor," I said. "My brother got a last-minute internship at the Perez Art Museum in Miami. It's okay if he sleeps on the couch for a month, right?"

"Sure. I don't expect to be here that much anyway. When does he get in?"

"I'm picking him up Wednesday at the airport."

Jonas shrugged and said it was all the same to him, and he left a few minutes later. I tidied up the house, then greeted Lester at my front door with a big kiss. It felt so good to be swept up in those powerful arms of his. After all I'd been through it was a relief to just be a guy with his boyfriend. I loved the sense of connection to him that the kiss provided.

We finally pulled apart. "I missed you," I said. "I loved being in Venice with Danny, but I kept thinking about how awesome it would be if you were there with us. So you could see all the architecture and the art work in person." I smiled.

"We'll put it on our bucket list, then," Lester said, with a big grin. "Gondola cuddling."

I laughed, and the idea that Lester and I would have a shared bucket list made me feel warm inside.

We sat at the kitchen table with a pair of healthy salads studded with chickpeas, tiny sweet tomatoes, and strips of grilled chicken. As we ate, I told him about the art work I'd seen, how impressed I was with all my brother had learned. "Your brother sounds like a cool guy. Am I ever going to meet him?"

"You are indeed." I told him about Danny's internship at the museum. "He's coming in Wednesday. You want to have dinner with us?"

"Love to." He leaned back in his chair. "So is your brother as cute as you are?"

"He is. And straight, so don't get any ideas."

"You're all the man I need, G-Man," Lester said.

He told me a couple of stories about bars where he'd done demonstrations, and then I showed him the images on the brothel tokens, and we decided to see how many of the poses we could imitate.

Later that night, we were sitting up in bed, both of us on our digital devices, reading emails and following links and showing each other cute videos. "You going to be busy this weekend?" he asked.

"Not sure. Why?"

"There's an exhibit in the Boca Raton Museum of Art," he said. "Secular Art from the Islamic World. I figure since you're developing an interest in art we might go up and take a look at it. Take your brother, too."

He sent me a link to the exhibit and I opened it up. When I scanned to the list of patrons at the bottom of the page, I was surprised to see Ms. Evren Kuroglu there. "This is the woman we're investigating," I said. "Lester, you're a genius."

"Hardly. I just wanted to go look at some paintings."

I agreed to go with him, and made a note to myself to research Kuroglu's connection with the museum.

Lester stayed the night, and a short time after dawn we went for a long, sweaty run together. We kept to the residential streets where there were no sidewalks, dodging guys walking dogs, early morning delivery trucks and big plastic recycling bins. Could I see myself running like this with Lester by my side for the rest of my life? Maybe. I'd known him for less than a year, and there was still so much we didn't know about each other.

He was strong, kind, and smart. His body rocked my world and he'd wormed his way into my heart as well. I had never fallen for someone as hard as I had for Lester. But I was savvy enough to realize that we were both still young, and on the brink of our careers. What if the Bureau transferred me somewhere else? What if it was Lester who wanted to move?

I was getting way ahead of myself. And all that wool-gathering meant Lester had gained a big lead on me. I put on the gas and sped up to catch him, then pass him. "You want to make this a race?" he called to my back. "You're on, buster."

We raced each other all the way back to my house, where we collapsed on the front lawn next to each other, a mass of overgrown grass and sweaty flesh, and it was only the fear of giving the neighbors a show that finally motivated us to get up and go inside.

Jonas was in the kitchen having breakfast as we walked past on our way to the shower, and from the smile on his face I could tell that he'd had a good time with his boyfriend the night before. Lester and I showered together, and by the time we were finished Jonas was gone, which meant neither of us had to get dressed right away.

Eventually, though, we both headed out. When I got to work I reported to Vito's office. "Good work on that painting detail," he said. "Miriam Washington brought me up to speed on what you did. Nothing more than I expected of you, though."

I basked in his praise. "But now you've got to shift gears. I want you to gather as much background as you can on Evren Kuroglu and Turkish Time LLC. This woman is slick, so we're going to need as much data as we can collect on her if we're going to figure out her role in the immigrant smuggling and shut that operation down."

"Along those lines," I said. I told him about discovering her connection to the art museum, though I left out the part about Lester leading me to it. Let Vito think I was already on top of my research.

"I doubt any of the art she's loaned to the museum was stolen, but you ought to go up there and check it out anyway. See if you can talk to anyone there about her."

I agreed, and when I got back to my office I texted Lester and discovered that he was free that afternoon for a jaunt up to Boca instead of waiting for the weekend to go with Danny.

There was something else niggling at the back of my brain when it came to Kuroglu. How had I found out about her in the first place? I went back to the article that mentioned her, and journalist Luca Albrecht, who had died in a motorcycle accident like Larry Kane.

I placed a phone call to the police department in La Chaux-de-Fonds, the town in Switzerland where Albrecht had died. Fortunately, the receptionist spoke enough English that I could leave my cell number with a message for the detective who had investigated the case.

While I waited for a call back, I did some research on the museum in Boca. I found the name of the curator who had assembled the exhibit and made arrangements to talk to him that afternoon, though I didn't tell him I was investigating Evren Kuroglu. In case he had a close relationship with her, I didn't want to tip my hand.

And I didn't want him to end up like Larry Kane or Luca Albrecht.

I left the office early in the afternoon and picked up Lester, and we drove up to Boca Raton. It was another gorgeous South Florida day, with a scattering of puffy cumulous clouds against a blue sky, palm trees swaying in a light breeze, and of course, clusters of traffic all the way up the highway.

The museum was located in the faux-Spanish shopping complex of Mizner Park, a couple of miles east of I-95. I paid the admission for the two of us, and then asked at the admission desk for Dashiell Beckett, the curator I'd spoken with. Lester and I milled around for a couple of minutes until a thirty-something guy with a brown manbun came out from behind a door marked Private. "I'm Dash Beckett," he said.

I was reminded of a cartoon I'd seen, about how hipsters could die—things like being run over by a self-driving car, falling off a cliff while Instagramming, or being strangled by a smart phone charging cable. If I was ever tempted to grow my hair long and pull it up into a man-bun like Beckett, I hoped someone would put me out of my misery.

I smiled, though, and shook his hand, introducing myself and Lester. "What brings you up here today?" Beckett asked. "Not just an interest in contemporary Turkish art, I presume?"

"More an interest in one of your patrons," I said. "Evren Kuroglu."

He nodded. "The kind of woman who generates interest," he said. "Wealthy, beautiful, with an air of mystery. And an excellent eye for art. Would you like to see the painting she lent us?"

I agreed, and he led us to a watercolor about three feet wide and two feet tall. It was by an artist named Seref Akdik, a seaside view, looking across the Bosporus at Istanbul. "Akdik was one of a group called the *Müstakiller* -- Turkish for Independents," he said. "They were a group of young Turkish artists who studied in Europe during the 1920s, then returned to Istanbul inspired by European styles from the period between the wars."

"You can see the same technique used in *Ragazzi al Mare*," Lester said to me. He turned to Beckett and I could hear the pride in his voice. "Angus just retrieved a painting stolen by the Nazis."

"Painted by one of the Macchiaioli," I said. "Kind of like Italian impressionists."

"I've heard of them," Beckett said. "How similar?"

I let Lester take the lead, talking about the brush strokes and the idea of capturing nature. Beckett nodded, then asked, "You think Ms. Kuroglu had an interest in that painting, too?"

I shook my head. I didn't want to get into the stolen brothel tokens. "No, her name came up as an acquaintance of the man who brought the painting to the United States."

"And that led you to investigate her?"

"I'm really just curious about her connections to the art world," I said. "Do you know if she has a big collection?"

"She owns several other paintings by Akdik," he said. "Though in my opinion this is the best of them. It was kind of her to allow us to borrow it."

"Can you tell me anything more about her?" I asked.

"She drives a Bentley and always has a bodyguard with her," Beckett said. "And she wears a lot of gold jewelry. She told me once she has a mystical connection with gold. That it's the sun metal, connected to health, wealth, and growth." He smiled. "Seems to be working for her."

He left us then, and Lester and I walked through the rest of the exhibit. Lester didn't know much about the paintings we saw, but he did point out some similarities between the French impressionists, the Italian Macchiaioli, and the work of the artists like Akdik who had studied in Europe. It was interesting to see how those same ideas had moved across borders and been interpreted by different artists.

When we finished with the exhibit, we strolled through the

arcades of Mizner Park and looked at expensive stuff in store windows, and I picked up a bunch of free glossy magazines that showed rich people cavorting in Boca.

We ate dinner at a New York style deli, and then I drove Lester home so he could get ready for a night of trawling bars to push his whiskeys. Then I settled down in my bed with the magazines I'd brought home. In one of them I found a series of photographs taken at the opening of the museum's exhibit. Evren Kuroglu was tall, probably close to six feet, with glossy dark hair curled into an elaborate knot. She wore a low-cut dress in what looked like peach silk, with a necklace of hammered gold and several gold bangle bracelets. The sun metal indeed.

A broad-shouldered man lurked in the background of several shots. While she was in her late fifties, he was probably twenty years younger, with skin the color of a paper bag, dark hair and a nose that looked like it had been broken more than once. So more likely the the bodyguard Dash Beckett had mentioned than a romantic interest.

Did she need a bodyguard because of all the gold she wore? Or because she had made enemies through her illegal acts?

Either way, he was someone I had to consider if I ever met Kuroglu in person.

Chapter 30

Leap of Faith

The next morning the Swiss detective called me. "Why does the FBI in Miami care about the death of this motorcyclist?"

"Shortly before he died, he wrote a blog about the manufacture of counterfeit watches in Turkey. I am investigating the sale of those watches in the United States." I hesitated for a moment, then said, "And another man on a motorcycle died here in Florida, a man everyone says was a very careful rider. Your Mr. Albrecht—was he careful, too?"

"Yes, so his family and friends say," the detective said. "Everyone was very surprised that he would die that way."

"Did anyone mention Mr. Albrecht's blog?"

"Oh, yes, many people," he said. "He was always writing these very controversial things."

"And is there any chance he could have been run off the road?"

"Murdered, you think?"

"I'm asking."

He was silent for a moment. "You are not the first to suggest this.

But we had no evidence, you see. No one to investigate, no one to charge."

We talked for a few more minutes. Yes, watchmaking was a big business in their town, and Luca Albrecht had a particular interest in the industry. He had written about labor conditions and about the use of chemicals in manufacturing. The detective didn't know anything about the counterfeit watch blog, but he said he would ask the people who knew Albrecht if they had any more information.

Miriam called me at eleven. "Mr. Venable went out on bail yesterday, and he and his attorney are here for a meeting. He'd like you to join us."

I walked down the hall to the meeting room off the lobby, past the display that memorialized agents who had lost their lives in service to their country. Not a group I wanted to join, though I'd come close in the past. Miriam met me in the lobby. "What's up?" I asked her. "Why does Venable want to see me?"

"Caleb Lewin and I spent a long time last night first with Mr. Sandler, and then going over the evidence we have," she said, and my heart skipped a couple of beats. Had I missed something? Failed to document a piece of evidence?

"The bottom line is that Mr. Venable can't give us very much on Ms. Kuroglu at all. He can't provide us any proof that Ms. Kuroglu knows the brothel tokens were stolen, which gives us zero leverage against her."

I looked at her. "And?"

"So he's agreed to let us monitor his meeting with her in the hope that he can get her to incriminate herself on tape."

"You're going to wire up Venable?" I knew it would be improper to make a joke, but I had seen Venable shirtless, and I could imagine it would require all of Wagon's ingenuity, and an awful lot of wire, to hook him up.

"That's where you come in," she said, and the balls all dropped in place. I'd be wired, not Venable. I'd have to keep an eye on him, while trying to make sure I was close enough to Kuroglu to record everything she said. I might even have to steer the conversation, if Venable wasn't up to it.

"How does Venable feel about it?"

"He's the one who requested that you accompany him." Miriam looked at me. "You think you can manage this? It's an awkward situation given your past relationship with Mr. Venable. And you'll have two different suspects to keep an eye on."

"Not to mention the bodyguard who accompanies Kuroglu everywhere." I took a deep breath. Time to put on my big boy pants and be a strong, confident Federal agent. "Sure, I'll go along," I said.

We walked into the meeting room. Venable looked tired, with dark shadows under his eyes, though his attorney appeared to be well-rested. The difference between counselor and client. Sandler had undoubtedly gone home, confident in a big fee ahead of him, while Venable had probably not enjoyed his brief stay in the Broward County Jail.

I slid into the seat across from Jesse Venable. I wanted to hear from him why he'd asked me to be the agent who went with him, and I asked him that.

"I know you," Venable said. "And you always treated me like a human being the whole time you were doing your job. I admire that, and if I'm going against Evren, I want somebody I can trust by my side."

Well, I'd done the job Katya had spoken of. I'd gotten Venable to trust me. Then I'd betrayed him, but he still trusted me. Either that, or he was setting me up for some kind of betrayal of his own, to Evren Kuroglu.

We hammered out details of what we hoped to accomplish. We needed Kuroglu, on tape, acknowledging that she was receiving stolen property. Without that, all we'd have would be Venable's word against hers.

"What if we can't get her to admit that?" I asked. "We can't just hand over the tokens and walk away, right?"

"Our worst case scenario is that Mr. Venable has to hand them over in exchange for payment. Then I step in with a couple of guys from the SWAT team to back me up and announce that the deal is off because the tokens are stolen. We leave with Mr. Venable and focus on the case we can make."

Start here.

"But what about the immigrant smuggling? We just let that go?"

Miriam opened her hands to me. "We work with what we have."

I hated that, but I couldn't argue with her, at least not in front of Venable and his attorney. She was right; we couldn't go after Kuroglu, or the smuggling operation, without more evidence.

"But if Jesse or I get her to cop to acknowledging the tokens are stolen, then we have a chance to use that as leverage for these other cases, right?"

Miriam nodded, and I felt my pulse accelerate. The fate of unknown refugees could rest on my shoulders.

Wagon came in then and hooked Venable's cell phone into a gadget that would relay the conversation into headsets for me and Miriam so that we could hear the call he had to make to Evren Kuroglu.

The room was silent as Venable called his client, and the loud ringing in my ear startled me. I stilled myself and focused on the sounds coming through my ear. Kuroglu answered, in a gravelly voice like the purring of a cat, with the slightest hint of an accent.

Venable explained that he had the tokens and suggested he bring them to her house, but she said she was about to leave on her yacht for a cruise to the Bahamas, and she wanted to meet at the marina where her boat was stored.

Miriam nodded at him, and he agreed. They made arrangements to meet at one o'clock at the boat storage facility, just off the 17th Street Causeway. After the call ended, Venable and I made plans to meet at a restaurant called The Boatyard, next door to the storage facility, and he and Sandler stood up. Venable reached out to shake my hand. "You'll take care of me this afternoon, won't you, Angus?"

His hand was clammy and his grip was weak. I pressed my hand against his and said, "With everything I can."

He smiled, though his eyes remained sad, and he and Sandler walked out.

"How do you feel about this?" Miriam asked me.

"Honestly? I'm conflicted. I mean, I'm totally willing to do this for the Bureau. But Venable..." I shook my head. "I don't understand him. It was my job to get to know him, get him to trust me, and then to betray him. And he knows all that, but he still trusts me."

"Those feelings are all part of being undercover," Miriam said. "Can you get past any personal feelings you have and carry this operation out to completion?"

I didn't have to hesitate. "I can. I feel sorry for Jesse Venable, don't get me wrong. He has a lot of money and a fancy house, but fundamentally he's a sad guy, and prison's not going to be a picnic for him, even in one of the low-security operations. However, he picked this path, and he's got to pay for what he's done."

As I walked back to my office, I thought about that. Yeah, Venable was a sleazeball, but I still had no evidence that he'd been directly involved in any deaths. He'd probably negotiate a plea deal based on handing us Kuroglu, and maybe never serve any time at all.

Back at my desk, I pulled up images of the boat storage facility where we were to meet Evren Kuroglu, located on a canal that ran into the Intracoastal Waterway. It was a huge building, the equivalent of four stories tall, with automated lifts that moved boats up to slots where they were safe from hurricanes and other damage. The front of the building was on a narrow access road. A series of garage doors led to stalls where vehicles could be stored, and beyond that to the narrow piers where yachts could be docked.

The layout made me uncomfortable – there were too many entrances and exits, too many opportunities for Kuroglu – or even Venable – to slip away. I'd really have to bring my A game to make sure the operation went off smoothly.

I memorized the interior and exterior of the boat storage facility until I could see it with my eyes closed. The real thing would probably be even more complicated, with boats in some of the bays, the sound of machinery working, the smell of salt water and diesel fuel.

A short time later, Wagon called me down to the huge two-story lab. "These should fit your waist," he said, holding up a pair of cargo pants with big pockets. "We're going to need to hide whatever you carry out to this meeting."

I stepped behind a partition and changed from my dress slacks into the khaki-colored pants. They fit loosely, which was good. I wasn't out to show off my personal assets to everyone I met.

I left my shirt open so that Wagon could once again hook me up with a wire. One of the other techs was using super glue to lift fingerprints from a laptop computer, so the big garage doors were open and fans were running. It was hot and humid, and I was embarrassed when I started to sweat. Wagon had to hand me a couple of paper towels to dry off so the tape attaching the wires would stick.

"You're sure these will stay on?" I asked. "I'm going to be outside, by the water. What if start to sweat again?"

He turned to his cabinets and rummaged for a while. I remembered a sticker I'd seen on a refrigerator at a friend's house. *There are haves, and have nots. We're a can't find.*

Eventually, though, he came up with a small antiperspirant stick and handed it to me. "This is a pretty strong blend, all natural ingredients. Rub it into your armpits before you get out of your car and it should carry you for a while."

Should. But what else did I have?

He ran the wire to a transmitter at my waist. My gun slid easily into one of the side pockets, a pair of slim handcuffs into another. Plenty of room left over for my wallet, my badge holder and a couple of other small tools Wagon suggested I take with me. "Just in case," he said.

In case of what, I wanted to ask. But I had learned by then to expect anything and everything to go wrong.

Once I was hooked up, I returned to Miriam Washington's office.

"I reviewed the layout of the boat warehouse with the agent in charge of the SWAT team, and he's going to lend me a couple of agents to place in strategic locations within the boat warehouse. I don't want you walking into this situation without backup."

"I appreciate that."

Together we counted out the twelve brothel tokens, each of them still wrapped in their original paper, and placed them in a dark purple velvet bag. "I sprayed them with something to make them shine, though I wouldn't dare clean them," she said. "I suggest you hand the bag to Venable before you approach Kuroglu. Let him take the lead in showing the goods to her. There's a cloth roll in the bag, too, that he can use to display the tokens."

She handed the bag to me. "Just keep your eye on the tokens. We don't want any funny business."

I drove up to Fort Lauderdale with the air conditioning blasting and the velvet bag on the seat beside me like a prized passenger. After I parked I opened my shirt and applied the roll-on antiperspirant liberally. I gave it a moment to dry, then buttoned up, checked my hair in the mirror, and put on my game face.

Jesse Venable was waiting for me in front of the restaurant where we'd arranged to meet. He was dressed more formally than I'd ever seen him, in a pearl-gray button-down shirt that stretched over his expansive belly, a pair of black silk slacks, and shiny black loafers.

Looking beside him, through a screen of trees by the front, I saw a phalanx of round tables with umbrellas, lining the water's edge. I was reminded of Venice, the way that water was everywhere, that Lauderdale was often called the Venice of America.

I handed him the velvet bag and explained about the cloth inside. "Perfect," he said. "That's just the way I would do it."

It was a bright sunny day, and the heat beat down on us as we walked together down the one-way street that led to the boat warehouse. Up ahead of us, I identified Evren Kuroglu's SUV by the custom license plate, ALTIN, which I had discovered was "gold" in Turkish.

It was parked in one of the garage bays, with the back hatch open. "You think this will clear me with the FBI?" Venable asked as we walked. "I don't want to go to prison, Angus."

I wanted to tell him that if that was the case, he should never have broken the law. "I can't make any promises," I said. "I'm not the district attorney, and honestly, I haven't gotten involved in the charges for any of the cases I've worked so far. But Caleb Lewin seems like a straight-up kind of guy, and I know that the immigrant smuggling case is a big deal. If we can nail Kuroglu, then I feel confident Lewin will treat you well."

Venable blew out a big breath. "I guess that's what I have to count on."

Ahead of us, Kuroglu stood beside the SUV, looking like she'd just stepped out of a fashion magazine, in a beige linen dress, black ballet flats and that same heavy gold necklace around her neck.

The man I'd seen in the background of the art museum photos stood beside her. I couldn't help noticing his resemblance to Lester. At least six-three, broad-shouldered and muscular. He wore a tight-fitting T-shirt that showed off his biceps and had tattoos up and down his arms.

"Who is this?" Kuroglu said to Venable as we approached.

"My friend Angus. He's the one who brought the painting back from Italy for me."

She raked her glance over me in a way that immediately dismissed me as a brainless twink hanging around Venable because he had money. That was exactly what I hoped she'd see.

"You have the gold?"

He nodded and pulled the dark purple velvet bag out of the pocket of his silk slacks. We stepped into the shadows of the warehouse bay, up to the front of the SUV.

As he removed and unrolled the cloth with the expertise of someone who'd done this a thousand times, I looked around us. The building was dark and gloomy, and only a couple of the bays were lit. Directly ahead of us was the yacht I assumed was Kuroglu's, because it had "Altin" written in a curling script on the transom, with "Istanbul, Turkey," beneath it.

I wondered where the backup agents were. Everyone in the building looked like they belonged there, from a couple of guys in jeans and T-shirts polishing the brass on a yacht nearby to a man and a woman drinking wine on the transom of another.

I turned back to Venable as he carefully unwrapped the first token and laid it on the black cloth.

"Beautiful," Kuroglu said. She picked it up, and stepped toward the open bay to see it better. I kept shifting my glance from her to Venable and back. I didn't like having the tokens separated.

I couldn't tell which one she had, but the gold glittered in the sunshine. While she examined it, Venable unwrapped each of the other tokens and laid them out on the black cloth. The big bodyguard hovered by her side, and I felt the first trickle of sweat under my arms, despite the antiperspirant Wagon had given me. I had to hope we got this deal completed before the sweat reached my chest and possibly cut out my transmission.

I resisted the urge to look back to the street, to see if I could spot Miriam and her backup anywhere. They had to be close, if they were going to move in as soon as we had something incriminating on the tape.

When Kuroglu stepped back inside, Venable said, "You see I've got all twelve I promised you. You have some money for me?"

She picked up her cell phone from the hood of the SUV and began to tap keys. "I am sending the money to you now."

That wasn't enough to incriminate her, because she hadn't acknowledged that she knew the brothel tokens were stolen merchandise. She turned and motioned to a deckhand on the yacht behind us, and a moment later I heard the big engine begin to rev.

Kuroglu was going to get on that boat and leave the country, taking the tokens with her. There was no way we'd be able to retrieve them once she was gone.

She replaced the token she held on the velvet cloth on the hood of the SUV. She rolled the cloth up and placed it in the pocket of her slacks, the black velvet sticking out. I remembered the guy who'd tried to pick my pocket at Trader Tom's a few weeks before, and wished I had his skill.

In desperation, knowing I needed to delay her departure and get something incriminating on the tape, I asked, "You know those were stolen from a museum, don't you?"

She glared at me. "Why is it your business?"

"Just asking."

"I am a Turkish citizen, and I am not governed by the laws of this country. I can buy whatever I want. I want these, and I don't care if they were stolen or not." She pressed her thumb against her first two fingers. "It is the golden rule. Gold rules."

A Bureau SUV pulled up then, blocking Kuroglu's vehicle, and Miriam jumped out, along with two guys from the SWAT team. She looked cool and collected in her suit, a dark green that day. But then, she'd been waiting in air conditioning while I was sweating it out in the gloom of the warehouse.

"Evren Kuroglu, you are under arrest for the purchase of stolen antiquities," she said, holding up her FBI badge.

Kuroglu glared at me with a look of pure evil on her face, then spun on her right heel, the skirt of her beige dress flaring. She took off into the dark of the storage building, her heels clicking on the concrete as she headed into the light that came in from where an open bay faced onto the glittering water of the canal behind the warehouse.

Her bodyguard stepped up to block the two SWAT guys, and I exploited that moment to feint left, then dart to the right around him. Instead of heading directly for the water, Kuroglu turned right, then left along an aisle along one side of the warehouse. I took off after her. I was glad that I'd memorized the layout of the building before getting there.

Around me, I noticed the man and woman who'd been drinking wine jump off their boat and head toward me. The two guys polishing brass did the same thing, but because of the layout of the building, with slim catwalks between boat slips, I was the only one close enough to her to follow.

Kuroglu was surprisingly agile for an older woman in heels. She ran down that aisle between boxes of engine parts, knocking them into my path, and I had to jump around them. She reached the transom of the yacht as I was dodging the last obstacle, an open box full of aluminum hoses curled around like the shells of a snail.

The deckhand, another guy in a T-shirt and jeans, helped her on board, remaining on the dock to cast off the stern and bow lines. Too bad one of the other agents hadn't been positioned back there.

I sped up, determined to catch her. I couldn't let her get away with the stolen brothel tokens. If that boat left the warehouse, she wouldn't pay for her crimes, and we'd have no evidence to stop the immigrant smuggling out of Turkey.

I reached the end of the walkway as the boat began pulling out into the channel. I didn't have a choice.

I jumped.

Chapter 31

Right in the Middle

Evren Kuroglu turned around as I landed on the stern. I held my arms out and struggled to gain my balance as the boat rocked beneath me. The sun blasted us from directly overhead, glinting against a metal railing to the right, and a trickle of sweat made a trail down my right cheek.

Surprise was written on Kuroglu's face, but she reacted almost immediately. She cleared the few feet between us in a moment, her hands out to push me overboard.

I ducked below her approach and moved around her, so that I wasn't so close to the gunwales. I pulled my badge out of my pocket and held it up. "FBI. You're under arrest."

She laughed, and kicked out toward my hand. I pulled it back quickly before she could send the badge flying. I shoved it back in my pocket as she took on a wrestler's stance. The sweat had begun to drip down my sides. I doubted that anyone on shore was able to monitor my conversation by then, as we got farther from the warehouse and the dual engines thrummed beneath us.

The boat made a sharp right turn, heading east toward open

water. Both Kuroglu and I took a moment to rebalance ourselves. I wondered if I would have the chance to pull out my gun.

The bulk of the warehouse was still to our right, a condo tower with a waterfront pool on the left. The engines revved as we gained the center of the channel. The shore on either side was lined with condos and boat storage facilities, with luxury yachts and sailboats docked along the seawall.

I didn't know how many other people were on the boat. Kuroglu's bodyguard had been detained by the SWAT officers, and the deckhand who'd tossed off the rope had remained on the finger pier. I assumed there had to be someone up at the controls. Who else was with us? Anyone I needed to worry about?

I took a quick look around, and Kuroglu seized that moment of inattention to launch herself at me. She raked my cheek with sharp fingernails and attempted to knee me in the balls. But I'd trained too much at Quantico, and then with Lester, to let her get that advantage. I pivoted, trying to grab her arm with one hand and reaching for the cuffs I had hidden deep in the front pocket of my cargo pants.

She slipped away from me, but I did manage to get my cuffs out. "I'm going to take you down," I said. "We can do it the easy way or the hard way."

"You are a foolish boy," she said, in that gravel-laden voice of hers. "And if you are with that stupid Venable, probably a fairy, too."

"And you are an evil witch," I said. "I don't know what kind of fairy tales they have in Turkey, but in the ones I grew up with the witch always loses."

She kept edging around, trying to get my back to the water, but I wouldn't let her. Every time I moved in close she feinted back. The deck was coated with some kind of non-slip material, so the salt water that sprayed as the boat raced forward didn't bother us.

Over Kuroglu's shoulder, I saw that an island blocked our forward path. Unless the captain turned into a north-south channel ahead of us, we were going to ram right into it.

While I kept edging around Kuroglu, feinting and blocking, I remembered the aerial maps I'd looked at before I met Venable at the boat storage facility. If my memory was correct, a left turn would take us into the Intracoastal Waterway heading north. It would be a long time before we could hit open water that way.

A right turn, though, would funnel us toward the port. We could go under the 17th Street Causeway and into the cruise ship basin. Then the captain could gun the engine and we'd quickly be in the ocean, and then not too much later out in international waters.

I'd just been in a bunch of different boats in Venice, so I had the idea that the captain would have to slow down to make his turn. Struggling to remember my high school physics about the vectors of an object in motion, I thought that if I positioned myself correctly, I could use the turn to launch myself at Kuroglu, hopefully catching her off guard.

In the distance I heard the siren of a police boat. Had Miriam called in the Coast Guard or the harbor police? I hoped so, but I couldn't count on that.

The captain blasted his horn and we approached the turn. As I felt the boat skew toward the right, I launched myself at Kuroglu and knocked her down. I was on top of her, struggling to cuff her, as she kicked and clawed at me.

I took a deep breath and grabbed her side, flipping her onto her stomach. Then, as I'd been taught at the academy, I quickly slipped a cuff on her right wrist. She wiggled and screamed but I used my weight to force her down and drag her left arm up.

I was drenched in sweat by the time I snapped the left cuff on. At least I didn't have to worry about the wires of the recorder any more. I slid off her as I felt the boat begin to slow down. When I looked up I saw a small boat approaching us with sirens blaring. A police officer at the controls used a megaphone to direct the captain to cut the engines and prepared to be boarded.

I left Kuroglu on the wet wood, screaming epithets in Turkish, and walked to the stern, where I pulled out my badge and identified myself to the officer on the launch. I was surprised to see the boat read *Hollywood Police* on the side; we were in Lauderdale, weren't we? But perhaps the port itself was within the Hollywood city limits.

Another police boat pulled up with Miriam and one of the two SWAT agents, Mark Hawkins, as I was explaining the situation to the police officer. Hawkins looked like he'd stepped out of one of the *Terminator* movies, weighted down with gear, including an assault rifle over his shoulder, while Miriam could have been featured on the cover of *Vogue*, in her dark green suit.

I held out my hand to Miriam and she stepped on board, one sandal-clad foot after the other. I loved the way she was able to maintain her nonchalance all through an operation.

"You can run, but we'll catch you eventually," she said, as she knelt beside Kuroglu. "Once again, Evren Kuroglu, you are under arrest for the purchase of stolen antiquities."

Kuroglu kept her face to the deck, ignoring us, though that was hard as I grabbed her cuffed hands and tugged. Agent Hawkins and I combined forces to bring her up to her knees.

I turned to Miriam. "I know there's a captain up there but there could be someone else on board."

"You didn't search the boat already?"

I nodded toward Kuroglu. "I had my hands full."

Miriam laughed. "I guess you did. Mark, you want to handle that? Angus, you back him up."

I followed Agent Hawkins up a set of narrow steps to the helm, where the captain, a slim guy in his forties with slicked-back blond hair, waited for us with his hands up. "Anyone else on the boat?" I asked.

He shook his head.

Hawkins leaned forward and pointed at a long finger pier jutting off the island to our left. "Why don't you bring us over to that pier for now," he said. "Agent Green, you wait here until we're docked. I'll check out the rest of the boat."

"You might want to tell Agent Washington what we're doing," I said, as Hawkins went back down the stairs.

"Already on my to-do list," he called back over his shoulder, and I felt foolish, telling a more experienced agent what to do.

"Am I under arrest?" the captain asked, as we moved toward the dock.

"I'm not the agent in charge, so I can't say," I said. Partly because it was the truth, and partly because I didn't know. Was he an accomplice of some kind? Miriam would have to interrogate him to find out.

I watched as the captain idled the boat gently forward. Looking out the back window I saw that the police boat was following us, its lights flashing. When we got to the dock, Hawkins threw a rope over to the deckhand, and we tied up. The captain turned off the engine, and I followed him down to the stern.

I watched as Agent Hawkins forced Kuroglu to step off the yacht and onto the dock. Miriam said, "I'm going to stay behind until we can get a qualified pilot to bring this boat back to shore. You and Agent Hawkins take Kuroglu to Miramar and give her the chance to call her attorney."

Mark Hawkins and I led Kuroglu down the dock to the police boat, and the officer at the helm drove us back to the yacht storage facility. I stood at the stern as the stiff breeze wicked away a lot of my sweat, though my hair was plastered down on my head like a bad fright wig.

The other SWAT agent, Luis Hernandez, waited for us at the warehouse. He was dressed like Hawkins, both of them built for power, not speed, and he looked like a distant cousin of a couple of WWE fighters I'd seen. "Fancy footwork hopping on that moving boat," he said, as he shook my hand. "Better you than me. I'd have ended up in the drink for sure."

And made a huge splash, I thought, but didn't say. They took Kuroglu with them in their Bureau SUV, and I hurried back down the long alley to the parking lot where I'd left my car, sticking to the shady side of the street. I hoped I hadn't spent enough time out in the sun to burn—it would be embarrassing to show up at work the next day with my face as red as my hair.

In the car I unbuttoned my shirt and pulled out the wires, and whenever I was stopped at a light I leaned forward and let the air conditioning blast my chest. I caught up to the Bureau SUV on I-595 and followed them back to Miramar.

While Hawkins and Hernandez handled Kuroglu, I returned to my office and began filling out an FD-302 based on everything that had happened that day. It was long and tedious, and all I wanted was to get out of there, take a shower and have a beer to release all the tension of the day.

Close to five o'clock, Miriam called to ask how I was doing. "Revising and polishing," I said. "I want to make sure I get everything right."

"Put it aside and come back to it tomorrow morning," she said. "That's something I learned in my years in academia. You need a fresh set of eyes to review anything you write."

Was she criticizing the writing I'd done so far? Or just being kind? Either way, I was glad to escape. I drove home, where I took that shower and drank that beer, a Sam Adams Cherry Wheat from a nearly-depleted six-pack in the refrigerator. As I felt the gold brew wash down my throat, I thought about what had happened that day.

Once again, I'd acted without thinking, by jumping on Kuroglu's yacht as it pulled out of the warehouse bay. Would Vito yell at me? Or commend me for following my instincts? If I had waited for one of the other agents to reach me, the moment would have been lost, and we'd have been left standing there watching the yacht motor down the canal.

Had I put myself into a situation of excessive risk? Kuroglu could have knocked me into the canal. I could have drowned, or been caught by one of the yacht's engines.

Stupid, stupid. How would Danny feel if something happened to me? Lester? I had people in my life who cared about me, and I owed it to them to learn from my mistakes and stop taking big risks.

But with big risks came big payoffs, too. If I hadn't jumped on that boat, Kuroglu would have escaped, and our case would have dissolved. Now at least we had a chance to put an end to the immigrant smuggling operation, and potentially save dozens or hundreds of lives.

In the end, that was what mattered. I was an instrument of the law, and of God's purpose for me. I would have to trust in that.

∼

I spent Thursday going over my paperwork, adding details, reorganizing material until I was sure it was perfect. Early in the afternoon I emailed the forms to Miriam, who called and asked me to come down to her office.

Vito was with her, and I slid into the visitor's chair beside him. "ADA Lewin met with Evren Kuroglu and her attorney this morning and convinced her to give up information on the refugee operations in exchange for a lighter charge on the gold smuggling," Miriam said.

"Isn't that a bigger charge, though? The immigrant smuggling?"

"She insists she was just the financier, and she's already given us the names of several Turkish nationals who handle the recruitment and the boats. We've sent that on to Interpol, who will liaise with the Turkish authorities."

"That's great," I said.

"Your job isn't done yet, Angus," Miriam said. "I want you to get in touch with Leonardo Foa and make arrangements to return the brothel tokens to the museum in Sicily."

"I can do that. I hope they'll put in some enhanced security so this doesn't happen again."

"Not our concern, sadly," she said.

My phone buzzed with a text message from Danny, that his plane had landed at Miami International Airport. I turned to Vito. "Would it be okay with you if I cut out a little early today?" I asked. "My brother's at the airport in Miami and I'd like to get over there and pick him up."

"I think you've earned a little comp time," he said. "It's probably too late to get in touch with Italy by now anyway."

I thanked him and Miriam, and nearly forty-five minutes later, I pulled up in the pickup lane at the airport and popped the back hatch. I jumped out to hug Danny hello. "I'm so stoked to be here," he said. "Not just to see you, but to get this internship at the museum. I can't wait to get started there and—"

I interrupted him. "Let's get your bags in the car and get out of here before I have to show my badge to someone and pretend I'm arresting you."

As we negotiated our way to the airport exit, I let him talk about leaving Florence, his flight to Miami, and what he hoped to get out of the museum internship. When he'd finally run out of steam he said, "So, what's new with you, bro? Did you get the painting back to the guy who sent you to Italy for it?"

"Eventually. It turns out that you were onto something when you pointed out the different wood on the back of the frame. Our buddy Remigio Grassini hollowed out that wood and stuck a bunch of gold coins in there."

"Gold coins? How cool."

"Even more cool than normal ones," I said, and described the brothel tokens. "Stolen from a museum in Sicily."

"And you carried them into the United States without even knowing they were there."

"Yeah, my bad. I should have paid more attention to the way you pointed that out."

"It's still awesome. You solved a major smuggling case. My brother the hot-shot Federal agent." He reached over for a fist-bump. "You're rock, Angus."

I basked in my brother's pride as we kept talking, about his last days in Florence, seeing the girls we'd met in Venice. Lester joined us for dinner that night, and I invited Jonas, too, because I felt guilty that I'd been ignoring my friendship with him. And I wanted him to like Danny, too, because my brother was going to be camping on our sofa for the next month.

We went to a brewpub in Oakland Park, on the north side of Fort Lauderdale. They had twenty-one different beers on tap, from a Floridian Hefeweizen that smelled of bananas, citrus, and cloves, to a Piña Colada Ale aged in Jamaican rum barrels for months and then blended with pineapple and coconut.

My brother chose that one, in honor of his first day in Florida, and I went with the Devil's Haircut, a red ale flavored with ginger and cherry because, well, red hair and all. Lester chose the High West Whiskey Barrel-aged Mint Julep because the description said that it mirrored the recipe of a Bourbon mash.

Jonas was the only wimp, asking the server if they had anything that wasn't so weird. "I'd go with the Hop Gun India Pale Ale," he said. "It's one of our most popular, particularly with women who don't want a strong beer."

We ribbed Jonas after that, for ordering a girlie beer, and he laughed and let it roll off his shoulders. He'd changed a lot in the year that I'd lived with him—lost weight, gotten more confident, started dating. I hoped I'd had something to do with that, dragging him to the gym, bringing home healthy food, and focusing on his good points.

I was pleased that Lester and Danny hit it off immediately, although part of their bonding was because Lester demanded embarrassing stories about me as a kid, and Danny happily complied. We laughed, ate burgers and ordered a second round, and by the time we were done we were all mildly drunk, except for Lester, who held his liquor better than anyone I'd ever known.

He drove us all back to the house, and after making sure that Danny was settled on the couch, I took a couple of aspirins, drank a big glass of water, and retired to the bedroom with Lester for a long cuddle that eased into sleep. As I dozed off, I felt happy that Danny had slid into my Florida life so easily.

Well, he and I were brothers, after all, so it wasn't surprising, but it was still a great feeling.

Friday morning I met with Vito again after I'd contacted Leonardo Foa.

"Good job," he said. "This case keeps moving forward quickly. The Syrian refugee who gave us the initial information identified one of the men Kuroglu gave up as the one who arranged his boat trip, and the Turkish police picked them up."

"How's he doing?" I asked. "The Syrian guy. Elyas Ahmadi."

Vito looked at me, and I could see he was remembering the way I'd done an end run around him to discover Ahmadi's name. "Settled in Amsterdam," he said. "Grateful for the work we've done."

"What about Jesse Venable?" I asked. "Is he going to do time?"

"ADA Lewin is working with his attorney," Vito said. "I still believe he was involved in those stolen coins from the Atocha exhibit, and I'm not going to let Venable get off scot-free unless he can finger whoever he worked with on that deal."

That was up to Venable, I thought. He was a street-smart guy and I figured he'd do whatever he could to stay out of prison.

I felt great. Most of the time, I was a little cog in the big operation of the FBI, and I rarely had the chance to see the results of an operation I worked on. Usually the data I collected, from interviews or field work, was passed on to other agents, but this time I was right in the middle of things.

I had helped Frank Sena retrieve an important part of his family history, and through my actions had provided a prod to get Tom Laughlin out of the bars looking longingly at young men and into a relationship with a man I thought could cherish him. I'd solved a smuggling case with reverberations back to an ancient historical site in Sicily and the theft of art works from Venetian Jews. Frank would get more of his uncle's art, and perhaps others would retrieve their own patrimony as well.

Traveling to Venice on Frank's dime had spoiled me a bit, as had seeing Jesse Venable's lavish home and art collection, and Evren

Kuroglu's yacht. I doubted I'd ever make enough money as an FBI agent to live like either of them, but I didn't mind that. As long as I could pay off my student loans, buy a house or a condo someday and take the occasional vacation with a great guy like Lester, I'd be happy.

It was gratifying, too, to see how Danny had grown up to be a strong, confident man who didn't need his big brother always looking over his shoulder. I looked forward to being part of a team with him. Between him and Lester, I felt like I was finding my place in the world.

I was finding my place with the FBI, too. I had taken the job initially because I hoped to live the adventurous life my father had dreamed of, but I'd gotten so much more.

And my career was just beginning.

Survival is a Dying Art is the third of the Angus Green FBI thrillers, though he also appears as a minor character in my novels *Mi Amor* and *In His Kiss*.

Want to keep reading about Angus's next investigation? In the first three books of this series, FBI Special Agent Angus Green has demonstrated courage, intelligence and empathy. One of his core beliefs is the influence his late father has had on his life. But what if he learns that everything he believed about that important relationship might be false?

It's no secret that the relationships between fathers and sons are at the heart of many of my books. Angus Green lost his father at age ten, and the memories he holds of things like looking at an atlas with his dad have had a great impact on his life.

His new case involves a Cuban refugee who wants to trade knowledge of a stolen Old Master painting for his freedom. From the painting (a portrait I invented of Jesus as a boy with his earthly father) to the motivation of the bad guy, who seeks to outshine his father, to the secret that Angus's mother has been keeping for years.

I loved exploring this story and hope readers enjoy it too. Here's the first chapter of *Brackish Water*.

Thanks for reading! I'd love to stay in touch with you. Subscribe to my newsletter and I promise I won't spam you!

Follow me at Goodreads to see what I'm reading, and my author page at Facebook where I post news and giveaways.

If you liked this book, please consider posting a brief review at your vendor, at Goodreads and in reader groups. Even a short review help other readers discover books they might like.

Acknowledgments

This book would not have been possible without the insights I gained as a participant in the FBI's Citizen's Academy, as well as through my membership in the Citizen's Academy Alumni Association and attendance at InfraGuard presentations—where the idea for this story first began. I'm grateful for all the great speakers, the lab visits, and the chance to shoot and watch SWAT demonstrations.

Thanks to Randall Klein for his editorial input for the entire Angus Green series, and to Kelly Nichols for a terrific cover.

And of course, Marc, who makes it all possible.

Contents

Reviews	iii
1. Until the Nazis Came	1
2. Trader Tom's Market	7
3. Burning Love	15
4. Good Intel	25
5. Hiding in the Bushes	33
6. Agent Asshole	45
7. An Important Work	51
8. A Little Excitement	57
9. Wipeout	63
10. Daily Entertainment	71
11. Innocent Victims	77
12. Bathing Beauty	85
13. Sex in the Bushes	91
14. Dirty Job	97
15. Surprising Offer	105
16. The Art is in the Selling	111
17. Navigation	117
18. Business Class	123
19. Brotherly Love	129
20. Rendezvous	137
21. Deferred Plans	145
22. The Criminal Gene	151
23. Quite a Collection	159
24. Art Lovers	171
25. Motorcycle Accidents	177
26. Spintria	183
27. A Bitter Pill	193
28. The Glitter of Gold	199
29. The Sun Metal	207

30. Leap of Faith   215
31. Right in the Middle   227

    Acknowledgments   239

www.ingramcontent.com/pod-product-compliance
Lightning Source LLC
LaVergne TN
LVHW010315070526
838199LV00065B/5567